East West Odyssey

EVA LIVIA CORREDOR

ISBN 978-0-615-18350-3

Grateful acknowledgment is made to the following for permission to use
their photographs: Jane Hoffer, "Umberto Eco at Columbia University," and
Anna T. Rogers, "Pierre Boulez at the Maison Française of Columbia
University." The author thanks Jeff Rhodes for his technical assistance.

Cover photographs by Georges Mamorstein and Eva Livia Corredor. Author
portrait by Livia Corredor Duffee.

For information on ordering copies of this book:
elc49@columbia.edu or (201) 224-6939.

*To those I love and those who helped and
inspired me on my journey.*

Contents

Preface

I called it "my half-way rock." Deeply embedded in the white sand, close to the grass covered dunes and cliffs that border the magnificent beaches of the Atlantic Ocean, the presence of this massif piece of rock still surprises me. Has it been washed ashore by a powerful tidal wave or did it get loose after heavy rain softened the earth and made the rock tumble down from the narrow stretch of land that separates the beach from the highway? I discovered it soon after we came to this seemingly untouched corner of the world to escape the exhausting buzz of Manhattan. After a three-hour drive, we found ourselves in Montauk, Long Island, one of the eastern-most points of the United States. I immediately fell in love with the place, its natural beauty, radiance and tranquility. Since it was fall, there were only about 800 inhabitants, mostly fishermen, living in the village. Their weathered wooden fishing boats, with tall rigged masts, and picturesque nets, rusty anchors and metal containers filling the spacious hulls seemed ready to sail from their harbor on Long Island Sound out into the deep waters of the Atlantic Ocean to collect their daily bait of blue fish, flounder, cod, starfish, and an occasional trophy, a large shark, that they would proudly display in front of their boat at their landing station in the harbor. The bakery, the liquor store, the movie house, and most restaurants were closed for the winter. But it was one of those days in October on which you could see forever. The air was crisp and clear, and the wind almost imperceptible.

It was late afternoon, when I climbed to the top of the rock, pulled my feet up close to my body, and hugged my legs with both arms. In this sort of fetal position, as if I had to protect something precious inside me, I cautiously blinked—or did I wink?—toward the fiery orange ball that was slowly disappearing behind the green walls of the far-away cliffs. "This is magical," I whispered to myself, while I let my eyes wander up

Our little gray house in the Hither Hills section of Montauk, overlooking the Atlantic Ocean, did wonders for our happiness and paid for itself and my daughter's education from the rental income during the summer season.

and down the beach and out over the immense gray-green surface of the Atlantic Ocean that was gently rocking, throwing foamy ripples onto the pristine sand. As far as I could see, there was no one else around besides me. "Even the seagulls have deserted the beach," I thought, "but about three thousand miles from here, just over there in the East, there is my family and Europe." I suddenly felt an incredibly warm feeling come over me, a happiness I had not known for a longtime. As if suddenly all feelings of loneliness, my vulnerability as a young woman alone, my worries about survival in this big foreign country with my young daughter, without family, with very little money and an abundance of shattered dreams had been lifted and replaced by a feeling of hope and confidence.

I jumped off my perch and ran up the makeshift steps that made it easier to climb the sandy dunes to arrive at a small winding path that led through heavy brush to the highway, across from which, on a slight elevation, there was what I had rushed to see: a small gray-shingled cottage with a large window and a glass door that opened onto a cobble stone terrace. On that beautiful clear, sunny afternoon, the terrace provided a dreamy, enchanting view of the Ocean. Far away, a ship was fading into the horizon.

Just a few hours earlier, I had signed the purchase documents that made me the legitimate owner of this modest but for me uniquely endearing cottage. It was surrounded by Japanese pine trees, rows of forsythia and honeysuckle that would bloom and become fragrant in the spring, next to bushes of the typical big-eyed Montauk daisies that usually unfold their charming white blossoms later in the year, and in one corner of the terrace a large ceramic pot filled with geranium stalks to which stuck a few wilted leaves and a couple of dark red petals were reminders of the long hot summer we had just experienced in the city. The small structure fit perfectly into the natural landscape. Tears welled up in my eyes when I fully realized that this little house on the hill, the shy quarter acre on which it stood, the warm dark earth I had touched earlier that day, was now really ours. It was the first piece of land in the U.S.A. that belonged to us, where my daughter could jump and play in the backyard, watch the rabbits and deer that lived in the nearby brush, smell the flowers and invite her friends for the weekend, run down the steps to the magnificent beach, climb up on the big rock or play in the waves of the wonderful Atlantic Ocean that connected us with our family and the countries in which we were born. On that day, I felt ready to reiterate the challenge I had set for myself a couple of years back when everything around us seemed to crumble: I was going to do all I could, use my brains, talents, education and hard work not just to survive in this country but create a life for the two of us that would compensate for all the losses we had experienced. Only if I failed would I seek help from others or try to "return home."

Soon thereafter, on an early morning, I drove out to the tip of the island, as far East as I could go, to watch the sunrise from the foot of the lighthouse that

The path leading from our house to the beach.

From the small flagstone terrace in front of our house, it seemed that I could see all the way to Europe.

had stood there proudly ever since George Washington authorized its construction about two hundred years ago. Again, it was an exhilarating moment, a consecration of the change that had occurred in our lives in the past few days. I sat there for some time admiring the bright colors rising on the eastern horizon, flickering, changing constantly until they finally gave way to a clear blue sky dominated by a radiant sun I later saw travel to its zenith over the "half-way rock" and our little gray house to disappear behind the cliffs. On its course, the sun had spanned a bow from East to West, as if warming us, protecting us underneath its path. For lack of a better, less religiously laden word, I had often thought of my daughter as the only real manifestation of "grace" in my life. I now had experienced a second such "blessing," and it remained closely attached to the first: During the summer months,

The white sandy beaches around Montauk, often deserted during the off season, seemed to belong to us.

I still love to drive out to the Montauk lighthouse at sun rise and soak in all the beauty of the surroundings.

the rent we received for the little cottage paid not only for its mortgage but also for my daughter's tuition at a fine Manhattan school. There was no extravagance in our lives. No piano, ice-skating, ski or tennis lessons for my daughter. I tried to pass on to her the modest skills I possessed so she would not miss out on everything that other children took for granted. One thing though was sure: there was plenty of love and joyful affection in our lives, and now also a growing trust in our future. But, as it turned out, the road was often rough and unpredictable.

PART ONE

The Uprooting of a Family
by War and Exile

1

A Sheltered Childhood

Where are you from?

Still today, the first question I am invariably asked in whatever country or situation I find myself, after having uttered merely a few sounds, such as "hello," "bonjour," "guten Tag," "buenas diaz," or "jó napot kivánok," is: "Where are you from?" The question usually annoys and even hurts me a bit because in spite of my great efforts to integrate in a new community and trying my best to learn the language, I feel rejected as "another," a "foreigner," someone with an accent, someone who does not belong. If I respond truthfully, "Fort Lee," "Annapolis," "Cambridge," "Portland," "Seattle," "San Francisco," "Dartmouth," "Paris," "Budaörs," or "New York," which are some of the places in which I have lived at least one year, people usually just stare at me and say I thought you were German, Scandinavian, Irish, English, French, American, Italian or some other exotic nationality (very rarely Hungarian), until I explain, usually with a tinge of irony, or at least strained humor, that I was born in Hungary, lived in Austria, Germany, France, England and seven different states of the U.S., became a U.S. citizen maybe long before they were born and have lived and worked in this country most of my adult life. On days when I feel less provoked, less sensitive to a hurtful rejection, I just respond by naming the place of my current residence or the country of my birth and try to move on to the next person or at least the next topic.

But then, indeed, where am I from!? And why do people always treat me as an "other"? I have given the question more serious thought in recent years. I even went back to my home country to visit the places where my ancestors were born and many of my extended family members still live. In the cemeteries of my parents' birth places, Budaörs and Solymár, I found our name on tombstones which date back two hundred years. I asked lots of questions of cousins and aunts who probably remember things from our family history and searched my own memory for things I vaguely remembered from my childhood, or just pieced together from conversations I had overheard. Yet, at times, I felt that I should just give up. What does it matter after all, who really cares, and why should I care where I am from, having lived in countries that had fought us and each other, dropped bombs on us, raped my beloved nanny, beat my grandfather to death, took away all our belongings, my parents' houses, land and orchards, forced us to flee to escape the dangers of war and left us with a life-long desire for a place we could again call "home." In 1989, when the Wall came down and the borders opened, it was too late for my parents. Both had died in exile. They never again experienced the warm feelings they had cherished for their home, families and friends who have since died or dissipated all over the world. "What a waste of lives and families," I thought. Most of the members of my family, especially my parents, experienced literally the bitter truth of the saying that "you can never go back home again." But I still have not given up trying.

Beginnings

So, going back to beginnings, I found out that I was most probably conceived during my parents second honeymoon that took them to Austria and Southern Bavaria where they visited lots of baroque churches, castles, night clubs and expensive eating places. It most likely happened in a moment of abandon or passion, maybe excitement over their new experiences. Maybe they were simply not cautious as they would have been back home after their first two children who were already seven and eight years old. I don't think my mother was happy at the prospect of enduring still another pregnancy and the burden of caring for still another infant. A beautiful blond who at eighteen married a man ten years her senior probably hoped she had done her duty by bearing a boy and a girl and could finally enjoy life again as she did during their all too brief courtship. She enjoyed reading Balzac, Proust and some Hungarian and German poets and novelists. She was quite versed in art and music and was a talented crafts person who spent time stitching, knitting, sewing and creating beau-

My parents on the day of their engagement: my mother was eighteen, my father ten years her senior.

tiful dolls and dresses for her children, but it may not have bothered my father to see her again more tied down and occupied at home instead of indulging in the frequent visits with other young women from the family to art galleries, lavish bath houses, beauty parlors, cafés and expensive stores in Budapest.

My father's life, as is the case for men still today in most parts of the world, was hardly affected by my mother's condition. He carried on with his successful medical practice and, on weekends, continued to play cards with his friends, which usually included the local priest, my mother's attorney brother and the pharmacist. The men did not refrain from enjoying evenings out in Budapest. As a tall, dark and handsome young doctor, there were, I was told, female patients who fell in love with my father, even one of the nuns at the local elementary school who would blush all over her face whenever my father, in his duty as medical inspector, came to visit the school. She was young, beautiful, with an impeccable complexion, and my father may well have made some gallant remark. He sometimes stretched his wit. But soon after settling in Budaörs, my father also became known in the community for his social concerns that were connected to his medical profession. He felt that many children of day workers and peasants were neglected while their mothers had to labor on the fields collecting peaches and grapes, or cutting corn or hay for the farm animals. Young women who were still nursing their babies carried them along to the fields in crocheted triangular scarves fastened to their backs. As a consequence, they often suffered back and spine injuries from the frequent bending involved in their work while juggling the heavy burden on their back. The local costumes required women to wear multi-layered skirts held up at their waist with tightly strung ribbons, which made the women vulnerable to all kinds of gastrointestinal and circulatory disorders. My father used to tell us of these dangers which he tried to alleviate by educating the women. He also created what must have been one of the first child care centers in Hungary where children whose mothers had to leave their children home alone while they were working in the fields received food and supervised care in a friendly, clean environment. The community appreciated my father's efforts on behalf of the working poor and he was always happy to be able to help. Once a year, on my father's "name's day," Saint Michael, I believe it was September 29, the children from the nursery came to our house with their mothers and teachers singing little songs, saying thank you and revealing in their flushed faces their admiration for this nice, generous man as much as for the house in which he lived.

Our house, our castle

I was born in that house. It was the same large stone and brick house in which my mother was born twenty-eight years before me. In the stucco wall next to the steps leading up to the veranda and the main house, there was a relief depicting a mother holding a child. I loved to look at it. It was probably meant to represent Saint Mary and Jesus, but I thought it could have been my mother smiling at me. There was also a large garden attached to the house. A deep well covered with a thatched roof stood next to the paved path leading to the main house, and at the far end of the yard a

The house in Budaörs in which I was born, as was my mother 28 years before me.

garage and an annex could be converted into further living quarters or even a doctor's cabinet.

Since the house was located in the center of town, just steps away from the tall baroque church, the pharmacy and all the convenience stores, my grandparents passed it on to the young couple when they married. It seemed ideal in size and location for my father's medical practice.

It was in this historical family setting that I was helped into the world by a midwife assisted by my father, who had already delivered hundreds of babies since he settled in the area right after medical school, about ten years earlier. I was born at the end of a beautiful spring day, March 7, at eleven o'clock on Saturday night, just one hour before the clock struck midnight and would have made me a Sunday child. Later in life, I thought the timing was an omen for things to come. I was usually a good student, a good worker, fairly talented in several things, but not always a straight "A," a perfect Sunday child. I had to resign myself to this imperfection, just as I was frequently complimented for my appearance but never reached my mother's, I thought flawless, beauty.

A little angel?

It did not last through my teenage years, but at least at birth my father apparently could not find anything wrong with me. Minutes after I was born and cleaned up, he wrapped me in some diapers and rushed to wake up my brother and sister, telling them, beaming with joy and pride: "Look, we have a little angel." It was only much later that my sister related to me how she felt at that scary moment when she realized that she had become

The church in the center of town, steps away from our house, where my parents were married, my mother and all three of us children baptized, and where my mother, before she tragically lost her beautiful soprano voice, would sometimes sing at special occasions. Most requests were for her "Ave Maria."

the older sister to this baby who looked as if she were to become the incarnation of my father's love for my mother: "Blonde, a mere stump of a nose in a round face and eyes that reflected the blue of the sky," as my sister put it. Until I came along, my sister and my brother had been at the center of my parents' love and attention. This "angel," a second girl, was a threatening intruder especially in my sister's emotional harmony. The memory of the event, she admitted to me not too long ago, stayed with her all her life. While I myself have admired and envied my older, more accomplished, dark haired and dark eyed sister, she apparently has never been able to overcome a certain jealousy for her much younger and, she thought, prettier sister who had stolen her father's heart.

When I look at myself in the mirror, it seems to me that my eyes reflect the gray of clouds, mixed with the blue green of the eyes of my former kitten and the hazel in my father's iris, and only sometimes the "blue of the sky," as my sister had put it, depending on what I am wearing. As I grew older, traces of my father's independent thinking, rather than my mother's more submissive character, started to surface in my behavior. A typical teenager, I also developed quite critical views of myself and others which, decades later, I was often able to channel into professional recognition by distinguished individuals who appreciated my comments, allowed me to participate in their work and activities, but, I admit, this

Our first family portrait. I was about ten months old and my unruly behavior apparently interfered with the photographic session and resulted in wiping out all the smiles.

characteristic has also remained a point of contention with peers who competed with me and tried to stop me in my path.

My genes all the way back to my grandparents

I believe to be a true mixture of both my parents, not only in looks but also in my mind, character and whatever talents I might have inherited, but some of my characteristics seem to have come directly from both sets of my grandparents. Parents and grandparents provided the "raw material" on which I built my own self as an individual.

My paternal grandparents in Solymár

My father's paternal ancestors hail from Solymár, a small community North-West of Budapest. My grandfather died before I was born after having fathered thirteen children, among them three sets of twins but one of the twins in each set always died at birth. My father, "Miska," as they called him in Hungarian, was the youngest in the family. He, my uncles and cousins, as I remember them, were all broad shouldered, rugged, with dark hair and dark, bushy moustaches and sun burned faces, while the women, who all had married young, appeared more delicate and of lighter complexion. Because of the stories woven around my grandfather's life, I pictured him as resembling the Huns, the forefathers of Hungarians. From History books I learned that they had come from the steppes of Siberia and were known for their high cheek bones, broad faces and legendary savagery. In the course of their Blitz-conquests of several East European countries, among them Hungary, they inspired both fear and awe among the population of the countries they ravaged.

Grandfather Bernát was not a Hun but a respected, wealthy landowner and wine producer, who owned vineyards and many peach and apple orchards. He also ran a butcher shop across the street from his white washed stucco house in the center of Solymar. I remember the long, one-story building and especially the large, bare yard sloping down towards the stables and the barns and ultimately to a stream. There was no grass in the backyard, just the bare earth, often dusty in the summer. But each weekend the yard was swept clean, just as each spring the house received a fresh coat of white paint. I remember the veranda punctuated by columns that ran along the yard side of the house and from which doors gave separate access to each room. I liked this house, maybe because it was so different from the house in Budaörs where we lived. On the veranda, there were tall oleander trees that seemed to be in bloom whenever I visited. Sitting outside the living room, grandma would pull me on her lap and talk to me while stroking my hair and smiling. I remember the warm feeling her gentle touch and closeness created in me. I still love oleander trees, and when I lived in California, was delighted to see so many of them in that state because they reminded me each time of those precious moments with my grandmother.

My father adored his mother, and from the way she looked at him and spoke to him, I could see that she adored him as well. He was her last born, and out of gratefulness to God for her beautiful family, she destined him to carry on the work of God. Since he was a good student, the village priest was happy to take the young boy under his wings and nurture him spiritually and intellectually. Today, when I look at my grandson, at his big shiny dark eyes, dark brown hair and charming smile, I often think of the way my father must have looked at that age when my grandmother suggested what to her must have seemed a desirable destiny. But as my father grew into a tall, dark, handsome and witty young man with sparkling flirtatious eyes, he also discovered what delight there was in the company of girls. I was told that girls were not slow noticing him either. "Let someone else become a priest," he declared just before graduating from "gymnasium," the Hungarian high school, "I will be a doctor."

Grandmother was not too disappointed by my father's choice. She continued to take pride in her husband, her children and her status in the community, but also imposed immutable rules on herself, most of them inspired by her religion. Once a year, during Lent, she adhered for six weeks to a strict diet of soup and bread and recited daily long prayers in Latin. While we all were ready to see this as a saintly sacrifice back then, I now think that it may actually have helped my grandmother to stay relatively healthy and trim to the respectable age of eighty, while most of the men around her tended to indulge in the rich Hungarian diet of fatty meats and carbohydrates which early in their lives led to pot bellies and in some cases to premature heart failure. But grandmother's devotion to what she believed was admirable, and I sometimes wonder whether her example influenced my father's medical ethics which were equally strong and exemplary. His choice of the medical profession never surprised me, since throughout his life, as I remember my father, his interests were humanistic, social, down to earth, and "horizontal." His medical but also personal ethics were directed toward improving the life of human beings.

On Sunday afternoons, my father would sometimes put me next to him on the front seat of his car and we would drive to Solymár to visit grandmother, while "anyuka," as I called my mother in Hungarian, would usually prefer to stay home. She may have resented the very strong bond that existed between my father and his "saintly" mother, who, after all, was her mother-in-law. Freud's theory of the "Oedipus complex" may have found some validity in that relationship and in some others I have observed, even if I still keep thinking that Freud's theories were so wrong in most other areas.

One visit, though, will remain forever graved in my memory. A few months after Hitler had invaded Hungary, my father told me that we were going to Solymár, which was about 20–30 miles from our house in Budaörs. We were driving in my father's DKW, when he slowly began talking to me in an unusually low and strange voice but then suddenly told me rather abruptly that we were driving to Solymár because grandmother had died. He quickly added that grandmother went straight up to heaven and was now with Jesus and all the angels. I had a hard time comprehending and imagining all the things my father said, especially grandmother being dead. When we stepped into her bedroom where she lay all wrapped in white silk and tulle on her bed that had been pulled to the center of the room, her face blue-white, rather large eyelids covering her eyes, her fingers overlapping as if in prayer holding her rosary, my father had tears rolling down his cheeks. I held my father's hand and pressed against him. His face was red, his eyes veiled and moist. He looked so sad. I had never seen my father cry before. I could never have imagined him crying. My big, strong father, for me the embodiment of strength and authority, whom all looked up to and admired, and in whose glory I frequently basked as his youngest daughter, his "Lia," "Liácska," "Lics" or "kis Évi," as he sometimes called me affectionately, this father cried, as he cried again but much, much later when I left for America with my husband and baby daughter.

When I returned to my native Hungary for the first time, during the Communist regime and several years after my father's death, I visited my family in Solymár. Seeing me as a grown woman for the first time, one of my aunts exclaimed: "She looks exactly like Miska's (my father's) first love!" whom they all thought he would marry. I felt embarrassed and confused, both for myself and my mother. I thought they were tactless, but in some way it reassured me that my father, who I knew loved me, had probably thought I was also pretty—he never told me so, nor did my mother.

My maternal grandparents in Budaörs and Budapest
My mother's blood line, according to my spotty research, seems to

have spouted vertically, infused by artistic, metaphysical, lofty, creative movements of the soul, dreaming of things beyond the daily existence, a place among the stars that possess the mystery of truth, beauty and the "je ne sais quoi" of charisma. Talented, ambitious and quite easily successful, they became doctors, scientists, mathematicians and land owners who strove toward intellectual and social recognition and enjoyed luxurious, bourgeois life styles. Idealistic and romantic, trying to avoid the ordinary, even the average because it seemed to be lacking in style, elegance and distinction, they sometimes forgot the basic equalizing imperfections of the human condition and struggled to overcome self-doubt, disappointments and shattered dreams.

I am still grateful for having known both of my mother's parents, grandfather János and grandmother Suzanne. In a document, I found two birthdates which could correspond to theirs: his, 1882, and hers, 1883. They were both born in Budaörs during the Austro-Hungarian Empire and at the time of Bismarck, the Prussian chancellor who created the first German "Reich." When I first saw a picture of Bismarck in my History book, I thought it was grandfather: the full face and especially the graying but bushy mustache twisted upward toward his ears, except that I remember grandfather smiling and often joking, not stern and militaristic looking like the "iron chancellor."

When grandfather came to visit, he usually sat in the big comfortable armchair in the living room and quickly dozed off. Almost instantaneously, a slight snoring sound would follow. He looked and sounded to me like a big, cozy kitten enjoying a snooze, but it never lasted more than a few minutes. I loved it when he rocked me on his knees and sang children's songs to me both in Hungarian and German. I still remember the "Hoppa, hoppa, Reiter, wenn er fällt, dann schreit er . . ." which I have tried on my own grandchildren. Even when the words are incomprehensible, it never fails to provoke a smile or a joyful shriek at the final verse when "der Reiter macht Blumps" (the rider falls down).

Strangely, I have no memory of my grandfather János in his own home. When I visited grandmother, she would serve me hot chocolate or milk coffee with a buttered slice of bread, and we would talk, just the two of us, in the upstairs kitchen. I thought that her chocolate tasted so much better than the one I was served at home. I still picture her in my mind as a relatively tall, trim and dark haired woman with deep blue eyes, similar to those of my "Solymárer nagymama" (as I called my father's mother who lived in Solymár). When I was about four or five, grandmother looked at my skinny dangling legs and arms and said that I must be taking after her. I did not quite understand what she meant but in my efforts to get to know myself better, her observation has stuck to my mind. I sometimes look at a picture taken of me at about that time and which our nanny managed to save from destruction during the war by keeping it with her own belongings, but I still do not find any resemblance. Her recognizing herself in me nevertheless pleased me. It provided me with a sense of closeness and belonging, of having roots, and "nagymama" seemed to enjoy the link as well. My grandfather "János" was a gregarious and generally well liked man in the community, but I never heard him compliment his wife and show her any affection. His brother studied medicine and became the private physician of the archbishop of Budapest. This great-uncle and his family had their house high on a hill outside Budapest, in the exclusive area of Kalosvár. My grandfather's strength, contrary to this learned brother, seems to have been a sort of innate intelligence and knowledge he acquired as an autodidact which he used very well to advance his business but also to counsel and help the younger men in the family to "make it." My father (his son-in-law, a medical doctor!) and uncles and cousins from my mother's family, most of whom had received a formal education and professional degrees as well, spoke very highly of Janibácsi's (uncle János's) "wisdom."

Some of my earliest and fondest memories still go back to my grandfather Jani. He owned two massive brown and white working horses, similar to those in the famous ads for Budweiser beer. In the fall, they were used to pull the wooden carriages laden with containers full of harvested grapes from the fields to the deep cellar next to my grandparents' house. In large open barrels, the grapes then were pressed to yield delicious sweet cider or left to ferment and mature into the famous Hungarian dark red wine rich in fruity aroma that accompanies well the pork, beef and veal dishes which constituted the daily staple of wealthy landowners.

In grandfather's cellar there were lots of huge wooden barrels and hundreds of glass bottles stored on shelves against the wall. Whenever my father came to visit, grandfather would get a glass tube that looked like a musical instrument, siphon wine out of a barrel, let it flow into a glass and then, with a happy, proud smile, invite my father to taste it. My father seemed to enjoy the ritual and always complimented grandfather for his exquisite wine.

The heavy iron door to my grandfather's wine cellar where frequent wine tasting and celebrations took place.

Once in a while grandfather would take me in his horse drawn carriage out to the fields where day workers tended to the vineyards. We brought them lunch that usually consisted of salami, ham, a big round loaf of what was called "peasant bread" and a few bottles of wine. The workers seemed appreciative of "nagy-papá's" (grandfather's) gesture and had big smiles and nice words for me. Sometimes I was even allowed to take the reins on our ride home. I felt on top of the world. But I also remember wondering during these outings about the families of these workers, especially, since around that time, my father created what must have been one of the first child care centers in Hungary and over dinner sometimes told us how difficult it was to get financing from the community administration and the mayor for this worthwhile humanitarian project.

Among the other family members on my mother's side I admired most was a cousin of my mother, "Lipótbácsi" (uncle Leopold), whose dream—today we would maybe call it a "hobby"—was to grow the most beautiful rose. He won a few prizes with his beauties, but the whole family admired him most for his gentle, witty nature and his quiet intelligence with which he took care of his family. Later, I found a parallel to his special devotion in Saint-Exupéry's little prince. The prince's love for a rose immediately made sense to me when someone read me the story. So did much later Voltaire's philosophical conclusion in *Candide,* that the best thing we can do as human beings is cultivate our garden.

Lipótbácsi's youngest brother was rumored to be a child prodigy. As a very little boy he used to be intensely interested in the chemical reactions that occurred in cooking and at times became a nuisance in the kitchen. I forget exactly which reactions fascinated him but the interest was genuine. He became a distinguished bio-chemist who pursued his career at prestigious research centers such as the Max Planck Institute and taught at universities all over the world. He was my mother's youngest cousin and closest to me in age. Much later, after he had become a recognized scientist, he frequently traveled to international conferences, which allowed him sometimes to spend a day or even just a few hours with my daughter and me in New York. His visits were precious, especially during our most difficult years when I felt very alone in the United States and was seriously preoccupied with our future. He gave me encouragement and cheered us up with his amazing repertoire of jokes. I felt devastated the day I received a call from my sister in Europe that on that morning he suddenly collapsed as he was getting up to go to his research laboratory and died of a massive heart attack, without any health warning. It happened in the midst of the Israeli-Lebanon war, July 29, 2006. His daughter had married an Arabic Christian working for an Israeli pharmacist in Haifa who begged him not to abandon her. The young family escaped the worst bombings by fleeing with their three children to Cairo, Egypt, but they soon returned to Haifa only to learn that grandfather had died. He and his wife had just celebrated their fiftieth wedding anniversary in the company of their four very gifted children, five grandchildren, family and friends. His heart could not take the stress of knowing his only daughter exposed to the dangers caused by this short but savage war.

There was a third brother in the same family whom I adored as a little girl. He was tall, a handsome man with a warm smile, a school teacher and talented sportsman, but he also built and carved furniture, painted beautiful pictures and, most impressive to me, could imitate the sounds of many animals, especially the songs of singing birds. When I was already three or four, he used to throw me high up into the air and catch me just before I would fall onto the ground. I now think he enjoyed my shrieks and giggles as much as I did the excitement. After the war, this uncle visited us in Germany shortly before I had to retake a school entrance exam that I had failed after we had freshly arrived in the country because I could not identify the subject and object of a German sentence. While I had quickly learned the spoken language from other children, I had completely lost out on formal schooling in any language for several years. I was convinced that my parents were terribly ashamed of my failure; I certainly was. But I was lucky to have understanding and caring parents. For a whole year, they found me a private tutor, a fellow refugee who had also escaped from Hungary, but his German was perfect, so he was able to prepare me in all academic subjects for the retake of the exams before school started next fall. I was terrified I would fail again, but my uncle told me that he was sure I would make it. That's exactly what I needed: someone like this uncle, whom I adored, to build my confidence. It was easy after that, and by the end of the school year I had not only caught up but was first in Latin, grammar and all.

The three boys had an older brother, who was drafted into the Army after Hitler invaded Hungary. He never returned home. A sister who fled Hungary as we did, before it was occupied by Soviet Russia, later married a fellow Hungarian and had a son at forty-five years of age who is practicing medicine somewhere in Europe.

Finally, the mother to these four remarkable men and their little sister had the reputation of being very beautiful and always impeccably groomed, down to the tips of her fingernails. I remember looking at her, searching for the signs of what they called her beauty. She had spotless white skin, an oval face, dark, pulled back hair that framed her smooth high forehead and violet colored eyes, but I could not help thinking that my mother was more beautiful, with her bright complexion, warm, well shaped body, blue eyes and straight nose (quite unlike mine which looked to me like a plump button and subjected me to lots of teasing by adults even though they thought it was cute). Both women, maybe because of this aura of "beauty" that surrounded them in the family discourse, commanded a certain distance that at times made me feel uncomfortable, inferior, not up to the "beauty" of these women in my family. Amazing, what impresses a child and which characteristics of certain family members have stuck to my mind.

One cousin of my mother achieved what no other woman in the family had been able to accomplish before her. After having lost her husband, a member of the Hungarian parliament in Budapest, only a year or two after they got married, embarked on a professional career as a mathematics high school teacher. She thus became the first professionally independent woman in the family. Ironically, in spite of her brilliant mind and advanced training in mathematics, she was able to exercise her profession only after having endured the tragedy of her husband's death. Becoming a widow set her free of the social stigma normally attached to a bourgeois working woman. For the next fifty years, she then devoted her life to teaching at a "gymnasium" in Budapest but also helping the more needy members of the family throughout the war and the subsequent Communist regime without ever losing her positive attitude and class. Witty, elegant, and smart, I admired her already when I was only a little girl. She soon became my role model in the family for her independence, courage and many

With some cousins and aunts who survived the war living quietly at the outskirts of Budapest.

With my beloved aunt, my life-long role model, in her apartment at Molnár utca, in the heart of Budapest.

personal and professional accomplishments. Much later in life, whenever I visited Hungary, I stayed with her in her vast, formerly patrician apartment in the "Molnár utca" (Molnár Street), which runs parallel to Váci utca, the "Fifth Avenue" of Budapest, where all the most elegant stores used to be in the pre-war era and have sprung up again after the liberation from the Communist regime in 1989. My aunt's apartment building, which bears still signs of its past glory and has preserved the leafy reliefs around the windows and the entrance door, is still riddled with bullet holes inflicted during street fights and bombings in World War II. Its winding marble stairs with black wrought-iron railings have not been repaired, nor was an elevator added, but the faded elegance of it all has always fascinated me and made me feel as if I were "home again." Whenever I was getting ready to leave after my short visits, she usually squeezed into my hands one or the other little piece of a family heirloom, such as little embroidered handkerchiefs or hand crocheted napkins that either she or her mother had made in their much younger years. At one of my last visits with her she insisted I accept what she had carefully placed in a jewelry box. It was a rather large size square cut ruby that dated back to her own grandmother. We both cried. It is now waiting in my safe deposit box until I can decide on the best and safest way to pass it on to my daughter, and hopefully to the generations after her, together with the little ring with the ruby my sister gave me as a Christmas present in 1944 when we had no Christmas. Until my aunt died at ninety-three, almost blind, and no longer able to climb the stairs to her top floor apartment, or venture down into the street for fear she might be falling, she still sent me cards or pictures of the family on which she managed to scribble a few greetings. After she had become a widow, she adopted the autistic little boy born to her brother and his wife and took care of him, teaching him as much as she could the basics of life so he could become self sufficient once she was gone and he reaches adulthood. He did manage to reciprocate her love and devotion and take care of both of them until her death.

My mixed bag

The mixture of my inheritance has thus been both a blessing and a burden. Reinforced by my upbringing, it influenced not only my early years but explains much of what happened to me later in life. The solid realism and clever business sense of my father's ancestors was offset by the more complex, individualistic, artistic nature of members in my mother's family who often distinguished themselves intellectually and artistically but could be moody, dissatisfied with themselves and depressed, characteristics that are often found in creative personalities. The world of literature, science and art seems to be populated by troubled figures. In my family, all this happened at a far lesser scale. There have been no geniuses or world famous figures except possibly my mother's youngest cousin whose work in cancer research was highly recognized and praised at the time of his death. After having moved around in the professional and business world, I now think that several others could have reached a higher level of recognition had they been coached and promoted professionally as so many, even quite mediocre people are today, especially in film, literature and so-called "creative fields." I had to come to the United

States and start working in New York before I became aware of the seemingly necessary practice of "marketing oneself." Previously, as a result of my upbringing by my parents, school, and even my nanny, Mariska, I assumed that modesty was not only a virtue but also a sign of good taste, and that it was enough to obey certain rules and do a good job to be rewarded, automatically, by one's superiors. Deep down in me, I still wish this were true and consider self-promotion somewhat morally reprehensible and in poor taste even though I occasionally had to engage in it myself to assure our survival in America, not only in my profession, but, sadly enough, even in some charitable organizations to protect what I had worked for. Too often there were wolves ready to devour or profit from other people's accomplishments.

Mariska and Nánny

I was by far the youngest in the family and benefited from the supportive, often playful attention of my older siblings and the adults around me. I had an extremely loving and caring nanny, called "Mariska," who came to my family when I was born. She was affectionate toward me, as if she were my second mother, but was also an excellent cook and baked the most delicious pastry, the famous Hungarian túrós and mákos csusza and mákos peigli to which I still feel addicted. Best of all, she knew how to keep me happy. To this day I cannot find any fault with her. Steeped in her deep religious beliefs, she made me believe that all people were basically good, whether they were rich or poor, and that ultimately the good will always be rewarded and in the end will always win over evil. When I was little, I spent much time with her and often took my meals with Mariska in the kitchen. When we fled home, she and her sister, Nánny, who had been our cleaning lady, stayed behind. Mariska was cruelly abused shortly thereafter by local Communists who were intent by all means to get to my father's money. But loving and faithful to our family, both young women rejoined us a few years later in our new home and country. When they arrived, we made sure that they take their meals sitting with us at the dinner table, not in the kitchen, even though out of the modesty they had practiced all their lives they agreed to do so reluctantly. My parents also

My sister and brother surrounding my beloved nanny Mariska holding me in her arms.

gave them time off on Sundays and paid for their yearly two-week vacations, a thing unheard of in the pre-war era. The two sisters usually spent their money on a yearly pilgrimage to Lourdes, in the South of France, organized by the local church diocese.

Mariska and Nánny stayed with us until my father retired from his official medical practice and my parents moved to a large city to be closer to my sister and their first grandchildren. Mariska had married toward the end of the war and had a son who grew up in our household next to me, but her husband, drafted into Hitler's Army and shipped to the Eastern front in Russia only days after their wedding, was soon missing in action and has never been heard of again. Mariska's son born from their short lived happiness has done quite well in life and now has his own family. Both Mariska and Nánny have outlived my parents and have enjoyed their retirement years far away from my own home. I have always considered them part of my family and shall always miss them. It was not long after my visit with them in October 2006 that Nánny passed away peacefully in her 96th year. Mariska's mind no longer controls her life.

Her big blue eyes stare into a world that she no longer understands but she is still gentle and still close to my heart.

Sheltered and alone

Those who knew me as a small child say that I was pretty, with long blond tresses usually tied back behind my ears with two white ribbons. Since I was a bit shy with people I did not know, they interpreted my timid smile and tendency to hide halfway behind my mother or my nanny as coquettish behavior. Dressed in short pretty dresses, white socks, leather sandals or black patent shoes that did not hide my lanky limbs, I was often complimented. Adults liked to talk to me, tease me and engage me in playful banter. But one day, playing in the attic with my brother, one of my older cousins ran his hands down the front of my body and briefly lifted my dress. I never told anyone about this but have not forgotten the uneasy emotion it stirred in me and that made me run down the steps and cling to my mother as if I needed her protection. Other than this incident, I do not remember any situation in which as a child I felt that I had to defend myself. No wonder I never became very good at doing so, even as an adult.

The family veranda

My early childhood universe was my family and my garden where nothing was threatening. But since I was extremely sheltered from the outside world and only seldom played with other children, I was also forced at an early age to learn how to be alone. I had many dolls and doll dresses my mother sewed for them and spent much time in my fantasy land inspired by fairy tales and my own dreams. After dinner, the whole family, including my father, would sometimes play cards and games with us. During days when the weather did not allow me to play outdoors, I filled lots of coloring books and was happy to find someone willing to read to me. I remember in particular the tales of the Brothers Grimm and of Hans Christian Anderson which I asked my mother to read to me over and over again while sitting at the large round table on the airy veranda safely and cozily cuddled in my mother's lap. It was on that veranda that

I was often happy to find my father around ten o'clock in the morning having his "second breakfast," of some slices of salami, bread and tea. As he was getting ready to make his daily house calls, his big brown leather bag filled with medical instruments and medication was sitting on the floor next to his chair. Since my father rarely left home without saying good bye to my mother with a kiss on both cheeks, I tried to be there to catch one too.

Much of our family life unfolded on that large, airy, marble laid veranda and the wide stairs that from there led down to a rose covered trellis and the garden. It was an ideal setting for family pictures. Yet, one of the first tragedies in my life also occurred there. When I was about three, my parents decided that I should get earrings "like all little girls." This, like the big white bows on my tresses, and teaching me embroidery and knitting, was part of their fashioning me into a female. My father, who was used to ear piercing, was asked to perform the operation. What a mistake that was. The puncturing procedure must have upset my father more than it actually hurt me, because I remember screaming, my mother crying, and the temporary earrings I was supposed to get flying through the air. I have no idea what the final outcome was of the mishap but I have worn earrings ever since.

A few years later, when I was about six and my sister fourteen, the veranda became the dance floor for my sister's first "house ball," a semi-formal teenage party, typical of the times and society to which we belonged. One of my sister's big friends in jacket and tie must have noticed my wide-eyed wonderment at what was happening. He grabbed me by my arms and swirled me around in a circle. It was my first experience on a dance floor with a handsome young man. I felt initiated into a mysterious new world.

Lots of questions in a little girl's mind

In those years, there were so many things I would have liked to understand about other people and myself but I also thought that grown ups had no idea how much I had already figured out by myself, just by observing them, listening to the nuances of their words, observing their glances, witnessing some harsh exchanges, hearing about their personal problems. They did not realize that in the cute little girl's body there was a mind eager to go beyond the limits they perceived as natural for her age. I did not know what my father was doing to my mother one night when I woke up to some noise and walked into their bedroom. It looked as if he were hurting her, lying on top of her, while she was moaning. But they quickly reassured me that everything was OK and that I could go back to sleep, so I stumbled like a sleepwalker back to my bed. I had no idea what I had witnessed. Words such as love, sex, sin, passion invaded my imagination at an early age but remained mysteries, romanticized by fairy tales, opera arias, folk songs even the catechism once I was exposed to it. Complicated emotions and acts, some of them forbidden, started to preoccupy me, but posed no threat.

My pets

I loved to spend my time in the garden, it was like an escape and also a refuge, but even there I was shielded from the outside by the tall stone walls which had only a few window-like openings filled with wrought-iron decorative motives that allowed glimpses onto the street. I did not on my own venture out into the street, but inside my confines I soon developed my own tastes and preferences. I felt less impressed by my mother's elaborate rose garden than by the tiny blue violets and snow-white lilies of the valley that, around the time of my birthday in March, started to pop up from underneath the leaves close to the walls and around some of the trees. I loved the little animals and insects I found in the flower beds, frogs, ants and worms, for which in my fantasy land I tried to build castles and carriages. During one hot summer, I felt sorry for the frogs and thought they might like to swim in the well. My nanny found them the next morning, bloated and dead, and the well spoiled for a long time, but nobody mentioned the disaster to me until I had become much older, knowing how devastated I would have felt about having caused the death of my beloved frogs. At about the same time, I lost another one of my pets, a big long-haired white and gray sheep dog, called Palytás (friend), whom I loved to hug, but with his exuberant movements and joyful barking he often frightened my father's patients until we finally had to give him away. He was entrusted to my grandparents who let him roam around the enclosed yard under the chestnuts trees that covered my grandfather's wine cellar. He was still alive when we left home.

Enjoying a sunny day in our garden in Budaörs with my only childhood friend Jóska.

Jóska

The only real playmate I had as a child in Hungary was Jóska. I don't remember ever playing with little girls. Jóska was the similarly privileged, similarly protected pharmacist's son. His parents were my parents' best friends. Like his father, Jóska was dark-haired and olive-skinned. He was about my height but broad-shouldered, only a year older than I, but already trying to act "macho." Because of his dark eyes, and straight dark hair, I used to tease him, telling him that he looked like a gipsy, but I liked his looks. In contrast to him, I was fair, freckled, lanky and coquettish. While he tried to walk "like a man," I typically cuddled against someone or squeezed myself into the corner of a big chair and blushed a lot. We were stereotypical opposites in gender, temperament and complexion, but developed a strong, exclusive friendship that survived our years as fugitives in several countries and lasted until I moved away to still another country. When we were little, our families strongly encouraged the friendship and kept jokingly suggesting that we were destined ultimately to get married to each other, but my playmate insisted that I first had to get rid of my freckles. Later on, my sister told me that she surprised me one day standing

At my sister's "house ball," I am the little girl in the front row.

on a chair in front of the bathroom mirror desperately rubbing my cheeks to wipe away these ominous spots from my face that could stand in the way of my ever marrying Jóska.

Privileged childhood before the war

Among the treats our parents offered us children were visits to Budapest which usually included a stop at Gerbeaud's, the famous French ice cream parlor at Vörös Marty Square in the center of town that sold delicious Italian ices. In 1991, when I visited Budapest after my mother's death, I sat for a long time at one of its outdoor coffee tables and had the chestnut ice cream that used to be my favorite. It tasted just as good as it did many years earlier and brought back sweet memories of times past, an experience that reminded me of Proust's "Madeleine." During the summer months, our parents used to take us to the famous Roman baths at the Gellért Hotel. One pool was agitated by artificial waves in which we could frolic every half hour when they were activated; another pool was very

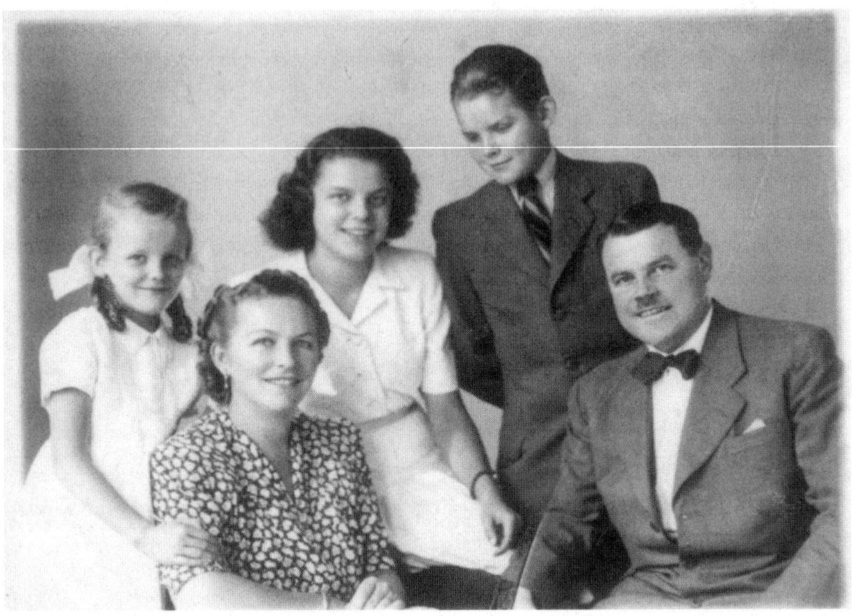

The last portrait of our beautiful, happy family in Budapest, shortly before we lost our home to WWII.

shallow, built in the form of a maze where refined gentlemen and ladies sat reading their papers and sipping a drink. Jóska and I roamed around naked, as was the custom for young children in those days. Some of the more mature readers flashed angry glances at us from above their reading glasses when we jumped around too close to them and splashed water on their papers. In 1991, I sat in that pool by myself with closed eyes remembering my young parents and our lighthearted joys with Jóska. My father had died seventeen years earlier. That happy life was gone forever.

Learning to swim in Lake Balaton

Nearly every summer, as I can remember, several of our family members with young children spent August in summer cottages on Lake Balaton. My mother and the three of us children usually stayed at an aunt's house. Since my father was the officially appointed community doctor for our region, and medical partnerships were unheard of in those days, he usually had to stay behind in Budaörs and joined us only for a few hours on Sundays after he had done his house calls and if there were no emergency cases such as imminent deliveries among his patients. We missed him but nevertheless enjoyed our vacation. During a boat outing on the lake, one of my uncles suddenly threw me into the water. He felt that it was time for me to learn how to swim. I was five. In no time, though, he jumped after me, holding me afloat, teaching me to "survive," as he put it, by simply lying rigidly on my back. The experience had no lasting trauma for me. On the contrary, I learned to swim that summer and have loved being in the water ever since.

A growing self-consciousness

In many ways, Jóska and I discovered the world together. Yet it was also early in our friendship that I became aware, in spite of all the efforts to guide me toward a "feminine" existence, that boys were not smarter than girls and that it was OK for women to work and still be beautiful and elegant. One day I bet a penny that my friend's maid would soon have a baby and, to his surprise, I won. I never felt inferior to Jóska in understanding the world around us. Due to a strange, phallic reasoning process, I felt quite equal to my boy friend in intelligence and social status maybe because I believed my mother to be more beautiful and my father to be more intelligent and more powerful than his—a seemingly typical Freudian reasoning in little girls. In fact, there was a mutual attraction between all of us, Jóska, me and our parents, across the genders. My father quite liked his mother, and his father felt apparently attracted to my mother's fair complexion and warm smile. I also admired Jóská's mother, Ilonkanéni (Aunt Ilonka), who spent most of the day working in the pharmacy but still received lots of compliments from my father. She was a stylish, shrewd business lady, who liked to direct everything at home and even in their pharmacy, while my mother, ten years younger than my father, was of a softer, more submissive nature and showed talent in arts and crafts and a quiet appreciation of literature.

The appeal of independent women

Yet, it became clear to me early in life that I was going to have a profession in life. As admired as my mother was for her beauty, her charming singing voice and her many other talents, I never envied her homebound existence. I knew when I was only about five or six years old, when there were no married women in my family who could even dream of achieving professional independence, with the exception of my aunt Mancinéni who was a widow, that feminine attraction and intellectual distinction were not incompatible. I often thought that the adults who treated me simply like a cute little thing, more like a pet, had no idea of what I was thinking and what I already knew and had observed in my short life. I remember a song I heard and immediately adopted as my own. I loved its lyrics that stated: "My thoughts are free and no one can ever take them from me . . ." No catechism lesson or religious sermon could ever change my mind about this presumably heretical rejoicing in my intellectual freedom.

The first taste of the real world

At six, I was finally released into the world of other children and entered first grade at the nearby Hungarian elementary school. For the first time in my life, I felt my "difference," the burden of a sheltered, privileged upbringing. It did not take long before I was challenged to take a fresh look at myself. I loved school and made good grades. The nuns teaching us continued the praise to which I was accustomed at home. But one of my classmates, the local mayor's daughter, who sat in the first row as I did, soon took exception with both my performance and my looks. One day, after my father had completed his medical inspection of the school, listening to our lungs and hearts, checking our teeth, telling the class to wash hands before every meal, the little girl told me that I got good grades only because I was the "little daughter of the doctor," "a doctor úrnak a kislánya," and that I was really a "büdös Schwáb," a dirty Schwabian," an ethnic slur she might have heard at home. Her parents belonged to a different ethnic group and may have envied my father's financial success and popularity in the community. I was distraught, but did not know how to respond. I hurt but also started to examine my personal worth and intelligence. At the same time, I developed a strong need to prove my worth to myself and to others. When I asked my parents why my classmate would have said those ugly words, I was told not to worry about it. The girl, who wore glasses and was invariably dressed in drab, long dresses and aprons, was probably envious of me and our life. The event remained without further consequence at that time, but it was the first really nasty thing anyone had ever said to me, and I still remember how it felt.

Similar incidents occurred throughout my life. Some people, especially in the U.S., seem to have a chemical reaction against tall blonds who are not dumb. One of my first colleagues loved to tell "dumb blond jokes" in my presence. They were obviously aimed at hurting me and airing some of her resentments against me because of my Arian looks. Years later, another colleague insinuated that my professional success was due to my looks, in particular my height, blond hair and "blue" eyes. Both women were short, dark and, I thought, quite attractive but also insecure and probably jealous, but I did not confront them. Little did they know how much I actually admired dark haired, dark eyed individuals.

2
World War II

The end of Paradise

The idyllic, protected childhood I had shared with Jóska in Budaörs quite abruptly came to an end. The summer and fall following my first year at school brought much turmoil to our lives. I noticed that my father and other adults in the family usually stayed up late to listen to a mysterious, forbidden broadcast on "Radio Free Europe." I remember them being upset about the easy way Hitler had conquered Hungary. "He simply ran over the country with his tanks," I heard them say, "shameless women even threw flowers on his path," said my father. Once in a while, they pitied us children because we were increasingly deprived of some of the goodies typical of their own childhood, such as the nut- or poppy-seed filled "kifli," a kind of croissant very popular in pre-war Hungary.

Nazis in our house

Not long after Hitler's invasion of the country, German soldiers appeared at our door and told us that parts of our house had to be turned over to the occupying military forces. Two officers soon moved into our "salon," where my mother used to welcome guests, and the dining room in which stood our baby grand piano on which I loved to play the children's songs "Boci, boci tarka . . ." and "Szeretnék szántani . . ." that my mother and sister had taught me when I was barely five years old. One of the German soldiers was a pediatrician, and as a fellow physician he tried not to be offensive to my father. He was generally respectful toward everyone in the family, but my father became suspicious when he noticed some of the glances the officer threw at my teenage sister.

As it turned out, my parents soon had to credit that same Nazi officer with quite possibly having saved our lives. Arriving back at the house in midday and looking quite concerned, he warned my parents that the Russians were rapidly approaching and that there likely would be heavy bombing and fierce battle between Germans and Russians in our area because we lived only a few miles away from the center of Budapest and very close to the airport. "If you want to save your family, grab them and leave immediately," he urged my father. My father, surprisingly, accepted his advice and acted quickly.

The last minutes at home

That same evening, while the soldiers were away, my father and grandfather dug a big hole under the apricot tree that shaded our veranda and buried the beautiful old silver cutlery, jewelry, some precious porcelain figures and even some cash in that hole, trampling the earth on top of it, covering it with leaves and snow to mask the freshly dug spot, believing that they could thus save the precious family heirloom from looters until we returned. "Wake up the children," I heard my father call upstairs to my mother, "and dress them warmly. The little one (meaning me) can take one doll, nothing else." Nobody would know this until months later, but after clutching a doll, not even my favorite one, under my arm, I quickly ran to the kitchen and grabbed the six little mocha spoons my mother used when she entertained her friends in the bright sitting alcove of our living room and stuck them deep into my coat pockets. For whatever strange sentimental reason, I just could not leave them behind that night and have kept them to this day. Maybe I felt the finality of the departure and tried to preserve a bit of the world I was about to lose.

Into the cold night—but where to?

Around midnight, December 8, 1944, it was freezing cold and snowing, when all five of us, dressed in heavy winter coats, crammed into my father's old DKW, which used to be his pride and joy, and just drove away, leaving behind my grandparents, our home and all our belongings. My brother and sister had squeezed onto the back seats among bags of food, a few bottles of wine, water, and blankets, while my mother held me in her lap on the front passenger seat and guarded underneath her legs a big bag stuffed full of paper money. My father did not use banks in those days and kept his money quite openly in a closet. I remember trembling and being scared of what might happen next as we reached the large road driving toward a vague destination, which my father simply described as "in direction of the border." We drove, not knowing whereto, believing that we would soon return after all the horror of this war was over.

A few hours into the drive, I must have fallen asleep but suddenly woke up as our car came to an abrupt stop. It was dark outside but I saw heavy smoke pore out from underneath the hood. The car had obviously overheated and threatened to catch fire. My father rushed to empty one of the wine bottles and ran to fetch some water from a road side pond he had noticed as we were driving by. He then poured the water somewhere under the hood. After the second attempt, the motor cooled and we were able to resume our journey and did not stop again all night until we ran out of gas the next morning. At that stop my parents told us to hide behind some bushes to relieve ourselves. Terribly embarrassed having to do that in the open, on snow covered grounds, we rushed back to the car the minute we were done.

Later that morning, we made it to the small Austro-Hungarian border city of Sopron where a man my father met in the street let us have the large basement room of his house and said we could stay there for a couple of weeks if necessary. But life continued to be a nightmare. Just days after we arrived, we received news from back home that my grandfather had been beaten to death by local Communists the day after we left. They had ransacked our house and could not find what they were looking for so they beat him because he could not tell them where my father was and where he had hidden his money.

No-Christmas 1944

It was shortly before Christmas. Completely exhausted both physically and emotionally, my mother suffered a stroke and slipped into a deep depression or coma (I never knew for sure what it was) for several days. I was bewildered. Even though all five of us shared one room, I felt very much alone. My brother and sister were seven and eight years older and tried to spare me their worries and grief. They hardly talked. I was left to make sense of it all for myself with the limited knowledge I had from books, religion and former experiences. I remembered thinking of the time when I was only about three–four years old and my mother was taken to a hospital for an operation that resulted in her losing her beautiful singing voice. In the course of that operation, the surgeon had inadvertently damaged her vocal cords, so that she could not talk for several months, and had completely lost her warm soprano voice. She never again sang the "Ave Maria" she had occasionally sung at special occasions at church or at a friends' wedding. The experience and the consequences of my mother's first "absence" had been devastating for me and added to my present fears. Years back, during her hospitalization, my nanny Mariska and my grandparents were at least there to reassure me that it had nothing to do with me. I had feared that she had left because I had misbehaved. This time, I felt alone. Everything was upsetting and unknown. My father had lost a lot of weight and became extremely tense. He did not want any questions and could not tolerate any noise. I was terrified that I had contributed to my mother's condition with my constant fears and frequent crying, but my sister tried to reassure and comfort me. During those weeks, my older sister was the most important person in my life, the only link between the past and this frightening present.

Finally, it was Christmas Eve, when we usually celebrated the birth of "little Jesus" and also received presents "he left" for us children. But this Christmas there was not even a Christmas tree and obviously no presents for any of us, so my sister pulled off a ring she wore on her left ring finger and gave it to me. It was a simple gold band adorned by a small round ruby set in a narrow gold leaf frame. I still have the ring and to this day, overly sentimental as this may seem to some who might read my story, the ruby has remained my favorite stone, even in its cheaper version, the garnet.

A special patient

During the weeks in Sopron, my father occasionally was called to help some sick person in the nearby area who had learned of his presence in town. One day, he was rushed to the monastery that was run by a very strict religious order; I think they called themselves Benedictines or Cistercians. My father was not allowed into the room of the dying nun. Instead, they had brought her out to him into the reception area on a wooden stretcher, without blankets or pillows, while she was barely clinging to her life having contracted a severe pneumonia. There was no heat in the entire monastery, and antibiotics were not yet available to the general population even though penicillin had already been developed. My father could prescribe only conventional medication but had little hope that the poor nun would survive in the given conditions.

Chain bombs

In January, our pharmacist friends from back home joined us in Sopron, the border town where we had sought refuge. We all hoped that the war would be over soon and that we could then all return home together. But there seemed to be no end to the raging war around us and the horrifying experiences we had to endure. British forces engaged in bombardments of our area nearly every evening. One night, my father stood in front of the basement door, watching the chain bombs rushing over his head with a thunderous noise, lighting up the sky as they hit the ground only a few hundred yards from where we had sought shelter. Inside the basement, our eyes fixed on my father, begging him to come inside, my mother clutched me tight in her arms, while my brother and sister huddled against her on the floor. My mother prayed with us. I was afraid but did not realize at that time that the bombs could have hit us any minute; how close we came to dying. On this Austro-Hungarian border, we were attacked from all sides, by all nations involved in this terrible war. Several came close to killing us. I didn't really understand who and why they would all want to kill us, so I just prayed for the end of war, for victory over war itself.

Apocalypse

After the bombing stopped that night, my parents immediately decided to move on as soon as possible the next morning, maybe to a small mountain village in Austria where they thought it would be easier to find a safe heaven for our family and escape the constant danger to our lives. When morning came, we were all exhausted from what had happened the night before. My parents were preparing to leave, but since Jóská's parents had decided to stay and see whether the fighting would stop and they could possibly return home to their pharmacy, Jóska and I used the last minutes we had together to run over to a nearby forest where we had noticed some activity close to a huge, old barn. A few yards away from that barn, we were suddenly confronted by some emaciated figures, wrapped in blankets, staggering out of the forest, from behind the trees. They wore no shoes, just pieces of cloths tied around their feet on a day of bitter cold and snow in the middle of winter. Some of them turned toward us. Long, pale, bony faces, large hollow eyes staring at us, like skeletons. Some soldiers in uniforms seemed to chase them. One of them hit the figure closest to us on the head with his rifle. I think it was a man. He stumbled and fell to the ground but the soldier immediately started kicking him with his boots, yelling "büdös Zsidó" ("dirty Jew" in Hungarian) and other things we could not make out. For a minute we just stood there frozen, baffled, horrified, as if we had just seen scenes from another world, a world of absolute evil and suffering. It was not the hell we knew from descriptions in the bible, where all would be burning while devils would be dancing around poking people with their forks. These were real-life soldiers, speaking Hungarian, who seemed to hit and torture frightened, death-like creatures, who looked like figures from Dürer's paintings about the apocalypse that I had seen in one of our books. Was this the end of the world? One of the soldiers promptly came over to chase us away. "Go home to your parents," he yelled. "What are you doing here? It's forbidden. Go! Quick!" As we ran across the fields as rapidly as our feet would take us, more frightened than we had ever been, we heard shots that rang out from the forest but did not turn around to look back.

Aphasia

When we reached our parents, they were already saying good bye, kissing and hugging each other. My mother put her arms around me and asked why I was shaking, but I could not respond. I did not know myself what it was that we had just witnessed. Breathless, unable to say a word for a long time, I just fell silent. My parents thought that it was the aftermath of the bombings we had experienced the night before or the impending separation from my best friend, Jóska, whom once again I had to leave behind. It took me a few hours, once I felt sure to have escaped the danger and the horrifying vision, and once my parents were able to cope with the new problems that arose at our departure, before I could describe to my family what we had seen.

Hitler, Jews, Aunt Livia

It was then that my father tried to explain what he thought we had run into: it must have been a concentration camp where Jewish prisoners were driven to work in the forest. He told us that some people in Europe were called Jews and that Hitler for some strange personal reasons hated Jews, and blamed them for the evils in society; that Hitler wanted to get rid of Jews in Europe and force them to live in a separate country. Later on, my father also told us that his best friend and his beautiful wife, Livia, whose name I had been given at birth, had both vanished without a trace shortly before we left home. She was Jewish and had disappeared with her husband. To this day, we have not heard from them again, but I passed on her name to my daughter and in the next generation it became the middle name of my oldest granddaughter. I dreamt that some day I would suddenly come upon them in the United States or Canada. Just recently, at a Paris exhibit commemorating the Holocaust, I found a book about the war whose author, a survivor of Auschwitz, bore our name, "Livia," but I did not get an answer to the letter I sent to the publisher, and the college in the United States where the author had been employed had no information about her whereabouts. She apparently was disliked at that place by both her colleagues and her students for what they said was her arrogance and capricious behavior. I am convinced that it was not my aunt Livia, who was much admired and loved in the family for her refined elegance and kindness, but this Livia may have encountered my aunt in a concentration camp or in Auschwitz, if that is indeed where she and her husband were deported and possibly died.

The end of innocence

My experience near that ghostly forest in Sopron has remained a recurring nightmare in my life. It still feels, as if on that apocalyptic morning, I had lost the innocence of my childhood. For the first time in my life I had seen evil.

Exodus

On that freezing, terrible January morning, when we tried to escape from Sopron, we soon discovered that all gas stations were empty. In his desperation to move us away from danger, my father managed to buy two long-horned oxen and, with the help of the farmer, tie them in front of our car. For a couple of days, they slowly pulled us along the caravan of refugees that by then had formed on the roads. As we passed Vienna, the whole city seemed to be in flames. It looked like a real life picture of the inferno.

To lighten the load in our car, my parents bought a bicycle for my teenage sister who was to ride alongside us, but the next day we somehow became separated from her and had to endure endless desperate hours until some one traveling in the opposite direction told us that he had seen a young girl sitting on the roadside next to her bicycle sobbing. My father managed to stop a motorcycle and asked him to let my sister know that we were behind her and would try to reach her as soon as we could.

Not long after this frightening incident, we were running out of food for both the oxen and ourselves and had to abandon our car and animals to seek refuge for the night in a camp. To our horror, the first gesture of the personnel was to "entlouse" us, pulling away our clothes and spraying a white powder down the front and back of our bodies. I heard my mother cry as we tried to fall asleep on the cots we were assigned in a large school gymnasium where they let us stay for the night to rest and to escape the bitter cold outside.

Like cattle

The next day we were all hoarded into some dark brown, dirty looking cattle wagons lain with straw that must have been used to transport animals or merchandise. Once we were all inside and the large doors slammed shut, the train started to ramble along noisily, and we were left only with a few window slots near the top of the wagon to provide us with air and some light. People got sick and needed to relieve themselves, but the train did not stop for hours. There was hardly any room to sit down, and it started to smell like in a latrine. Someone sitting in the dark encouraged us children to sing hoping it would stop the constant screaming in the wagon but nobody had the heart to do so.

A sign of humanity

After two days stuffed with many other refugees in this smelling, rattling train that stopped only a couple of times a day to give us some bread and milk for the children and allow us to relieve ourselves in the nearby bushes but not long enough to clean out the human waste that had accumulated in the train, we finally arrived at a station where we were allocated our next quarters. Luckily, our family was sent to a small village, Maishofen, near the town of Zell am See, in Austria. It was situated in a wide plain, surrounded by hills and snow covered mountains and near a picturesque lake. I thought it was quite nice and romantic, but my mother soon felt claustrophobic due to the many unusually tall mountains that surrounded the village, so unlike the plains of Hungary. Even though all five of us were given just one room in the only hotel there was in the village, the owners immediately took us into their hearts and helped us as much as they could. I had grown rapidly since we left home, "like starved weed," as someone said jokingly, and could no longer fit into my shoes and coat. I will probably never forget the day soon after our arrival when the owner brought me a warm pair of winter boots, "Stiefel," as she called them, and draped one of her large ponchos made of thick green loden wool over my shoulders. They kept me warm throughout the freezing winter months.

Food and shelter

With the help of the village priest, the owner also informed the community of the presence of a doctor in their midst. There were no physicians in town since all had been drafted into Hitler's Army. Soon town's people and nearby farmers came to call on my father, sometimes picking him up in their horse drawn carriages, so he could assist in delivering a baby or relieve someone else's suffering, even pulling teeth in a few cases. Fortunately, he had brought with him the big brown leather bag with medical instruments that back home he used to take along on his house calls. Returning from his visits, my father usually brought back some eggs, a piece of ham, milk, or butter, whatever his patients could spare to express their gratitude. By then, the big bag of money we had brought from home had lost all its value, and my parents were happy whenever they could offer us a real healthy meal instead of the daily ration of boiled potatoes or some form of pasta.

Spring came late in the mountainous area where we found refuge, but once the snow had melted, we were able to go out on the fields that had been harvested in the fall and find left over potatoes, beets, or corn. Some apples and pears had survived under the trees and in the ditches lining the roads. We used certain green leaves that started to grow for soups and salads. A few weeks later, we were able to pick blueberries and wild raspberries on the surrounding hills and once in a while, to our delight, we even found a patch of Edelweiss which was said to be a sign of good luck. Slowly, our humanity returned. My father also told us that Hitler seems to be losing the battle.

The end of the war!?

Soon after we heard the encouraging news, a German officer and his family moved into the hotel room next to ours. According to my father's assessment of his uniform, he was a high ranking officer. My father thought that he probably wanted to find a quiet refuge for his family. I was actually quite happy to see his two little girls who were about my age. We quietly smiled when we crossed each other in the hallway. I still felt uncomfortable speaking German. Then, on May 8, 1945, as we rejoiced at the certainty that the war was finally over, we heard from neighbors that the father had taken the family for a walk high up on one of the mountains. After a picnic, he shot them dead, his wife first and then the two little girls before pulling the trigger on himself. When the hotel management heard the news, they opened the room and found all kinds of food, the kind we had only dreamed of for weeks. There were also some pancakes left on the table which the hotel keeper offered to me. Not knowing where they came from when he gave them to me, I ate some and gave the rest to my brother. Only later was I told that the two little girls who had stayed in that room were dead. "Maybe it was the best thing for them," my father said to comfort me. "Who knows what would have happened to them after Hitler's defeat." Thinking back, I still feel a pinch in my stomach, not just because I ate the pancakes but at the thought that the father of these nice-looking little girls, with whom I would have liked to play, was a Nazi.

The American victors

The same morning of May 8, 1945, tanks appeared on the road and then stopped in front of our hotel. People shouted, "The Americans are here! The war is over." There were rumors about Hitler having committed suicide. Nobody spoke of "victory." It would not have meant much to us children. All we wanted is to go home and no longer fear for our lives. When I saw some children dare approach the American tanks, I followed them timidly. One of the soldiers was black, and I had never seen a black person. I remember looking at him for a while. He smiled and threw us candy which we children joyfully picked up. I saved some for my brother and sister. We were also watching the soldiers having breakfast sitting on top of their tanks: fried eggs, toast and orange juice. One of them tossed his whole plate over a fence. I felt like screaming "no," but we children just stared at them incredulously. I could maybe have salvaged the tray, and eaten the delicious looking eggs, but was too ashamed and afraid to do so. The soldiers had no idea how we felt about their throwing food away while we were hungry most of the time. It was cruel; "a sin," I thought.

My brother later joined me downstairs to look at the soldiers and the tanks, but my sister, who then was a young teenager, would not leave the room for days, until the soldiers and their tanks had moved on. There had been rumors of rapes, even gang rapes and she was extremely afraid. We had heard that back home my sweet nanny, Mariska, a pretty, deeply religious young woman, had been brutally raped by local Communists. It has now been documented (J. Robert Lilly, *La Face cachée des gi's: Les viols commis par des soldats américains en France, en Angleterre et en Allemagne pendant la Seconde Guerre mondiale,* Payot, May 1, 2003) that in the conquered, so-called liberated countries, allied soldiers engaged in victory celebrations, which involved heavy drinking, and then went out to search for women to rape. In Germany, they considered women their bait, to which victory entitled them. Sometimes they shot the fathers and husbands who tried to prevent them from taking their women. They even abused mothers in front of their children. Thousands of such horrors happened immediately following the end of the war, even though commanding officers did not want to tolerate them. Under Eisenhower's command, lots of soldiers were court marshaled, hanged or shot, while their families back home thought they had died fighting as heroes in the line of duty.

News about these atrocities toward women, though, was not made public in the United States until more than half a century later when the government in Washington finally released the files. The Allies did not want to overshadow their victory and their greatest accomplishment, which was the opening of the concentrations camps and liberation of those who had managed to survive the Holocaust. I, as an eight-year-old child, my brother and sister, and even my parents, were hardly aware of all the atrocities that had occurred other than from rumors and the ones we had experienced ourselves. Later I read in Elie Wiesel's *Night* (Hill & Wang, 1960): "People (even Jewish people) refused not only to believe his (Moshe the Beadle) stories, but even to listen to them," (p.4). In the Spring of 1944, Wiesel writes, "it was still possible to obtain emigration permits for Palestine," (p.6) but "the older people wanted to stay." "Optimism soon revived," (p7), he writes, "the atmosphere was peaceful and reassuring," (p. 9). People could not imagine, until it was often too late, that such horrors as the Holocaust could exist. They were unthinkable, even to Jewish people. It took months and years until we all learned what had really happened, reports George Konrad, who survived the Holocaust in Budapest while waiting for his parents to return from deportation. He confirms in his recent book *A Stranger in My Own Country* the lack of information about the Nazi horrors in his own part of Hungary, Transylvania. It is amazing to me how he and his parents did survive and finally return to their country.

$$3$$

Exile

There was no way to go back home again.

World War II was officially over, but, painfully, there was no question in my parents' mind of returning home to Hungary as long as it was under a Communist regime. As liberal as my father was in many respects, devoted to his patients, concerned about the health of children and selflessly caring for the poor in the community, he was also steadfast in his opposition to all totalitarian regimes even when they promised more social justice. In my father's mind, Communism and Nazism were among the greatest foes of mankind because they denied freedom to the individual and threatened to enslave entire nations as was the case in Stalinist Russia and in Hitler's Third Reich. The local Communists "back home," most of them quite uneducated, poor and living at the lower echelon of society, were hoping for a takeover of Hungary by the Red Army and swore that my father would be among the first ones to hang after the victory because he was wealthy and lived in a big house in the center of town. Just as he was opposed to Communism and feared that Hungary may fall prey to the fast approaching Red Army, as it had only about a year earlier to Hitler's tanks, my father's humanistic idealism clashed with both ideologies. I was told after the war, that my father was much appreciated in the community as a very capable and dedicated physician but he was also recognized for his social and charitable activities. His enemies were a handful of local Communists, most of them lazy and given to alcohol, who resented and envied this young doctor's success in the community and more than anything else wanted to get to his money and possessions. As soon as we had left home, leaving everything behind, these local Communists, we were told, beat my grandfather who died soon thereafter. They broke into our house to loot and to party, destroyed our piano and ransacked most of the furniture. Some neighbors later told us that they led a horse into our living room—I still don't know how it made it up the stairs. Worst of all, they raped my beloved young and beautiful nanny who had stayed behind.

Our home, lost forever

Once the Communist administration had seized power in the community, our house was given to a Communist doctor and his gypsy wife. They have been living there, as far as we know, to this day. When my sister and I dared to make two separate visits back home to Hungary during the Cold War, in the 1970s, the house was completely run down, there was hardly any paint left and stones had been pulled out of the walls, the two once beautiful wrought iron gates, one small one leading to the main house and the large one opening to the garage, were rusty and damaged. Tall grass was wuthering where once there were my mother's well tended flower beds. The trellis, that used to be covered with roses, was gone. During one of my first visits "home," the gypsy lady spotted me in the street staring at the house and asked who I was. To my great surprise she then invited me into our former living room where I recognized one of our old paintings on the wall. "They must have liked it, "I thought," therefore it survived," but I also felt a weight filling my chest that made it increasingly difficult for me to breathe. I quickly I thanked the woman after only a few minutes and rushed out into the street, sobbing in the bus all the way back to my aunt Mancinéni's apartment in Budapest where I stayed for a few days.

After the fall of the Soviet regime, I returned to Budaörs and again stared at our house from the street but did not see anyone inside. I even had dreams at that time of getting the house back and fixing it up to its former beauty, but my family dissuaded me fearing that I would have to tear it down almost completely and ultimately may be disappointed living there with all my sad memories and amongst people most of whom I did not know. While most of my father's family still lives in Solymár, my mother's family in Budaörs had left soon after the take over by the Soviet regime to move to the center of Budapest or cross the borders and are now spread out over several countries and even continents. I still exchange year-end greetings with a few cousins who are living in Sidney, Australia, Exeter, U.K., and Strasbourg, France. They were university students when they fled Hungary risking their lives during the 1956 uprising in order to escape from the country. They managed to complete their medical training abroad, marrying women of their host countries and settling down with their new families in diverse places of the world. My sister married a fellow medical student of Heidelberg, continued living and practicing medicine in Germany, and was thus able to be near my parents, taking care of them until they died. I envied her for being able to do so while my daughter and I were the only members of our family to have ended up living and working in the United States.

My mother's cousin, a noted bio-chemist in cancer research, with his wife in Strasbourg, France. On his frequent trips to conferences in the U.S., he paid brief visits to my daughter and me that made us feel less alone in this big country far away from the rest of the family. He also cheered us up with his endless repertoire of jokes.

Another cousin of my mother who escaped from Hungary in 1956, became a child endocrinologist in London, U.K., and finally settled with his family in Sidney, Austra-lia. His occasional stopovers in New York—sometimes only for a few hours at airports—helped maintain the family tie lost with many other members of the family.

Life in exile

As I was growing up, and especially after leaving my family to study and live in France, it continued to disturb me that my father, after all these difficult years during and after Hitler's terrible war, should have decided to accept the offer to run a hospital in Germany and later settle into his own medical praxis there instead of attempting a return back home to Hungary. For the rest of their lives, my parents chose to live in exile. Neither of them ever set foot in Hungary again but whenever "home," "otthon," or "zu Hause" was mentioned in the family discourse, it referred only to one place, our home in Hungary. My father's life in Germany consisted essentially of work, caring for his patients and his family, usually in that order. I don't remember his taking a vacation or ever again having a close friend as he did in Hungary. In taste, emotions and temperament, my father remained forever a Hungarian. After 1989, when Hungary was liberated, it was too late for both of my parents. My father had died and my mother was dying. "What a waste of lives and families," I thought when it was finally all over. But wars were still raging in other parts of the world, Africa, and soon also in the Golf, then in Iraq, and as I am writing today, in Lebanon, where innocent people, many of them children, are killed by Israelis, supported and financed by American money. How could I see the humanistic superiority of one nation over another?!

Today, looking back at my parents' lives, I feel more reconciled with my father's decision and believe to have understood his reasoning. After World War II, there was devastation all over Europe, but particularly in Germany where there was hardly a house or building that had not suffered from bombs or gunshots. There was hardly a family that had not lost someone to the war, the population was needy and suffering in many ways, and there was also an extreme shortage of doctors, many of them having been drafted into Hitler's Army, were killed in the war or sent to prison camps and never returned to their families.

In some ways we were fortunate. In World War I, when my father was eighteen years old, he had been drafted into the Austro-Hungarian Army and sent to fight against the Italians close to the Piave River. As he climbed out of a trench one day, he was shot through his chest, a bullet entered his body close to his left shoulder and exited in the back, but he survived. This time, in World War II, no longer a young man and also the only physician left in a wide district at the outskirts of Budapest, he was able to escape the draft. When the war ended in 1945, my father was in his late forties. He had lost everything he had worked for or both of my parents had inherited, but was not ready to return to a Communist state whose ideology clashed with his own. My parents's dearest wish at that time was to find a place where we could reestablish some normalcy and peace in our lives, where my father would feel needed, was likely to be appreciated, would be able to make a living and provide us children with a decent education. A few family members and friends from Hungary had emigrated to England and even Canada. My parents, who knew German but no English and only a little French, accepted the first best offer that had come their way, the one that was also closest to "back home."

It takes a family

After we arrived at the hospital in Wertheim am Main, which was essentially a refugee hospital, our family was given separate physician's quarters near the main building. It was a small gray house, full of bullet holes from the war, but with large windows and a garden. For many years, we lived a very frugal life while my father worked hard to find the means to care for his patients and also provide for his family. He talked to us frequently at great length, reminding us of what really mattered in life. "As you have seen," he would say, referring to our recent experiences and his own example, "education and skills are the only treasures you can take with you wherever you go, something nobody can take away from you, and you never know which of your skills or what knowledge would allow you or someone you love to survive." I thought of his words often when, as a student in Paris and later, alone with my daughter in a foreign country, living near the poverty line, I had to accept a variety of jobs just to make a living. In the first years after the war, while busy at the hospital all day, my father tried to have dinner with us as often as he could. We played cards and social games together in the evening, and always had animated discussions about lots of things, special occurrences in my father's medical practice, our lives at school, the German people, and always, still, about "back home in Hungary." My father truly enjoyed his family and we all cherished these moments of togetherness. It created a strong bond among us in the foreign country in which we tried to settle, even though, in typical teenage fashion, I soon began to resent what I felt was my father's excessive domineering and paternalistic attitude. The resentment passed as I grew older, and during my many years struggling to make a living in the United States for my daughter and myself, alone and often lonely in a far away, foreign country, I deeply missed our family gatherings, especially those that later attracted other family members who had also fled Hungary and joined us abroad. Our moments of togetherness had given me a sense of belonging and even pride to be an offspring of this bunch of people. Later, as a mother, I would have liked my daughter to experience and emotionally benefit from such wonderful family gatherings.

Settling into a new life

In the years after the war, when my family first arrived in Germany, we had to struggle to fit in, to make it among the Germans, to create and feel at home. We were lucky to have had each other, which I again remembered later when my daughter and I had only each other to depend on for support and company. I tried to be cheerful and positive, as my father had been toward us. For as long as I can remember, my sister aspired to study medicine, so when we arrived in Germany she soon had to pass her exams to get ready for university. My father was there to encourage her. My brother's learning disability prevented him from ever mastering German and allow him to pursue academic studies. He was hoping to learn a trade, so my parents introduced him to several possibilities but they were all disappointing. He simply did not fit into any of the available opportunities and, in spite of a phenomenal memory, stumbling on a linguistic predicament, became discouraged and finally withdrew into a religious order. I often felt guilty of not having been able to help him and always thought that in our family, he was the saddest victim of the war. I had not attended school for more than two years after my first elementary class in Hungary, but had quickly learned to communicate in German during our months in Austria. I lacked any formal training in grammar and mathematics and, to my shame, failed the entrance exam to what should have been my first level at the "gymnasium," the German high school, but I was able to catch up. My parents provided me with a tutor for a whole year who drilled me in all the academic subjects. At the same time, I found time for piano lessons on our newly acquired but really old, upright piano, improved my swimming and began to play tennis. In the fall, I was ready to join my grade and even pulled first in Latin at the end of the school year. To my delight, my piano teacher allowed me to participate in the yearly recital he organized for his students in a pretty castle and told my parents that I showed much promise and should be encouraged to pursue my lessons. At school, my teachers and classmates for a while still made fun of my accent and enjoyed my distorted pronunciation of certain words, for instance, the priest who taught us the catechism just loved to hear me mispronounce the word "Engel" (angel) by splitting it wrongly into two very distinct syllables, "En-gel." Their bemusement hurt me deep inside, but I did not let them know because I knew that they did not mean to be rude to me intentionally.

Boys

I felt comfortable with my new classmates and had noticed with some secret satisfaction that the boys in my class did not object to me either. As we grew, and in those years I shot up to almost my adult size and towered over many of the boys in class, I never lost my popularity with them. On our field trips, they frequently wanted to have their picture taken with me. One day, after some of us went on a daring swim in the river Main hanging on to a traveling barge, one older boy, after we returned to shore and I stretched out to rest in the grass, leaned over me and tried to kiss me but succeeded only in giving me a buzz on a cheek. Later that year, he wrote me poems, sent me post cards depicting sculptures of beautiful women or photographs of movie actresses whom he likened to me. I usually blushed and enjoyed his flattery but remained distant in my feelings for him.

Another move, another school, nagymamá's death

After a few years as director of the hospital, my father wanted to move away from the somewhat depressing environment and the difficult and frustrating administrative position he had accepted because it was nearly impossible to get funding and medication to care adequately for his patients. He longed to return to a solo praxis which he had enjoyed in Hungary, where he had the freedom to devote himself entirely to his patients without state interference and useless paper work. His other dream was to build us a new house with a large garden.

My grandmother from Budaörs had recently joined us from Hungary where she felt very lonely after my grandfather had been beaten to death by the local Communists. We were delighted to have her with us, but soon after her arrival, in the midst of our move to our new environment and hopefully our own new house, she was diagnosed with ovarian cancer.

Since school started in September, the pharmacist in the new town, whose daughter was to be in the same grade as I, accepted to take me into their family until my parents could follow a few weeks later. My grandmother was also moved to the hospital in the same town since her condition quickly deteriorated but it meant that my mother could not be there to care for her mother every day. My parents usually came for a visit on Sundays. I was the only one to be able to visit grandmother regularly and, as it happened, was the last one to see her alive. A day or two before she died, I went to her room at the hospital but could hardly recognize her. She had shrunk to a mere skeleton, appeared heavily sedated, still moving slightly but did not seem to recognize me. Seeing her in that state terrified me. This was not my grandmother. It was like death looking at me. She reminded me of the skeletal figures I had seen near the forest in Sopron during our flight from Hungary. I was alone with her in the dimly lit room and the sight of what was left of her was nearly unbearable. I stayed a few minutes and tried to speak to her but she did not respond, so I just ran out of the hospital into the street and the sunshine where I was able to regain my composure. How insensitive I was, I told myself soon afterwards and was wondering whether she had recognized me, but I think she was too far gone to have even noticed that anyone was there next to her in the room. I was ashamed and guilt ridden but could not decide to go back into her room. I had loved "nagymama." How could I have abandoned her like that in her last minutes? I did not know much about cancer. Did she get sick because we had not been good to her, had left her behind in Hungary? I should have shown her more affection after she arrived from Hungary and during the last weeks at the hospital! Did she want to die? When I saw her last, her watery blue eyes just stared at me. Her mind had drowned. There would be no more answers.

Settling into still another "home," making new friends

It was difficult to be alone, without my parents, after grandmother died. My hosts were nice to me but there was frequent tension between the parents and their daughter whom they constantly criticized at meal times because she was slightly chubby and enjoyed food, especially whipped cream. I had reached my adult size and was rather trim since I played tennis and swam quite regularly. I felt embarrassed and sorry for my friend who later developed an eating disorder and has suffered from poor health ever since. Fortunately, my parents arrived a few weeks later, so I could be back with my family and concentrate on my school work. I was also anxious to make friends with my new classmates.

To my surprise, I quite rapidly became a popular student and a year or two later was even voted class representative. Still remembering the nasty comment of the mayor's daughter in elementary school, I first thought that my classmates voted for me for some ulterior reason, maybe they felt sorry for my having lost my home, country, and now also my grandmother, or that I just "looked right for the job," but they assured me that they really thought that I would be the right person because I was "nice and smart." I felt relieved that my classmates did not favor me because I was the daughter of the medical doctor. Such doubts and insecurities about my qualifications continued to surface occasionally in the years to follow, but then I just tried to live up to people's higher expectations of me. It often worked. At other times, when I noticed that someone simply tried to be nasty to me, for no apparent reason, because I was blond or the daughter or wife of a doctor, or something else they resented, I often just walked away. I still do. When I feel that people just do not like me for some obscure, seemingly subconscious, chemical response in their own disposition, I do not fight, just try to move on to a better place. More often than not I was lucky enough to do so.

Polio

Soon after our move to our new location, I had to cope with still another quite unexpected tragedy in my life. I had signed up for a Red Cross swimming course because I wanted to become a strong swimmer and also learn how to save someone if necessary. Since I was the youngest girl of the group to pass a rather tough test, my picture appeared in the local paper. It was a flattering surprise but I could enjoy it only for a week when I suddenly became paralyzed on the entire right side of my body, from my vocal cords to my leg. Since it was not immediately clear what had caused the paralysis, my father took me to the most famous experts in the field, all the way up to Hanover. I still remember how embarrassed I was when they examined me, lying there, or being asked to walk and bend while all naked in front of my father and other physicians and nurses. It was determined that I must have contracted polio from spending a lot of time in the infected local swimming pool. There were several cases diagnosed in Europe at that time but there still was no penicillin or other antibiotics available to the average German citizen for a cure of this contagious, debilitating disease. I don't know what made the symptoms disappear after six months during which time I lay in bed at home, trying to study the class notes and homework my school mates sent along with the local bus each day. They also sent lots of funny get well cards to encourage me, telling me that I was missed. I still feel grateful for their warm support.

When it was finally over, the only sequel I immediately noticed was that I could not run as fast as I had before which affected my tennis game. Tennis was the "in sport" at my school, and I felt crushed by this debilitating condition and envious of my healthy classmates. During a skiing trip with our sports teacher and classmates in the Black Forest, I also had a knee injury on my weaker right knee that never really healed. I was never again excellent at any sport, just managed to hang in there. The veins on my right leg had weakened as well and suffered considerably about ten years later when I became pregnant with my daughter. But I was grateful that I had not become a cripple. I had survived, and at school could continue my afternoon program in painting which I loved, and, at home, playing the piano, even though I never again took formal lessons, which I regret to this day.

On a ski trip to the Black Forest with my German schoolmates. I am second from left.

Silence about World War II

At high school in Germany, I became very interested in History but we received hardly any instruction in recent History or political events. Our manual stopped at World War I and the Weimar Republic that followed it. The experience of World War II was maybe too new, raw and undigested to be formalized in textbooks. The trauma that had marked me during the war thus remained buried and cloaked in silence at school but still never left me. It gradually strengthened into a mere personal commitment to oppose evil until it became more defined during my years as a student at the Sorbonne in Paris and through personal discussions of the Holocaust with my Jewish friends and fellow students who had suffered from it. I read Elie Wiesel's books and saw documentaries that are now shown in all schools in Germany but were not available to us in the immediate post war years.

While in Germany, it never occurred to me to associate my classmates and even most of their parents with Germany's Nazi past. I was happy to have them as my friends. Hitler, Nazism and the events of World War II were hanging over Germany like a gloom that everyone wished had never existed. I remember parents criticizing the sports teacher for lingering Nazi methods when he forced the boys to jog barefoot in the snow. Most other teachers who occasionally made comments about the war seemed devastated by the horrors that had occurred. I never heard anyone downplay or excuse the role Germany had played in World War II, but I clearly remember many people distancing themselves from and express anger about Hitler's "shameful regime" which, they felt, wronged not only millions of innocent people but did also unfair and irreparable harm to the German people itself. They frequently talked about their own suffering during the war, the bombings, the lack of food, the constant fear of being arrested or deported into camps, the loss of their homes and belongings, gang rapes after the war, the cruelty of interrogations by the Allied Forces, the years spent in French and American prison camps, and especially of family members, simple soldiers, lost on some foreign battle field in Russia, forever missing in action or maybe buried in mass graves or under the rubble of their own towns and villages.

Vacations to expand our horizon

After the war, during the years that I lived in Germany, my life revolved mostly around school. Those years were still sad, but relatively peaceful. In his new medical practice, my father was soon recognized as a capable and devoted physician. Even some of his former patients from Hungary searched for him and came to be examined and treated by him. But my father always lived modestly. My parents never took a vacation, and only rarely could afford offering one to us children, but they tried. I remember the time when I was entrusted to my eight-year-older sister for a trip to an island in the Baltic Sea, called Sylt, where we one day came upon a nudist colony playing volley ball. We saw them from high above the cliffs where we had gone for a walk in the dunes. Once I got over my initial shock, I thought they actually looked more disgusting than immoral jumping around naked with their fat bellies and other body parts wobbling.

Another time, my sister and I were allowed to spend some time at the Italian Riviera, where my sister started to worry when she noticed a much older man circling around me and singing to me while I was sitting at the beech. This aging Italian man from Sicily, who introduced himself as Mario, was not easy to shake off. For the whole week we spent there, he came every day to the stretch of beech allocated to our hotel to look for us. One day he arrived with a rather large photograph of himself that he insisted I should take home with me. He said he had fallen in love with me and had already told his mother that he wanted to marry me. He seemed particularly stimulated by my youth and the fact that I was a virgin which I one day admitted, stupidly, believing that it would deter him from pursuing me any further. I think he also believed that I had a wealthy father, so the whole package seemed irresistible to him.

My sister was very annoyed at this man since she had met someone she liked who proposed to take her for a ride in his Porsche on one of the elevated roads that run along the Mediterranean coast and provide "a unique view of the sea," as he put it to convince her to accept. But my sister did not dare leave me alone at the beech, so the man agreed to take me along. I am sure to have spoiled their fun, but for me it was also one of the scariest rides I remember. I think it was to impress my sister that he drove his Porsche at high speed on the narrow winding roads high above the cliffs from which Princess Grace of Monaco years later fell to her death. I felt shaken and relieved when we finally got out of his car un-harmed.

My nicest summer was spent on a youth exchange my father had arranged with a fellow physician in Lugano, the Italian part of Switzerland. I was learning Italian and this was supposed to help me "improve my skills and see how families in other countries lived," as my father put it. The Swiss doctor's family, especially their slightly older daughter, was very nice to me. I felt spoiled, couldn't believe I was allowed to occupy such a pretty room with my own bath in a stunningly beautiful home. They had a full time gardener for their lush grounds and a cook who prepared the most delicious Italian food. I had "prosciutto" and "carpaccio" for the first time in my life and loved the "pasta sciutta" that introduced every meal. I also had my first taste of olive oil and parmesan cheese. Their neighbor was a Frenchman from Paris who used to drive me every morning in his white convertible sports car to the swimming pool in town and bring me back in the afternoon. He complimented me a lot but, to my hosts' relief, remained a perfect gentleman.

I felt bad for the son of the family who later in the summer came to live with us in Germany where conditions could not compare to the wealth and luxury of my Swiss hosts. We tried to make his stay pleasant, but I think he must have been disappointed. I know my father felt unhappy, probably embarrassed, when I later told him of all the luxury that had surrounded me during my stay in Switzerland. He even became angry when I pointed out, unfairly, some of our own shortcomings. The Swiss doctor and his family lived in a house untouched by war, that they had inherited from the wealth of previous generations, while my poor parents still had a hard time making ends meet in our new country, constantly juggling priorities, having lost everything that they had inherited or worked for.

Non scholae but vitae discimus

Only after leaving school did I realize how much my father's educational principles had influenced me and continued to do so later in life. We all had some knowledge of Latin, my father from his gymnasium and medical training, the three of us children learned it at school and, like our mother and even my nanny, were exposed to some Latin vocabulary and phrases in church and religious manuals. But Latin never became some snobbish practice for its own sake. It had its practical purpose as did most of what we were to learn both at and outside school. Similarly to mathematics, my father said, Latin grammar taught us "to think logically" and, together with Latin vocabulary, helped tremendously in the study of foreign languages. "Non scholae but vitae discimus," (we do not learn for school but for life) was my father's motto. We were encouraged to look into all fields of knowledge, develop all skills available to us and try to excel. Still somewhat traumatized by the war experience and the complete loss of everything he had owned except his trained mind, my father wanted us to be ready for every eventuality, able to survive in any situation without any material support, using only what we knew and had trained ourselves to master to the best of our ability.

This extended to moral questions. We should always be ready to help those in need but not rely on others, be ready to help ourselves. This is why for years I thought it immoral to apply for scholarships as long as one was able to earn the money for tuition during vacations or have parents who could pay for it. Scholarships, in my mind, should be given only to the needy, not to those who thought it would bring them recognition and look good on their curriculum vitae. To my surprise, most of the wealthiest students in the United States did not share such views. I tended to despise them for their attitudes and had to get used to what I felt was a selfish, materialistic culture.

Aesthetics

For as far back as I can remember, at my home and at school, I was led to acquire an appreciation for the various forms of aesthetics, in the visual arts, music, and later in literature and poetry, the changing styles in architecture, fashion, and even the physical beauty of people of all ages, genders and origins. Originally, this interest may have been passed on to me and my sister by our mother who was introduced to the study of aesthetics at the fashionable finishing school she attended in the hills of Budapest before marrying, at barely eighteen, a man who was ten years her senior and did not share her devotion to the "beaux arts." Amazingly, though, once he had retired from his medical practice, my father developed quite an artistic interest in creating his own sculptures out of ordinary pebble stones.

From the Greeks and Romans to the Existentialists

Among my favorite academic subjects at school soon emerged History, especially of the Greek and Roman era, and its relationship to later kings and emperors who tried to emulate their power and style in other European countries. I remember looking in the mirror to see whether my body could in any way compare to the beautiful Greek and Roman goddesses pictured in my Latin manual and decided that only my mother's straight nose, oval face and well proportioned body had any resemblance to these classical beauties.

In my early teens, I devoured Karl May's books about Indians and reports about other native civilizations, even reading them during class, holding the books on my knees to hide them from my teachers. Toward the end of high school, under the influence of an excellent, young teacher, I discovered contemporary literature and became fascinated by the work of the French existentialist writer Albert Camus. I felt that his protagonist in *The Plague*, Dr. Rieux, embodied some of the humanistic medical ethics with which I had grown up at home: the absolute professional commitment, the unselfish deeds and sacrifices required in helping others even when faced by despair over the final outcome. At the same time, I became more and more critical of inauthentic "bourgeois" values, based on money, which had no intrinsic humanistic validity. Camus's famous anti-hero and protagonist in *The Stranger*, Meursault, led me from my classical to a more modern humanism which I embraced a few years later as a student in Paris.

Teenage years after World War II

As was the case after World War I with Dadaism and Surrealism, the post-World War II generation in Europe was eager to attack the conservative bourgeois values of a civilization that allowed Nazism and Fascism to be born and degenerate into the horrors of World War II and the Holocaust. The displacement of traditional values occurred more rapidly in countries such as France than in Germany which for years lay in ruins, physically, spiritually, and politically, and only slowly regained some independent thought, dignity and respect under the leadership of its Chancellor

Adenauer. Germany had no voice on the international scene, and the whole world combined under the auspices of The United Nations wanted to make sure it never again regained its past destructive power.

No wonder, German youth felt similarly silenced for many decades and did not dare engage in any creative activity or even rebellion until a few writers and novelists had the courage to publish the first indictments of Germany's shameful role in the recent onslaught on humanity. Even among teenagers, who were too young to have experienced the war, the mood was more reconstructive than destructive, and it was more materialistically oriented than spiritually and ideologically. At school in a small town, proving intellectual excellence by getting good grades or, maybe more so, by impressing fellow students by one's knowledge, talents or wit, earned the greatest recognition but was definitely enhanced by the parents' status and their professional success in the community. It seemed to guarantee that their accomplishments had grown on solid grounds. This value judgment was clearly conservative and raked of a past bourgeois and even aristocratic value system.

Since I lived about ten miles from school, after class activities were restricted by the need for transportation which was scarce. The local bus made only a few round trips per day, and school buses did not exist. I often drove my bicycle on the days I wanted to play tennis, attend painting courses or go to the swimming pool, unless I resigned myself to taking the later bus which risked to interfere with my usually heavy load of homework and forced me to stay up late. We had no television, only a radio and a record player to listen to music, which included also American music and Jazz. Some magazines we could buy included pictures of American gadgets and the "new look." From his occasional trips to a large city, my father sometimes brought me back beauty magazines for teenagers that explained how to apply "make up" and use creams against acne of which so many of us suffered.

Ami go home

After May 8, 1945, I never again encountered any soldiers of the American, French or English occupying forces, except when we saw them occasionally in convoys traveling through our area. My father both despised but also felt sorry for women who socialized with soldiers since he often witnessed sad consequences of such associations in his medical practice. Despite the welcome help from the Marshall plan, the population wished for the retreat of the occupying forces that too often engaged in reprehensible and even criminal behavior with women, especially after heavy drinking. Black babies were born to white women, sometimes as a result of rape, many pregnant women were abandoned. Women who befriended American soldiers and left to marry them in America, did not know what would await them there as "war brides." Understandably, parents were fearful and upset whenever they had to cope with such situations. "Ami Go Home" graffiti appeared on lots of walls, mostly in the big cities and near the casernes where soldiers were housed or nightclubs that played American music and attracted a military clientele.

Teenage social life

In my small town, the social life of a teenager evolved close to school. We staged plays by Schiller, Shakespeare and Molière, sang in choirs and attended concerts that often took place in nearby castles or elaborate medieval town halls. We met at sports events, especially tennis matches and soccer games. Our parents, at least those like mine who had the willingness, place and means to do so, offered us "house balls" at which we danced to records that I bought from my allowance or my friends brought along. The repertoire consisted mostly of waltz, tango, foxtrot, occasionally a piece of Jazz or a more daring American import. The girls dressed in cocktail dresses—mine were usually sewn by my mother or handed down to me by my sister—the boys wore jackets and ties. The food consisted of fancy hors-d'oeuvres artfully prepared by my mother with the help of our maid. We drank fruit punch which was usually spiced up by a bottle of champagne, but nobody ever got drunk, even though some pretended to be tipsy. Youthful hormones were no doubt raging, but did not get assuaged by more than a slight kiss, a touch or rubbing against each other's bodies in a slow dance. Nobody sneaked up into a bedroom or a dark corner of the house. I believe that all the girls and maybe even all of the boys did not engage in sexual intercourse before graduating from high school. I don't remember any teenage pregnancies occurring at my school. Our parents and teachers provided us with firm rules and vigilant supervision. If the ball took place in someone else's house, my father, who was used to be called to a patient in the middle of the night, came to pick me up exactly at midnight rather than entrust me to a student who maybe just received his driver's license and, borrowing his parents' car, dreamed of some tangible rewards for his chauffeuring. If one of the upperclass men invited me for a date on Sunday afternoon, my parents made sure to sit down and talk to him before we took off. The pretext was to be civil and get to know him but they also wanted him to feel that he did not have absolute license to go as far as he pleased with me. He had to abide by a higher authority.

Was it an easier way to grow up?

Sheltered from illicit behavior, we did not feel deprived of fun. In many ways, our lives were easier and maybe happier than the ones of today's teenagers. While there were hushed talks, especially among the boys, about sex, venereal diseases such as syphilis and gonorrhea, drugs, HIV and AIDS had not arrived yet to threaten our lives. Since most of us were virgins, we had nothing to fear, at least not physically, from our para-sexual activities, except maybe a broken heart, which, I suppose, happened to most of us. In a class of thirty, the ratio was one girl to two boys, so girls did not lack attention. I don't remember boys being rude to us girls. Some were shy and just watched the more outgoing in action. During class, recreations, field trips and social gatherings, we enjoyed an "esprit de corps."

First love?

And yet, the day I set foot into my new school, just before my bout with polio, I noticed that one of the boys was just a bit taller than the rest, wore a nice shirt and blazer, spoke without any regional accent and displayed an ease in his manners that revealed that he had probably moved in select circles. When he looked at me with his dark brown eyes and smiled I knew right then that I wanted him to find me different and special as well. I never confided my feelings about this boy to anyone, but they must have been written all over my face when a few years later, once we turned eighteen and could drive, he picked me up for a date in his father's Mercedes. My parents worried and later encouraged me to get over this infatuation. There were rumors about his family. His parents were divorced and the father lived with a mistress, which was considered immoral. The father had the reputation of being arrogant and ruthless in his business and, even among my classmates, it became known that he beat his son with a belt whenever he failed to win at a tennis match. But all this did not change the way my body and mind remained captivated by the young man for several years.

Dating

I went out on dates with others. There was this handsome upper class man with dark brown hair and dark blue eyes and a mathematical mind. My parents did not mind seeing him around and liked his family. There was also the older brother of one of my classmates who was already studying medicine and, I think, he felt that his future profession gave him an advantage over other possible suitors, and my father would not a priori disapprove of him. But all this was just play compared to the one who had stolen my heart.

At the School for Interpreters in Munich

After our "Abitur," which is the diploma we received at the end of high school after a grueling written and oral exam, my special friend and I, without prior agreement, ended up studying in the same big city. I enrolled at what was considered the best school for interpreters in the country, only Geneva placed higher, and chose to study French and Italian, two Romance languages which were easy for me because of the many years of Latin I had at high school. Among my classmates in my Italian class was an opera singer, a heavy set older man, who invited me for coffee in one of the famous coffee houses in town where he suddenly started to serenade me with "Dunkel Rote Rosen schenkt man schöne Frauen," but cooled considerably when I told him that I was a virgin and not interested in having an affair. I enjoyed the big city life, the many art galleries, theaters and concerts, but I had very little money left after paying my rent and for the whole semester lived mostly of cornflakes and hard boiled eggs. Somehow I still managed to join my friends for evenings at night clubs where sensuous singers swayed us with their mellow Jazz and recent American hit songs. We had fun at "Fasching," the German carnival, attending the famous masked ball at the Fine Arts Museum.

Fireworks and finale

After the Christmas Holidays, my friend from home invited me to go skiing in the Austrian Alps and listen to a Mozart concert in the beautiful baroque castle of Salzburg, perched high upon a hill. After so many years building up to it, I realized that I was living my first love. Yet soon after its unique apogee, I decided to spend the Spring semester in Paris to perfect my French in a situation of total immersion into the language and culture of France. For several months after I left, my friend and I exchanged the most tender love letters which I later stored in a far back corner of my parents' attic even after the affair collapsed and left me devastated. My friend came to Paris to tell me that his father objected to our all too serious relationship at such an early age. His father first wanted him to become "somebody," at least earn a doctorate. Whether it was true or not, it hurt, but not forever. A wise man who got to know me quite well told me much later, that I always seem to jump back on my feet again, whatever happens. How right he was, but also what a surprise I had, about twenty-five years later and after many ups and downs in my life, when there was a call late night, followed by a transatlantic visit and a dinner at the Plaza in New York that somehow reconnected the thread that had been cut decades before after hundreds of promises of "eternal love." The first emotional fireworks must have been real, since they still linger a bit today in yearly phone calls exchanged on our birthdays. Munich, Salzburg, Paris, cities that witnessed our youthful emotions, still echo in our conversations.

PART TWO

The Ups and Downs of
My So-Called Best Years

4

Studying in Paris

Paris, here I come!

I had truly extraordinary parents and don't know how I deserved their unconditional trust and support when during my Christmas vacation I dared ask and they consented to let me study in Paris for the spring semester. I was twenty years old and had never traveled or lived by myself when I prepared my little suitcase, and said goodbye to my parents at the train station after they had handed me my passport, some French Francs and a round trip ticket to the East Train Station in Paris. With my toothbrush I had packed a few blouses, sweaters, two skirts and a pair of flat "ballerina" shoes, but also a little black dress, a fashionable hat and a pair of low-heeled pumps my mother thought I should have in Paris. It was the first dress she did not sew herself and that was not handed down to me from my sister's discarded outfits. I also stuck a small dictionary into my blazer pocket, just in case there was a word I had not learned at the school for interpreters. I felt ready. I did not realize then that the most useful and precious baggage I took with me to Paris was the education I had received from my parents, at school and good people around me.

Not quite a year earlier, I had passed the German "Abitur," a rigorous examination at the end of "gymnasium," the German high school. I had studied nine years of Latin, some French, Italian and English, was still fluent in my native Hungarian, had learned to take stenographic dictation in three languages and, as a hobby, played the piano and tennis and was interested in art, music, literature and history. Fortunately, and without any credit to myself, I also possessed a young tall trim body and a fair complexion that seemed to attract the attention of enough French men, notably of a few tall dark handsome ones, to keep me reassured that even though taller than the average French person, I enjoyed a favorable reflection in their eyes. Their reassurance made me immediately feel at home in this enchanting cosmopolitan city. Also immediately, I felt ready and eager to plunge into my studies, perfect my French and visit all the museums and historical sites that I knew only from school manuals or books and brochures that I had received from my parents and friends as presents for my birthdays or at Christmas.

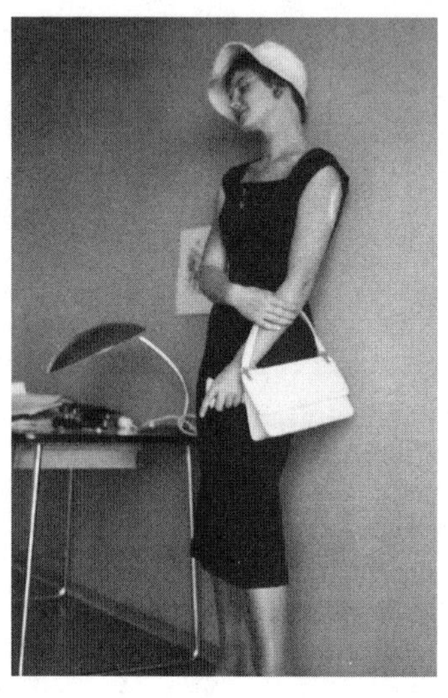

As I was preparing to leave for Paris, my mother insisted that I should have a little black dress, hat, handbag and pumps.

Life at the Cité Universitaire

The Schmidt School for Interpreters, where I had studied in Munich, had helped me with reservations of a room at the Cité Universitaire, registration at the Sorbonne for a French Civilization Course, and even provided directions how to get to these places from the Gare de l'Est, the East Train Station in Paris, where I would arrive.

In those days, registration at the Sorbonne cost about $25 for the semester, my dorm room $5 per month, and meals at the various student restaurants in the Latin Quarter, 25 cents for a well balanced four-course meal that sometimes included delicious "moules meunières" as a first course and always plenty of baguettes to fill up on. A little bottle of wine cost less than water, so I became soon used to having dinner "à la française." This left me just enough French Francs from my modest allowance to buy a "carnet de métro," an occasional lipstick or have "un petit café" with my friends.

I had found a room at the Cité Universitaire. There were about six thousand students housed in many "pavilions" built by nations from around the world who wanted to send their students to study in Paris. Several of them were designed by famous architects such as Le Corbusier. In the course of my five years studying in Paris, I was assigned rooms at the Pavillon Franco-Britannique, la Maison du Cambodge, la Maison de la

My international tennis partners at the Cité Universitaire in Paris.

Suède, la Maison d'Allemagne and for several years at the Pavillon Deutsch de la Meurthe, where I shared a room with a Vietnamese student, called Marie Beaubois. Unfortunately, our life together soon ended in the worst tragedy of my student years. Marie died suddenly, within forty-eight hours, after she got pregnant and her boyfriend, a medical student, had taken upon himself, with the help of a fellow medical student, to perform an illegal abortion on her. Since in an attempt to protect her lover from being expelled from medical school she had sworn not to tell anyone why she was bleeding profusely, and the hospital personal was not well staffed during the Easter weekend, she simply bled to death. I saw her hours before she passed away at the student hospital, shortly after I returned from having spent the holiday with my parents and could not find her in our quarters. She looked very pale and complained from severe pain in her lower abdomen but did not tell me about the bleeding. She implied that it might be due to some bad food poisoning and hoped to get over it soon, especially once the doctors returned to the hospital Monday morning. I don't know what happened to the men who performed the abortion, but I still feel guilty about not having done anything to help save her. She and her little sister Pauline had been sent by their parents, a Vietnamese mother and a French father, to study in Paris to escape the Vietnam War only to experience Marie's tragic death in France a few years later. Marie was very smart, a third-year law student, beautiful and elegant, and was hoping eventually to return to practice law in her country. I tried to stay in touch with her little sister and see her as often as I could while she lived with a family in Paris, but then she was placed in a foster home in the south of France from where she still wrote to me for a while, bitter-sweet letters that I have kept to this day, but soon stopped answering my letters. She may have returned to her country.

I continued living at the Cité, pursuing my studies as best I could and also enjoying what life had to offer me. It had not taken me long to make friends. I played tennis with a Chinese student, Kim, and Ali, who was from Tunisia. Both were excellent players, and I was flattered that they would want to play with me while my game was average at best. There was also an Olympic size swimming pool where I enjoyed swimming, and a large "amphithéâtre" for plays and lectures. Women had to be careful not to show up in curlers or wearing a hat at any of the public places, including the restaurants. If they did, students broke out into a frenzy, pounding with hands and feet until the ominous object was removed. I saw this happen numerous times, but most shockingly to the wife of an ambassador who was forced to remove her coiffe.

Years later, my husband and I lived in the relatively luxurious student quarters at the Cité that had been built by Cuba before its economic collapse in the 1930s, during the Depression. In the Tunisian pavilion, opposite our building, Farah Dibah, the later queen of the Shaw of Iran, lived just like another student. We frequently saw her at the student restaurant. At that time, nothing to us predicted her future role in the limelight and the later tragedy of her family.

Studying at the Sorbonne

The first day I walked into my classroom, a large auditorium of the Sorbonne, the venerable Paris University dating back to the twelfth century, a blind professor was led to the pulpit from where he lectured for about fifty minutes on Romans, Gaulle and Vercingétorix to a full house of over one hundred students. I did not miss a word of what he was saying and then rushed to my second class, called "Travaux Pratiques en Phonétiques," to which I devoted my greatest effort during my first semester in order to rid myself of any trace of a foreign accent that my intensive course at the School for Interpreters in Munich, Germany, had not been able to eradicate. In the evening, in front of the small mirror in my room, I practiced the sounds and words we had studied and couldn't wait to finish this course and then, hopefully, speak French like the natives.

After class, I usually walked from the Sorbonne up to the Jardin du

Luxembourg where, on sunny days, lots of students sat around the water basins and their decorative, spouting fountains seemingly reading their notes and textbooks, but also leisurely glancing at each other and the children who delighted in maneuvering remote-controlled small boats, sometimes eagerly encouraged by their fathers. Since I did not want to squander the little money I had, I sat down on the edge of the basin instead of paying ten cents for a chair. After I felt rested, I continued my stroll down the Boulevard Saint-Michel, then walked alongside the banks of the Seine, where I loved to scrutinize the treasures of the "bouquinistes," and, if I still had some energy, I climbed up the Champs Elysées all the way to the Arc de Triomphe before, exhausted, taking the métro back to my dorm.

During one of such walks, about a year after my arrival, I ran into hundreds of very tall French policemen marching down the Boulevard Saint-Michel. It turned out to be the day Charles de Gaulle was instituted as President of the French Republic and had sent his tallest policemen to the Latin Quarter to guarantee against any revolt by the more left-wing oriented student body.

Living a dream

I lived my days like a dream and knew after a few days that I never wanted to leave Paris again, that after having lost my home in Hungary, I finally had found my new home in the beautiful, historic and romantic capital of France on the Seine. Paris reminded me of Budapest, its stately, solid, decorative buildings, and the beautiful bridges across the Danube. The joy in living, food, playful romance, creative arts and interest in fashion resembled the life style Hungarians enjoyed as a complement to their daily existence. I was eager to plant roots and integrate into French society but knew that it would not be easy to blend in and make the kind of living I desired. I would need to work on bettering myself, have more money and ultimately land a real profession.

Accumulating diplomas and certificates

My French Civilization courses taught me much about literature, art, architecture and history but, with my goals firmly established, I also signed up for two additional six-week courses to earn a certificate as commercial interpreter for French and English at the British Chamber of Commerce, and for a similar diploma at the Alliance Française. From courses taken at the Interpreting School in Germany, I was already quite fluent in French, had become a good typist and knew to take stenography in German, French and English. After having convinced my parents to let me continue studying in Paris, I signed up for a three year program in Hungarian at the prestigious Ecole Nationale des Langues Orientales Vivantes, rue de Lille, where I managed to obtain my Diploma after only two rather than the three years required of most French students. At twenty-one, I was thus fluent in four languages and knew the proper form and expressions of business correspondence in addition to having earned a prestigious diploma from the Sorbonne and deepened my knowledge of French civilization and history. I continued taking courses at the Sorbonne in French and English literature and visited lots of museums and special exhibits on the days of the week when they were open to the public without an entrance fee.

Oh, to become a Parisienne!

In order to become socially acceptable in select French circles, I was also eager to familiarize myself with what was considered proper behavior and started to observe the ways and style of distinguished French people I met or came across at public events. I wanted to blend in and show that I had a sense for style and fashion which later turned out to be a plus in gaining the approval of the French. I tried to figure out how to look a bit fashionable even on a very small budget. I found an inexpensive twin set in the color I had noticed was popular among young women on the fashionable Grands Boulevards and also among my fellow students at the Sorbonne. From my next savings I also replaced my flat ballerina shoes with a pair of high heeled pumps that I could afford only after my friend introduced me to an outlet close to the Place de la République. I was surprised how well I managed to walk in them and what they apparently did to my appearance, tested by merely walking down the Boulevard Saint-Michel after my courses. French men do not hesitate to throw not just glances but also compliments at you. To me, who had barely emerged from my teenage years and was still insecure about my looks, noticing such attention, even though I was a bit shy and tended to lower my eyes or just look straight ahead not to meet the eyes of the passers bye, such uninhibited expressions of approval felt quite flattering. Men tended to be much more reserved at the places where I had lived before.

My best friend

I was lucky. During the next few summer vacations, my linguistic competence in several languages, and possibly also my looks, led to jobs that helped me improve my financial situation. The greatest gift of fate to me, though, was that I had also found an excellent Parisian friend. She was of Hungarian descent, kind and very intelligent and became not only my classmate in studying for a diploma in Hungarian but my soulmate for the years ahead. A few days after we met, she invited me to visit her family. For decades we shared all the significant events of our lives, vacations, marriage, the birth of our children and even our divorce, until nearly twenty years ago melanoma robbed her of her relatively young life. She had to leave behind two sons, her mother whose only child she was, and a very caring cousin who became like a brother to her after he lost his mother and little brother to the ravages of the Holocaust. I still miss her and will forever feel devastated by the loss.

A variety of jobs and bosses

While my friend was the only child of relatively wealthy parents, I continued to live on a very tight budget and had to find work during summer vacations and sometimes even in the course of the school year. It did not affect our friendship. It was then that my parents' educational principles, my international training and background, combined with my lucky genes and early ambitions started to pay off. Most of my life, it has been relatively easy for me to find a job, albeit not always the best paid or the most interesting one, including the ones I found during my student years in Paris. I spent one weekend wrapping medication ten hours a day so that I could purchase food tickets for the rest of the month until my parents' check would arrive in the mail. During one long hot summer, I worked as a secretary-receptionist for a large European airline. Hours were from 8 a.m. to 6 p.m. with a two hour interval at noon. Not ideal timing for me. I could not afford having a two-hour meal at a restaurant and would much rather have ingested a sandwich or an apple and gone home two hours earlier. My boss occasionally invited me for lunch, assuring me that even though he found me very attractive, he loved his wife and his intentions were entirely honorable, which was fine with me.

A creepy boss harassing me

Not so another boss I experienced. I was recommended to this lawyer by one of my fellow students at the Sorbonne who had worked for him but had to return to Argentina. She did say that he was looking to hire an attractive young student and seemed delighted at my knowledge of Hungarian and German since he was engaged in requesting German restitution funds for Hungarian Jews who had lost everything in World War II. It seemed an ideal job that would allow me not just to earn money but contribute to a good cause. For a week, I did my best to take careful dictation and type his letters in perfect form. Mr. Koenig seemed very satisfied but soon, calling me to stand next to him while he was signing the letters, made attempts at touching my breasts and made quite explicit propositions as to how I could increase my salary, "buy nice dresses on the Champs Elysées," and more, if only I conceded to a "few favors," as he put it. In his twisted mind, he advanced the argument that "he was too old to hurt me." I also thought that he was too ugly and disgusting to get near me. As he was talking to me his wife walked in and I thought of letting her know what an ugly creep she was married to but felt sorry for her. I simply took my purse and walked out before I had received my first paycheck.

In the spotlight with Pathé Marconi

My next job was both glamorous and exciting. The famous music company Pathé Marconi interviewed students at the student center of the Sorbonne for a job as receptionist-interpreters at a fair at which they launched their brand new transistor radios. They hired me without asking many questions and sewed the names of all the languages I spoke onto the sleeve of the elegant uniform I received for keeps together with daily make up and hair dressing provided by Revlon for the entire period I served. A French TV channel taped me while I was showing the fancy new radio to a few children who were visiting the fair. The shot appeared at the evening news. The next day, a father called the music company to enquire whether I would be interested in spending several hours on weekend afternoons and evenings babysitting their children and practicing their foreign languages with them while he and his wife could have time to themselves. He assured me that he would drive me back to my dorm after their night out. When I talked to my parents, my father immediately nixed those plans, telling me that he did not want me to be a servant, what a "babysitter" represented in his mind, nor did he want me to be driven home by a strange older man in the middle of the night. His arguments were similar when I was thinking of applying to Pan Am as a stewardess. "Stewardesses are just better maids," he said, and "easily fall

My first "glamour job" in Paris that got me onto French TV and travel in the fast train "Mistral" to Marseilles to present Pathé Marconi's new transistor radios.

into traps and acquire a bad reputation traveling from one country to another, staying in a different hotel each night." Instead, he would try sending me a higher monthly allowance whenever I had special expenses. My father, I think, had no idea how easy it would have been for me to "misbehave" right there in Paris. At my job for the music company I met and had my picture taken with several of the renowned stars such as Charles Aznavour and Yves Montand, but fortunately the company had explicit rules for its employees that prohibited any private socializing, especially with us students. The same protective rule was in vigor when we were sent via the fancy rapid train called "Mistral," which later became the present TGV, to exhibit their transistor radios also in Marseilles. We regularly dined with celebrities at restaurants around town who were quite charming, but the motto "N'y touche!" (don't touch) prevailed in all circumstances and I did not deceive my parents' trust.

German conversation lessons for a professor—what a treat!

The student services office referred to me a professor who was teaching German at the University of Montpellier and wanted to practice speaking German during his frequent visits to Paris. Since his request came from an official source, I accepted. The lessons usually took place over dinner in a nice restaurant where I was treated to my first truly delicious French meals. Once in a while he also invited me to a theater or a show before he deposited me by taxi, very properly and politely, in front of my dormitory at the Cité Universitaire. One day he took some photographs of me which he apparently showed to a sculptor friend who soon thereafter proposed to hire me as his model, but I did not want to get into a potentially messy situation with this sculptor and even less the professor who had become a trusted friend. My parents must have done something right in keeping me on the right track.

Friends from Hungary and Germany visiting

There were former friends who came to visit when they heard that I had moved to Paris. Jóska, who for years was my only friend in my childhood and was with me on that horrible morning when we nearly ran into a forest near Sopron where Hungarian soldiers mistreated emaciated, barely clad Jews in the middle of winter. There was still a certain closeness we felt twenty years later and, I think, we still found each other attractive—I for his dark eyes and hair, his tall muscular built, his broad shoulders, and he complimented me for my figure and fair complexion. But we had grown apart while attending high school and university in different places and did not marry each other as we had promised when we were children at home in Hungary.

My so-called "first love" from high school and my semester in Munich also came, but I was not too happy, since I felt cheated by him—I should not have. We were barely twenty when his father did everything he could to prevent his son to become too serious about our relationship. Still, I resented his coming to Paris and was relieved when he left. Nevertheless, both these young men constituted a link to my past. At one point, each of them told me that he wanted to marry me, the first when I was about five to seven years old, the second when we both entered the life of adulthood, freedom and sex. Since then I have completely lost track of Jóska. My so-called "first love," or was he the "second"?, surprised me with a phone call about twenty-five years later and came to visit when he was on a business trip to the United States. We still exchange souvenirs and update our news over the phone, usually on our birthdays.

My black and red Beetle

When I was still at high school and not allowed to do so, my father started to teach me how to drive so that I could have my driver's license for my eighteenth birthday. For my twenty-first birthday, while I was already a student in Paris, he surprised me with a brand new black Beetle with red leather seats and sent me coupons to buy a limited quantity of gasoline each month. I loved that little car and so did my friends in Paris who forty years later still remember our drives around town, the little Beetle stuffed with my friends to its capacity. My sister was very jealous, but a few years later when she inherited my car because I left Europe, it took only a few weeks before she totaled it. I felt sorry for her and embarrassed. The accident had not been her fault.

A summer course in London that ended with a marriage proposal

Always intent at providing us with the best possible education and expand our horizon, the year after I met my Hungarian girlfriend in Paris, our parents sent us to study English for a month at the Cambridge School for Languages in London. We lived in a boarding house in Hampstead run by a rather unpleasant, overweight lady who usually received us while she was having breakfast in bed. She was quite nice to my friend but unfriendly to me and made sly remarks about my "looking German" which seemed to disturb her. My friend and I determined that the food we were served at dinner must have originated from the combined gutters of France and England and, at breakfast, we usually enjoyed the ritual of throwing the dirty brown liquid the cooks called "café au lait" into the sink.

Our stay evolved into an unexpected development. My father had entrusted me to a distant cousin, by then a medical doctor, who had left Hungary in 1956 and settled in London. While my girlfriend spent some of her time with a nice man she met in our Hampstead boarding house, my cousin took me to concerts at Albert Hall and to London museums such as the Tate Gallery. Toward the end of our stay, to my surprise, my cousin called my father telling him that he had grown very fond of me and was thinking of asking me to marry him if my father had no objections since we were distant cousins. My father, quite surprised but non committal, said that it would be ultimately up to me to decide. When I talked to my parents later that evening I learned that my cousin's father had been an extremely authoritarian and jealous man who tormented his beautiful wife, a second cousin of my mother, to the point that it became nearly unbearable for the whole family. I liked my cousin, still do, and thought that he was very intelligent and cultured but told him that I needed time to think about his unexpected proposal. In those days, especially after having lived in Paris, London seemed to me a rather stiff, boring city where most men wore pin striped suits and tall hats and the meals were built around boiled meat, potatoes and cabbage. I couldn't wait to return to Paris and left my cousin with a very uncertain response.

The irresistible charm of Paris

Back in my favorite city, my black and red Beetle added to my sense of freedom and also to my popularity. My girlfriend and I traveled to visit my family in Germany where my sister had already finished her medical studies and married a handsome, talented colleague who was fluent in French. My friends long auburn hair and beautiful Semitic features attracted much attention wherever we went. My family was charmed by my guest. They appreciated her intelligence, refined, and gentle manners and felt reassured about my company in Paris, telling me that they could not have wishes for a nicer friend for me. But when we continued our travel to Bavaria, the manager of a youth hostel took offense at our short pink shorts and told us that we should try to find quarters at the Folies Bergères in Paris. In the end, he nevertheless provided us with two bunk beds for the night.

The fall semester in France begins in October, so there was time after work, to enjoy the long evening hours. During the summer months, daylight in Paris often extends to 10 p.m. With my friends we sat in one of the open air cafés in the Latin Quarter, sipping "un petit café," the typical strong French coffee, for hours without being chased away by the establishment. For publicity purposes, some nightclubs featuring fancy shows and well known "chansonniers" frequently distributed tickets to students asking them to dress nicely and just sit there at a big table close to the entrance where they could be seen by passers bye sipping a glass of champagne. Naturally, we were delighted to comply.

A significant encounter

During the semester, I took most of my meals at the restaurant of the Cité Universitaire where I lived. After returning from England, I noticed that a tall student with short curly dark hair, broad shoulders and powerful arms, dressed in unusually loose clothing, frequently waited at the door and then sat across from me at the large dining table. Unlike Europeans, who eat with fork and knife, he used only his fork, putting down his knife as soon as he had cut his food, which to me meant that he lacked manners. Whenever he made an attempt to talk to me, I felt uncomfortable and did not respond. I guess today we would say that I felt as if he were stalking me, until one day, he suddenly displayed his white teeth in a broad smile and seemed overjoyed claiming that I had smiled at him as well. I am not sure I did, but I did start to find him cute in his persistent attempts to break the ice between us. I also admitted to myself that he was rather good looking and finally quite charming when he tried to pay me compliments in a heavily accented French. In any case, on that day he claimed victory and hence felt entitled to speaking to me at every meal. Soon, he would accompany me back to the entrance of my dorm where one of the cleaning ladies one day paid me a terrific compliment in front of him and told him not to let me escape. Although born in Spain, before coming to Paris, he had lived on a far away tropical island which provoked both apprehension and a certain curiosity in my mind. My hesitant attitude toward him gradually dissipated as I learned more about his tastes for classical music, his all star basketball performance and his fine mind that allowed him from a financially and socially mixed background to pursue successful medical studies at the distinguished university of Paris. He also seemed to have an excellent sense of humor. Still, my friends and family to whom I introduced him in the next few weeks tried to cool our relationship. They felt that he might not be the right man for me, that we were culturally and socially too different to find happiness together.

A carefree summer at La Côte d'Azur

At the beginning of the summer, my girlfriend and I decided to celebrate the end of the school year by taking another trip together, this time to the French Riviera, where we spent an amazingly relaxed and enjoyable month at the beech, not eating much and shedding our bikinis only in the evening to put on some chic outfits, silk dresses for my friend, cotton skirts and tops in my case, for our nightly promenade along the Mediterranean or an occasional meal in a pizzeria.

My new friend had decided to drive his scooter all the way from Paris to Rome that summer but, on his way back, stopped alongside the beeches of the Mediterranean to search for us. He knew approximately where we would be and indeed found us in Juan les Pins and spent a few days with

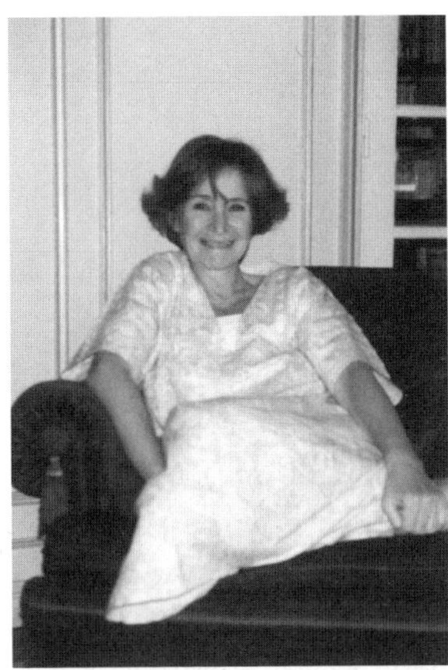

us at the beach. My girlfriend was not too happy about the intruder on our vacation, but I had a hard time getting angry at him. It was too late. I had been charmed. As it turned out, it was to be the last carefree summer my girlfriend and I spent together.

She was my best friend ever, a Parisian of Hungarian descent, whom I met only days after my arrival in Paris.

Enjoying a walk alongside the Mediterranean in Nice with my friend a few months before my marriage.

5

Marriage and Motherhood

Wedding bells were ringing

A few months later, my tall, dark and handsome "chevalier servant" and I decided to get married. We prepared a two day celebration. My family, somewhat surprised by the news but cheerful, made the long trip to Paris in my brother-in-law's Mercedes. They arrived one day early and, instead of going out to have dinner at a restaurant, feasted on French baguettes, cheese and red wine in their hotel room. My future husband's family lived too far away to make the trip but he was surrounded by several of his fellow medical students who hailed from his home country. The next morning my brother-in-law and a colleague of my future husband served us as best men at the civil ceremony conducted by the mayor of the Quatorzième Arrondissement, the 14th district, where we lived. My mother had lent me her beautiful fur coat and a nice hat which made me look more grown up than my twenty-three years. For the church wedding the next morning in a small chapel at the outskirts of Paris, I wore my sister's sweeping white marriage gown that we rapidly adjusted to fit my slim, slightly taller frame. The wedding reception and sumptuous meal was held for about

After solemn wedding ceremonies at church, festivities continued at the historic Closerie des Lilas in the Montparnasse district of Paris.

thirty guests at the famous historic restaurant called La Closerie des Lilas, on the Boulevard de Montparnasse, at the edge of the Luxembourg Garden and the Latin Quarter. In the evening, a smaller group of the wedding party joined us in listening to a great performance of Gounod's *Faust* at the dazzling opera house of Paris, the Palais Garnier. The following morning, after all our guests had departed, the two of us were left to enjoy our newly married life. Since the wedding had taken place in the middle of the school year, and we had spent most of our savings on preparations for the big event, we postponed our honeymoon till a later time but enjoyed our life together, still living in university housing, yet this time in my husband's much larger, more luxurious quarters with private bath. Incidentally, Farah Dibah, the later Queen of the Shah of Iran, lived in the building across from ours, and we often saw her, totally unaware of her future role and social status, enjoying dinner like the rest of us. Since we continued to eat at student restaurants and had cleaning ladies who took care of our room and bath, it did not matter that I had not learned to cook yet and was not anxious to assume housewifely duties. We both continued our studies and quizzed each other before exams. On weekends we gathered for fun with our long term friends, and those who joined us later such as Denise, George, Jean-Claude, Suzanne, Michel, Guillermo and others. We were extremely fortunate that our families generously agreed to continue sending an allowance, even though a modest one, until we graduated and landed a real job. My father's medical practice had picked up, and I was his last child who still needed support. My older sister and her husband by then were practicing physicians and had become self-sufficient. Until a revolution in his country made it impossible, my new husband's allowance, a gift from his extended family, arrived in American dollars which in those days went far in the exchange into French Francs. Once this abruptly stopped, we became entirely dependent on my father and were anxious to finish our diplomas, especially since I had become pregnant with our first child.

My female body: mother, wife, woman

In my early twenties, it seemed to me that my body asserted itself excessively and threatened to gain unwelcome control over my mind. Reason and desire at times seemed to battle each other. Marriage for a while provided a safe heaven. I remember thinking that it felt good to have a husband and being in a union sanctioned by society. The thought that in a few years, once my husband would have finished medical school, we could establish ourselves somewhere and live a nice, pleasant life provided me with a quiet contentment. A husband was also supposed to provide protection to his wife and family against bad people and dangerous things in life. I enjoyed having his strong arms around me even though they did not really protect me from anything. They did not have to. We sometimes attended political gatherings where they discussed Fidel Castro's "maquisard" revolution and then his turn for help to Communist Russia. We were both interested in world politics but never got involved in manifestations. Not much happened early in my marriage and even in the months of my pregnancy to threaten my dreams of a happy future. The nausea in the morning made me look pale and my hair became a bit limp. The veins on my right leg, which had suffered from polio, showed stress from the hormonal change but protective stockings and the fact that I hardly gained any weight made it all bearable. My husband was sure we would have a boy who looked like him but had my eyes.

It's a girl—Daddy's girl

In the early hours of a summer morning, my waters broke, and my husband, trembling, rushed me to the hospital Palais Royal, near the Boulevard Montparnasse, where he had reserved a room but for a month later. They did accept us anyhow. We had driven to the hospital in my black and red Beetle. Just a few weeks before, upon my father's urging, I had taught my husband how to drive, and he passed his driver's license with flying colors. Later his brother made fun of him because he had allowed a woman to teach him driving. "Strange," I thought. "He must have macho hang-ups," which I had not noticed in his brother.

My husband had picked the hospital Palais Royal after having trained there in gynecology, and while I suffered through my contractions for nearly twenty-four hours, he renewed his former acquaintances with a student nurse who periodically came to check my pulls and temperature and the midwife who finally, late Saturday evening, lifted my baby from my body and exclaimed that she was a picture of her dad. The baby's vigorous screaming seemed to indicate that she had also inherited his strong vocal chords. I felt numb and just empty for a while, still suffering from the tears and sutures the doctors had administered, until a warm feeling inundated my body and I was finally allowed to hold my baby close to my heart. She still had her eyes closed but agitated her slender long fingers, and my husband told me that she was a healthy, beautiful little girl. He did not seem disappointed about not having a boy.

For weeks before the baby was due, we had been searching for names that would sound good in all the languages to which our child was likely to be exposed. We had agreed on Roland for a boy but remained undecided between several choices for a girl, among them Caroline, Isabelle, Margarita and Livia. The next thing I heard after her birth was that her father had named her after me, because she was going to be "a strong, big girl like her maman." At that moment, I was not absolutely sure it was meant as a compliment but now I think it was.

Motherhood

Caring for my little baby was not easy at first, it probably never is unless you receive a lot of guidance and loving support. Even though I had read some books about mothering, I felt totally unprepared and fearful of doing things wrong, causing irreparable damage to her. It would have been good to have my mother or sister nearby, since they had gone through the experience. On the second or third day after giving birth, I developed an infection on my left breast, which meant that I could not continue breast-feeding my baby. I felt guilty, lonely and depressed, longed for comfort and affection but also did my best not to reveal my feelings to anyone. It was pretty awful. I had to stay at the hospital for ten more days while my mother, who finally made the long trip to Paris, took my baby and cared for her in our student quarters. My husband moved in with a colleague, which provided him with welcome companionship. It was a difficult time for my mother, not just for me. I finally returned home, practically as slim as I was before getting pregnant, which reassured and pleased my husband who thought that I was back to my wholesome self. But it was deceiving. I was not. He just would not have it otherwise. I felt as if I had been raped.

Caring for our baby

My husband did help me with feeding the baby in the middle of the night, and bathing her in a little plastic tub we had bought. Our daughter became more beautiful with every day that passed. Her skin cleared up. Her face looked like a little heart. She opened her eyes widely and seemed to smile even before babies usually do. She may have felt some cramps in her stomach which twisted her lips into a "smile." We were just typical silly, proud parents.

Baby's first trip abroad

When we went to visit my parents, my father was overjoyed about our gorgeous, healthy baby who, I think, he thought took maybe after him with her dark brown eyes, round face and lively disposition. To me she looked, as the midwife had exclaimed at her birth, exactly like her father, only more finely chiseled, more delicate. She had his relatively broad shoulders, a long torso, beautiful hands with long fingers and her father's full lips. Her face was shaped like a little heart, but there was nothing anyone could detect that she would have inherited from me. I was just a bit disappointed. During the visit to my parents, Mariska, my former nanny who came to us when I was born and now again lived with our family, confirmed that the baby had no resemblance to me. For the first time, that I can remember, Mariska also scolded me and called me irresponsible for not having baptized my little angel before taking her on a perilous, eleven-hour car ride from Paris to Germany. So we rushed and managed to have her baptized a few days later, surrounded by the family, with my sister serving as her godmother.

Poor but still happy

Back in Paris, I experimented with cooking on our "réchaud," a small electric cooking device, and months later was into preparing pureed baby food while my husband and I continued to eat at the student restaurant. One of the most exhausting chores for me was washing diapers in our bathtub and disinfecting them in a big pot of boiling water that took a half an hour to reach the boiling point on our tiny heating unit. Fortunately, we could take showers and did not need the tub, but when I started to feel rheumatism in my hands, we decided to subscribe to a diaper service and a few months later switched to plastic diapers even though we could hardly afford the expense. We lived extremely frugally and yearned for a bit more luxury but that was not soon to come. During the day, we continued to attend our classes and pass exams, taking turns to babysit. In the evening, my poor husband sometimes studied in our bathroom so the baby could sleep and I could rest undisturbed by the light. We did not get much sleep, and I often felt exhausted by my duties with the baby and my courses. When I took my baby for a ride in the fancy stroller I had inherited from my sister, I was sometimes asked whose baby she was since I was so slim and she did not look like I did. It was a good time for us, even though we were poor and could not afford much more than pay for food and the one room and bath we had at the Cité Universitaire. But that was the beauty of Paris. You could be happy there without much money, it was not a materialistic country but rather governed by humanistic ideals, something that is being threatened by the recent election of a president who seems more in love with America and neoconservative politics than the traditional values of France.

Good-bye Paris

When our daughter was about eighteen months old, my husband received his medical diploma from the University of Paris. It was a great accomplishment, but in order to practice in France, he would have had to live in France for five years, preferably between the age of fifteen and twenty, pass his "baccalauréat," the comprehensive examination at the end of high school, and do French military service. My newly minted "medical

With my sweet daughter, saying good bye to the beautiful Gardens of the Tuileries.

doctor" husband was not ready to subject himself to all those demands, and started to propose that we should immigrate to the United States. I think it was something he had wanted to do all along but knew that I would not be happy about. I wanted to live in Paris, but for all practical purposes I agreed to give it a try. We set out to search for an internship in a U.S. hospital. I wrote lots of letters since my proficiency in English was a bit superior to my husband's. We had to petition not only for a visa but also a job offer, since both of us were born in countries that fell under an existing quota system. East Orange General Hospital in New Jersey soon sent a contract, and we spent our remaining months in Paris getting ready for the big day. We took pictures of our baby at various historical and picturesque sites of Paris, such as the Place de la Concorde and the garden of the Tuilleries. She was a happy, bouncy little girl with a ready smile and a lively interest in her surroundings. People in the street told me how beautiful she was. I knew it but loved to hear it nevertheless.

Last goodbye to best friends and family

We got together many times with our friends to say good bye. My best friend had married an intelligent, good-looking man and they promised to come to see us in the U.S. We also paid one more visit to my parents who were heartbroken about our moving so far away. I have felt guilty toward them for the rest of their lives. As we were ready to leave, my loving, generous father, tears rolling down his cheeks (only the second time I saw him cry since his mother's passing), squeezed some money into my hand. He also presented us with a brand new, white VW Beetle with a beige leather interior, so we would not have "to worry immediately about buying a car in the United States." My sister inherited my beloved black and red Beetle, but as I recounted above, did not enjoy it for long.

A last stroll through the familiar streets of Paris.

6

Life in America?

On the high seas

July 1st, 1962, we boarded the German ocean liner *Bremen* in Cherbourg, the outermost tip of Brittany. We stopped in Southampton, U.K., to pick up more passengers and then spent nearly a week cutting through the high waves of the Atlantic, admiring romantic sunrises and sunsets, trying to have fun and not allow any anxiety of the unknown spoil our joy of being together, playing with our daughter who would soon be two years old but hung on to me during the whole voyage rather than play with other children and the many wonderful toys in the nursery. Having our meals at a round table for twelve was hard on my husband whose English was still very halting. There were several loud and embarrassing interjections he would make, such as repeatedly saying "what?" with a very audible "h," when he felt particularly frustrated. I just pretended not to have heard them but told him later, when we were alone, to use the interrogatory word more cautiously. We made friends with an American couple who had a child of our daughter's age. Since they had spent a year in France, they pointed out some of the differences between Europe and the United States, and made recommendations what to do and not do once we had arrived in our new country.

America, here we come—hello Lady Liberty

As we approached the coast of the American continent, my husband stood on deck with his camera ready to shoot the first picture of Lady Liberty as soon as she appeared in New York Harbor, surrounded by the majestic skyscrapers of lower Manhattan in the Empire State. He used up several rolls of film, and we ended up having about one hundred pictures of the Statue of Liberty and lower Manhattan before our ship signaled its

90

arrival by a loud blow of its horn and gently glided alongside the piers before, finally, throwing its anchor in front of Pier 48—or was it 58? After the constant rocking of our stomachs for several days, I was very happy to finally step off the ship and touch solid ground.

On Pier 48 or was it 58?

It was a very hot and humid day in New York when we arrived. I had never experienced such oppressive heat made even more unbearable by high humidity. The pier looked dirty and uninviting to me, but my husband seemed happy. He was searching in the receiving crowd to find his cousin whom he had not seen in years and who had offered to drive us to our destination in New Jersey. They soon spotted each other and flew into each other's arms, exclaiming words I could not understand. She then marveled at and hugged our daughter and, after throwing a probing look at me from my blond hair to my high heels, extended her hands to me and said, "welcome to America." I have no recollection of the immigration formalities to which we were certainly subjected, but remember a few days later when we came back to the pier to retrieve our car. On the way back to New Jersey, we stopped on West 42nd Street for our first American "hamburger" with "French fries." It fulfilled a dream for my husband, but I had no idea what the names referred to, why they were called "hamburgers" and "French" fries. To me it looked simply like chopped meat squeezed in be-

On the Bremen, sailing from Cherbourg, France, to our new home in the USA, with New York Harbor and Manhattan already in sight.

tween a little round loaf of bread and "pommes frites." I soon had a similar surprise with "French" cleaners and "French" dressing. I did not see the connection to anything I had experienced in France.

A real apartment

The apartment allocated to us by East Orange General Hospital, facing the hospital buildings on South Munn Avenue, appeared to us surprisingly spacious. This one had a fully equipped kitchen, a separate bedroom, and even air conditioning, luxuries we had not enjoyed in our student quarters at the Cité Universitaire in Paris. This was going to be our home for a year until my husband completed his internship and hopefully found other hospitals where he could complete his residencies toward his specialization in internal medicine, followed by a sub-specialization in nephrology and finally pass both the New Jersey and New York medical board exams that would allow him to practice in either state. The stipend for an intern was very low. Fortunately, we did not have to pay for our apartment and my father had given us a few hundred dollars that I hurried to deposit safely in a savings account.

A difficult routine

"Interns," as first year medical graduates are called in the United States, have a grueling schedule which is hard on their families as well. We hardly saw "papa" at home. In addition to his day's work, he was also on duty every other night at the Emergency Room. One day he brought one of his colleagues home to meet us. "Dr. Pappas" was Greek and quite short. He did not have much to say but told me that my husband was very popular at the hospital, especially among the student nurses, and would not be alone for a long time if I were not around. How tasteless and rude, I thought. He did not have a nice word for me. How different from the way men treated me in France. I later learned that he was in awe of my husband, mostly because of his size, looks and popularity with women, while the short, rather stocky Greek doctor felt he himself was much less in demand.

My first real friend in America, an Australian

I had to cope with many unexpected, often unpleasant situations and started to feel very alone and lonely most of the days until I met an Australian nurse with her little boy while sitting on a bench near our building. She immediately noticed that we were not from the area and started a conversation. Soon I looked at her as a trusted friend, my first friend in America, which helped me feel a bit more comfortable in my new surroundings. We talked about life in the United States, child rearing, places where to shop for food, and she explained to me why the other women at the near-by playground, as I told her, seemed to throw bemused and even hostile glances at me when I arrived with my little girl: I was dressed in the summer suit and shoes with two-inch heels that I used to wear in Paris at similar occasions. The next time I went to the park, I wore my tennis shoes which seemed to attract less attention. I thought that the lengthy shorts several, even overweight women wore looked very unattractive but did not dare venture out in the short shorts I had worn to play tennis in Paris at the Cité Universitaire.

Adultery, violence and abuse nearby

One evening we heard a lot of commotion coming from the street and then the apartment above ours, which had been allocated to a Pakistani doctor. He apparently had an affair at the hospital with one of the student nurses and was caught by a supervising nurse who called the doctor's wife. She was a very young looking, pretty, gentle lady who was always very kind to me and my daughter when we crossed her in the elevator, but when she arrived at the hospital and found her husband in a compromising situation, he fell into a rage, pushed and pulled her across the street and all the way back to their apartment where he chained her to their bed. A few days later, she was gone, sent back to her brother because she was "unfit to be a wife."

Is there a light at the end of the tunnel?

I tried not to let all these depressive events get to me. Once I had my car, I would put my daughter on the back seat and we would drive around, not venturing very far, just trying to escape from that hospital environment I had started to hate more and more. Meanwhile, ugly things continued to happen.

The first time I parked my car in the garage, the attendant, a Black man, asked me where I was from and then told me that he had been in Europe during the war and "had girls like you," to put it in his words. I got scared hearing him boast like that in a dark garage while no one else was around and was also glad my father did not have to hear this. He would have been outraged about such a comparison. When I went upstairs to our apartment, I locked myself into the bathroom and let my tears flow until I could quiet down a bit. Soon thereafter, I had to go to the basement to do my laundry, where an elderly lady, overweight, with very crooked legs, wearing an apron-like dress and pink slippers with pompoms—I cannot forget the way she looked—asked me whether I was a "war bride." She also wanted to know whether my family in Europe had a bathroom and a real toilet or just a hole in the ground.

I started to hate this country and its people before I had met even a dozen. I yearned to go back to Europe, to a civilized society where we would not be treated like dirt. There was nobody to defend me and I could not do it myself, especially not in my halting English, so I just froze and walked away.

As a doctor, immediately assuming a medical position at the hospital that provided him with respect from a large number of less educated personnel, especially the many student nurses, my husband did not experience the kind of humiliations I had to endure. He quickly made friends with his colleagues and often had meals with them at the hospital cafeteria while we were home alone. New in the country, on a very limited budget and without much social contact, days tended to be long and lonely.

A massive invasion of in-laws

In the months after our arrival in the United States, more and more members of my husband's family left their country which had recently known revolution and political upheaval. They came to gather around their "doctor" son, brother or cousin, to whose medical studies in Paris, unbeknownst to me, several had made monthly contributions to help one promising boy in the family "make it." They probably felt that the time had come for him to reciprocate. They had no idea of our financial situation, and in all fairness to them, I don't think they expected much money from us but rather an improvement of their own social status. They also had no idea of how lonely and unhappy I felt in those days. At weekend gatherings, the men would keep to themselves, drinking "coca" or beer, while the women, including me, were relegated to watching the children and preparing the meals. Whenever I tried to offer them dinner at our apartment, for instance a paella that took me all day to concoct, I was told that the way they cook it was different, I used the wrong recipe. In their country they did "not use paprika." The family complimented and courted my husband, not knowing that he actually provided very little to our living expenses. They seldom had a kind word for me. It did not occur to them that the meals I prepared for usually a large crowd, but which they did not appreciate much, were actually produced with the money my father had given us and I used only for special occasions or needs.

Sois belle et tais-toi!

There were days when I was ready to explode, needed some emotional support but did not know where to turn. I finally presented my husband with an ultimatum, "me or the family," which I immediately knew was wrong, unfair to him and impossible for him to carry out in my favor, but the present situation was too depressing and I couldn't see how it would change in the future unless we moved away. When I married him, I had no idea that this would be my life, a servant woman, sometimes complimented for her looks but immediately told that she was different, not like a "Latina," which they would have preferred. Yes, indeed, I was different. I would have loved to participate in discussions, the kind we used to have in Paris and in my family. I wanted to be a "subject" not a thing pushed into a corner. There is a saying in French: "Sois belle et tais-toi," be beautiful and keep quiet, but in France or in my family I had never experienced that kind of deprecating treatment, an objectification of who I was. I remembered what my friends told me about my being different from the man I was thinking of marrying. Having come to live with him here in New Jersey, I indeed felt very much that I was different. Here I was a foreigner not just in a foreign country but also in a foreign family and culture, trying to live with these two new cultures, one embedded into another, both foreign to me and, helas, both alienating. But I could not tell anyone how unhappy I was. I don't think anyone in my husband's family would have understood how it felt to be surrounded every weekend by all these people whose language I barely understood, whose culture was so different from mine and who, I felt, did not really want to know anything about mine. I missed my family and friends and spent much of my first year in the United States unhappy and yearning to return to Paris.

A new life in the Big Apple

The prospect of moving to New York City the following July, rekindled my hope that things would improve. I began to review my stenography books and practiced on the typewriter I had brought with me, confident that I could find a job next year, maybe in New York City, where we could have a better life. While my daughter still refused to let go of me and would not stay at a play school unless I remained there with her, I tried to help her overcome that fear which, I think, was due to the fact that she was exposed to too many different languages, French, English, even some German and now Spanish, before she could master even one. We continued to speak French at home, and she finally learned to express herself a bit in that language, but all the other children around her would not understand her nor she them. Fortunately, she overcame the predicament with amazing rapidity once she started going to school after our move to Manhattan.

The only pre-school we could afford—a nasty fat owner

With the help of an ad in the *New York Times,* I found a seemingly interesting job in midtown as a receptionist for a well known Bauhaus architect. This meant that I had only less than two weeks to find a pre-school for my daughter. There was one on Central Park West that promised good care and fell within our budget. My daughter cried the first day as I was leaving her and I felt helpless and guilty, but she seemed less unhappy on the days that followed and slowly seemed to warm up to the other children. Soon she came home speaking English but with the soft, singing Harlem accent of the lady who was taking care of her group. The middle aged lady was nice but had no professional training in child care as was required in Parisian nurseries. Since we lived on the Upper East Side of Manhattan, it was difficult for me to drop off my daughter at eight o'clock in the morning before going to work in midtown and then picking her up by six o'clock in the evening when the school closed. It added about an hour each time to my commute to and from work. Even though my husband was a medical doctor, we still lived near the poverty line and could not afford sending her to a pre-school closer to our apartment until I started to receive my paychecks. Yet, the day I met the owner of the school, who seemed to examine me from head to toe and then made a strange and I thought disparaging remark about my daughter, because she did not speak as well as the other children, I knew that I had to take her out of this place immediately. The woman reminded me in her attitude and looks of the one in England who had been rude to me when I stayed in her boarding house in Hampstead with my friend. They could have been twins, even though one lived in England and the other in France. I was anxious to remove my daughter from her school and influence.

At the Upper East Side

We had found an apartment at the Upper East Side, without being aware of its being a fashionable area. A doctor who had completed his residency at my husband's new hospital returned to Iran and was happy to simply pass his apartment on to us with some of his furniture. The rent cost a bit more than one third of our monthly budget. It was above our means, but I expected to receive a paycheck soon.

My first job in Manhattan—what an ordeal!

Once I had my interview with the Bauhaus architect, who was of Hungarian descent and seemed pleased to hire me, I began to feel much happier. I felt that there were nice, educated, civilized people in America, not just in Europe. But I soon realized that the job I took was not for me.

Working the phone should never be the first job of a recent immigrant who still has some problems with proficiency in the English language. It was very painful for me to admit that I simply could not understand the English pronunciation of certain names, especially the German-sounding names of several clients. I would sometimes try to repeat their names but with a more Germanic pronunciation which offended certain clients who did not hesitate to tell me so. Kinder callers, who noticed my difficulties, would offer to spell their names, but then rattle down the letters at a speed that still left me puzzled. It was hell. I felt like an idiot. I had never been trained to retain words that were spelled to me rapidly and in English over the phone. In Europe it is usually not necessary to spell your name, it suffices to just point out any deviations from the norm, for instance a double consonant or hyphenation. Even today, I am not entirely comfortable when people provide me over the phone with the rapid spelling of a lengthy name or address. It is a European weakness, as is the neglect to retain first names at introductions, since they are not used in formal conversation. No European political leader would refer to a visiting counterpart, as George W. Bush did, calling President Chirac "my friend Jaaacques," made worse by unduly lengthening the vowel, or calling his own Secretary of State "Condy" at a press conference in front of the Prime Minister of another country. He recently behaved just as inappropriately toward the new British Prime Minister Brown. President Raegan was heavily criticized by the British press when he "shockingly" put his arms around Queen Elizabeth's shoulders, as was George W. Bush when he gave the German Chancellor a "back rub" at the G8 conference. Such differences in etiquette and linguistic practices require a certain sophistication in the different cultures. I was eager to acquire it in the practices of the United States but needed a bit more time.

A first taste of discrimination at the job

At my first unfortunate job with the architect, there was also a young woman who gave me my first taste of discrimination at a workplace in New York. From the day I walked into the office, she seemed to resent the way I looked, dressed and even the fact that I was married to a doctor and had a cute little daughter which someone must have divulged to her before my arrival. The first thing she told me was that since I was the last arrival it was up to me to make sure each morning that there was enough toilet paper in the toilets. I thought that it was a strange welcome, but OK, she was right. In that office, I started at the bottom of the ladder. Yet several times she also seemed extremely bemused by my accent, especially my way of pronouncing certain names. She could have been told that I struggled with that aspect of my job and rubbed it under my nose. She did not take into account that each time this happened I also excused myself right after having been corrected and tried to improve as fast as I could. It was not so much what she said but more the way in which she said things to me that was hurtful. After a couple of weeks, instead of trying to survive at that job, dreading to pick up the phone or listening to the sly remarks of that co-worker, I decided to quit. I excused myself to the nice architect for having accepted a job that was obviously not for me.

Vive la différence!

Leafing again through ads in the *New York Times,* I soon found a job at Columbia University. This time it was the right choice for me and allowed me not just to function well but even grow rapidly in my new linguistic and professional environment. I was hired to help prepare an international conference that accepted papers in three languages, which meant that I could make use of the skills I had previously acquired while adding new ones, especially acquiring greater fluency in English in a positive milieu. At the beginning, my work consisted mostly of writing and answering letters from potential conference participants in various countries around the world. Soon I was promoted from secretary to administrative assistant which also meant an increase in salary. I had a wonderful boss, a long-time immigrant himself, who guided me and appreciated what I brought to the job, my linguistic and secretarial skills and especially my international know how in business correspondence and personal exchange. The conference was a great success for my boss and his partner, and they passed merit on to us who had helped them with the task, especially after the publication of the proceedings in three languages that needed much editing and proofreading.

A sensitive boss before the dictates of feminism

On a few occasions, my boss allowed me to bring my little daughter to work when she had a cold and was not allowed to attend school. She would sit at an empty desk coloring books, drawing people and landscapes, or quietly playing with toys, patient and well behaved until we could leave. Sometimes my boss would sit down to talk to her, tell her stories and make her laugh. All this, years before feminism came to fight for similar privileges in the treatment of women with kids. This fine man was also instrumental in encouraging me to continue my studies at graduate school, I should not "waste my mind," he said. I followed his advice a few years later when I decided to apply to the Graduate Faculties of Columbia University.

Our "blitz-trip" to Florida

We were eager to see more of the United States, and my husband was particularly attracted to Florida, which was similar to the country where he had lived before coming to Paris for his medical studies. During his summer break, between two hospitals where he was training as a "resident in internal medicine," we jumped in our little Beetle and just drove for hours, through Virginia where we visited a friend, a former medical student from Paris, then through the Deep South, where we were shocked to witness the poverty and discrimination against Blacks. Little skinny children were sitting on the porch of some run down homes just watching us drive by. Toilets had signs above the doors that read "Whites" and "Colored." On the second day, we arrived around midnight in Miami Beach, where we luckily found a room in a small hotel on the beach that was within our budget. Stepping on to our balcony in the early morning, we saw a dozen or so really old looking people doing aerobic exercises on the beach. After an improvised breakfast, we hurried to get to the swimming pool, where our little four-year-old suddenly took to the smooth, warm water and spent hours floating in her inflated life-saver ring, even ready to learn her first breast strokes after she had been terrified by the waves of the ocean and stubbornly refused to go even near the water at the beaches of the Atlantic in New Jersey. We teased her, telling her that she looked like a little turtle pedaling around in the pool, which made her giggle with joy.

House wife?

Since all the work for the international conference at Columbia University was completed, I took a few months to stay at home, trying to be the perfect wife and mother on a budget that, in spite of our vacation extravaganza, was still near the poverty line. I cooked, cleaned and even sew a few pieces of clothes for my daughter and myself. Our social life had picked up a bit, I would have liked to have something new to wear, but I could not possibly afford buying a dress. So, I asked my parents to help me purchase a sewing machine and, using Vogue patterns, was able to sew a beautiful blue taffeta tunic dress for myself which I wore, with some success, at a dinner held at the Plaza Hotel for the Mount Sinai Hospital medical staff. My husband seemed pleased both with how I looked and the low price of the dress. During a few months, sewing satisfied my craving for a creative activity, so I continued searching for fabrics in the lower Manhattan retail shops, making fashionable dresses and even capes for both my daughter and myself.

Frolicking in the warm waves during our "blitz trip" to Miami Beach.

Another baby?

Since my daughter was already four years old, we were thinking of having another child. It was not to be. After giving birth to my daughter, I had experienced several miscarriages which always left me devastated, and the surge of hormones caused problems with my veins, even phlebitis. Finally, I had made it to the fourth month when my husband decided to buy a new car—a big Buick that had belonged to one of his colleagues—and plan a long awaited vacation for the early summer to one of the beaches of the Atlantic. I did not feel well the day we left and was scared by the speed with which my husband drove his new car. I know this was annoying him and spoiled his pleasure of finally being able to drive a big American car on a long stretch of highway. When we arrived at Virginia Beach, I was in poor shape. My face looked gray and I had pain in my lower abdomen. My husband had noticed and told me that I looked terrible and would I please fix my hairdo and just try to enjoy the vacation he was offering us. He thought that dinner and a good night's rest would help me get over whatever my problem was. But the day we arrived back home after less than a week, I miscarried, a little boy they told me, and had to be hospitalized. I was blamed by my husband for having "willed" what happened. His words were cruel. I also developed a dangerous phlebitis on my right leg and had to be bedridden for several days. Since it was difficult and annoying for my husband to take care of our daughter, taking her to and picking her up from school while he was supposed to be present early

My sweet three-year-old showing off the dress I made for her. I made a similar one for myself while trying out being a "stay-at-home mom" and hoping for more children.

morning for his work at the hospital, he decided to carry me home from the hospital, so she could just stay with me all day until he returned in the evening and brought us some food. My doctor was very unhappy with his decision and asked him whether he knew that this could kill me in case the blood clot traveled to my heart or brains. I was scared but let my husband carry me in his strong arms from the hospital wheelchair to the car and then up by elevator to our apartment. I was quite impressed that he could do so, and so was our doorman when we arrived at the lobby of our building. Luckily, the inflammation subsided within a few days, and I could slowly resume our normal routine and try to assure some happiness at home.

Yes! the Lycée Français for my daughter

In the fall, my daughter was accepted for kindergarten at a distinguished French school in Manhattan. I was delighted that she was accepted but my husband thought that I was snobbish and my ambition for her future non realistic. Today, I am so glad to have persisted. It was the right first step to assure her future. She would attend a school where she would receive the kind of education I strove to offer her, where she would grow up speaking both French and English in a bi-cultural milieu, were academics, especially mathematics, were also of a high quality. In the back of my mind I kept the thought that any time we decided to return to France, she would be ready to jump in and continue her studies without interruption, since France has a nationally devised curriculum and the same final exams at all the numerous Lycées Français established around the world.

Encounters with the rich and famous

My daughter liked her new school and soon made good friends. Some of the parents of her friends became also my friends since we tried to help each other organize after school activities. Most children came from wealthy families but our modest income did not seem to matter much. We were readily accepted by everyone. While waiting for my daughter after school, I occasionally chatted with Otto Preminger whose twins, a boy

My daughter with her best friend from the Lycée Français of New York and the children of our next-door neighbors.

My daughter (left) with the four children of my first friend in the United States, an Australian nurse who lost her battle with cancer in the prime of life.

and a girl, were in the same class as my daughter. His son, who seemed to like my daughter and probably tried to impress her, made a long distance call from London to wish her "Merry Christmas." She was overjoyed. While waiting one day for my daughter to finish her solfège class at the Dalcroze School of Music, I sat next to Jackie Kennedy who was patiently waiting to pick up Caroline. At about the same time, we were shopping for shoes at Bloomingdale's when Grace Kelly arrived to do the same for her daughter Caroline. Unlike Jackie, and I am sure unintentionally, she caused quite a stir looking beautiful and regal. I guess, in New York, one is bound to run into celebrities.

The Kennedys

I had seen Jackie and President Kennedy in Paris, as they were arriving in an open car from the airport of Orly for a conference with Khrushchev. Having John Kennedy as my first president in the United States, made me feel that it might be OK to live in this country. His assassination soon thereafter was a terrible blow to my faith in this country. It was reinforced by a nasty remark from a Republican co-worker who seemed anything but unhappy about the loss of this great man. Bobby Kennedy's assassination added another blow to my increasing disillusionment with United States politics. Historically, the best and most beloved rulers have sometimes become the victims of murderous fanatics, such as the "Bon Roi

Henri IV," the Good King Henri the Fourth. The day of Bobby Kennedy's assassination, I was in the East 86th Street cross town bus, wearing a polka dot blue and white blouse, when a man started to attack me verbally and then stood up in front of me shouting that "blonds like you killed Bobby Kennedy, blonds in polka dot dresses; you will pay for this." Naturally, I became scared that he may actually hurt me, but even though there were several men on the bus, maybe a dozen people altogether, no one came to my defense. Fortunately, we were getting close to my stop at York Avenue where I got off the bus and rushed home. It reminded me of the non Samaritan nature of those who, not long after we moved into our new apartment on York Avenue watched as a woman was beaten to death under their windows and did not call police because, as we learned later, they "did not want to get involved."

The French adored the Kennedys, especially Jacqueline Bouvier Kennedy, whose elegance they traced to her French origins. To this day I still feel great admiration for both the President and Jackie Kennedy. Since I was less involved in national politics, I knew less about Bobby. By chance, I have several times encountered one or the other member of the Kennedy family while living in Manhattan. Jackie used to bicycle ride around the reservoir in Central Park, with John John sitting in a child seat behind her. One late evening, around midnight, I saw Jackie, who was already Mrs. Onassis at that time, cross East 86th Street by herself. The day Jackie died of cancer, I was walking down Fifth Avenue when I saw John Jr. rush toward his mother's apartment building. Jackie Kennedy was an inspiration to me at all phases of her life, as a mother, devoted, elegant wife of a great even though unfaithful man, and later a widow whose dignity moved the whole world. She possessed enormous qualities, unfailing class in overcoming so much adversity in her life, even after her failure to find happiness in the marriage to a rich man who was not quite worthy of her. Professionally, as well, she distinguished herself as a trusted editor for a very respectable publishing house. I have always admired women who managed to combine all their talents, character, beauty and intelligence to live complex lives as wives, mothers, and professionals with dignity and class.

Life with my mother-in-law

After my miscarriage and the hiatus of being a stay-home wife and mother, I longed to go back to some professional activity that would also make me less dependent on my husband's graces. My mother-in-law had moved in with us, the four of us were living in a one-bedroom apartment. She was kind and very quiet, often depressive and probably feeling displaced as I did, but the two us got along fine, even when she made me cook rice at every meal, even in addition to a spaghetti dinner. I cut, set and combed her hair to make her feel prettier and occasionally bought her a blouse or other piece of garment, which she seemed to appreciate. But none of us had enough privacy. My husband kept complaining about having to sleep on a sofa bed. My daughter had to share her room, the only bedroom we had, with her grandmother, and the living room also served as our dining room and our bedroom.

The U.N. General Assembly

In hopes of improving our situation, I started to interview and submit to IQ tests at places such as the Ford Foundation and the United Nations and was offered a position at both places but chose to start with a General Assembly at the United Nations to explore the possibility of eventually landing a job as an interpreter. My mother-in-law was to meet my daughter when the school bus dropped her off in mid-afternoon in front of our building and stay with her until either my husband or I returned home. It did not work out well. One day, I found them inadvertently locked into the bedroom for a couple of hours. The door lock could not be activated from the inside but this had never caused any problem before. Next, my neighbors complained that my daughter was driving her noisy little car back and forth in the hall and was sometimes sitting for hours outside our apartment door playing with her toys. My mother-in-law had felt sorry for her being too confined to the apartment. It was also the time of the great New York blackout, when at the United Nations we thought the Russians were attacking us, and I rushed home having to climb lots of stairs to get to our apartment and reassure my daughter and my mother-in-law who had become nearly hysterical.

Since for work at the United Nations I tried to dress as nicely as I could with what I had brought with me from Paris, my mother-in-law suspected me of cheating on her son on days when I had to work late. While it would have been easy to have affairs with these men from foreign countries who came to the U.S. without their families and seemed quite eager to find company, I was absolutely faithful. Toward the end of the General Assembly, though, I was invited for a lunch and interview by a close assistant of the then Secretary General. I do not want to name either one. He offered me a position in the Secretary General's office on the tenth floor, but I felt that my interviewer did not clearly spell out the nature of my position. In the course of the interview, he asked me, among many other things about my home situation, whether I loved my husband and whether I occasionally attended dinners without him and, if necessary, could work late. I was not quizzed much on my educational background and professional qualifications. Maybe my boss had already provided that information. I had always idealized the United Nations as a most noble institution created after World War II to prevent another Holocaust, but after a few weeks of working there I found the atmosphere a bit disappointing. While these men were supposed to devote their time to the good of humanity and assure justice and harmony in the world, many seemed more interested in enjoying a life of luxury and privileges provided and financed by their impoverished nations. Since I was not a native speaker of any of the five languages used at the United Nations, English, French, Russian, Spanish and Chinese, my dreams of becoming an interpreter were short lived. The rules would not even allow me to apply. So I thanked for the offer to work for the office of the Secretary General on the tenth floor but told my interviewer that my babysitting situation would not allow me to live up to the time requirements of the job. It was true. My mother-in-law no longer wanted to be there for my daughter after school. She did not want to be tied down every afternoon. So I left the United Nations, a bit disillusioned, at the end of the General Assembly that had lasted three months.

Signs of a failing marriage

The situation at home became increasingly difficult to bear even though my mother-in-law had moved away to live with her daughter. A two-bedroom apartment became available next door at that time, something we had hoped for, but my husband suddenly did not want to make the move. I was desperately trying to save our marriage, even though fights became ugly and started to affect our little girl. My husband's temper sometimes seemed out of control. He was a very strong man, and I became increasingly afraid of him and even feared for the safety of both my daughter and myself. He realized it himself that things were getting out of hand. But we always reconciled. After a particularly violent fight, I called my parents and begged them to send money for two one-way tickets, but then, after another reconciliation, used it instead to apply to graduate school at Columbia University.

Escape into Graduate Studies

At that point, I would have liked to sign up for medical school, but my husband was adamant about my doing so. "Having two doctors in the family," he felt, "would never work," even though my sister and her husband were both MDs and we knew several other medical couples, which all managed well. Since it was more acceptable to my husband and seemed less disruptive to our family life, in addition to appearing less difficult since I was fluent in the language, I decided to follow my former kind boss's advice and apply instead to the French Graduate Faculties at Columbia University.

The interviewing professor, who was close to retirement age, asked me "why in the world" I wanted to go to graduate school since I was married to a doctor and had a child. I was shocked by his question. He was obviously much behind his time. Contrary to him, my former boss was enthusiastic about my decision and whole heartedly supported my application with a glowing letter of recommendation. I was admitted after easily passing an English test, the first multiple choice test in my life, and accepting conditions that required a B-minus average in my first semester. I finished with a B-plus.

Denial of pleasure—refusal of help

I loved my studies, but soon my husband seemed to become jealous of everything I liked that was not traceable to him, even the books I raved about. Herbert van Karajan was scheduled to give a concert in New York, but my husband denied me, for no good reason, the pleasure of attending his concert, which had been one of my dreams. For the summer, we had planned to send our daughter to stay with her grandparents and cousins in Germany. My husband and I were to follow later to join them for a couple of weeks. But things between the two of us got worse with every day that passed. I ended up flying to Europe by myself while my husband decided to stay behind. He vacationed at the beaches of New York, as my neighbors later told me. As soon as I returned with my daughter from Europe, he left the apartment and moved in with his mother and sister's family.

The medical office he had opened on West End Avenue did not seem to attract patients. I thought it was because he opened it in the middle of nowhere. I had encouraged him to risk settling for a more plush location, even Park Avenue, where our new acquaintances from my daughter's school and my work would help him develop a clientele. Instead, he listened to his brother, and after closing the West End Avenue office opened another one in Brooklyn where he was hoping to attract a Spanish speaking clientele many of whom were on welfare and would be supported by government money, but it turned out to be a disappointment again and he had to close that office as well.

7

Suddenly Alone in a Foreign Country

The crumbling of my universe

Our marriage was definitively over. With it, the whole structure of my universe crumbled. At a time when I had finally settled somewhat in our new country, my despair hit rock bottom. My daughter and I had made friends with a family whose daughter attended the same French school as mine. Her generous kindness and sincere concern helped us survive the first desperate moments and weeks.

No maternal sympathy

I longed to see my parents. My father paid for a round trip, but as we arrived, my mother was extremely unhappy about the idea of a divorce. "How can you do this to me," she said, with little understanding of my desperate need for emotional support. I had "brought shame on the family," she said, "there had never been a divorce before." Her complete insensitivity to our needs was too much for me to bear. I grabbed my daughter and our suitcases and left my parents' house precipitously to move into a hotel for the remaining days until our flight back to the United States.

The most devastating months of our lives—fighting for survival

During the months that followed, I nearly broke down. It was my love and sense of responsibility for my daughter that kept me going. We had to cope with the most difficult times of our lives. No job, living off the savings from my father's money of which my husband before he left had quickly withdrawn one half for himself to buy a Mercedes and ski equipment so he could vacation with a new girlfriend in the French Alps. My daughter and I lived at the poverty line, but I was too ashamed to ask for help or any government assistance. How could I possibly go on welfare

110

and live off food stamps still married to a doctor. After the devastating months of my asking for a separation agreement that would have forced my husband to provide some financial support, his attorney responded with a threat of a final divorce, even the loss of my daughter, if I did not comply with his petty financial dictates until my husband himself intervened and told his attorney to stop harassing me. I had pleaded mental and physical cruelty, but at the hearing my husband told the judge that I was a good wife and mother and he just wanted to be a bachelor again. It was the first year after he had completed his residencies and had doubled his income. For the first time in his life, he earned some money and wanted to enjoy life by himself, without the burden of a family. One of the last things my husband said to me was: "You always wanted to work, now you can work, but make sure you soon find someone who wants to marry you. After you turn forty, it will be much more difficult." I had barely turned thirty. His sarcastic comment was meant to hurt me but also revealed his hope to rid himself the sooner the better of any obligation toward us in the future.

The day of the divorce

The day the divorce became final, walking out of the courtroom, I just sat on a bench for a while, all by myself, totally exhausted. For a few minutes, I couldn't even remember where the entrance to the subway was. Once I made it home, I took my daughter by the hand and went to Columbia University to tell my advisor that I had just been divorced and was ready to go back to my studies. He was very kind and rather sensitive, more than ever before or after. He also asked me whether I was quite sure of what I was doing since, he added in a rather low voice, "in the end it is always the same thing," but he also promised to support me as much as he could. My daughter had waited for me in the secretary's office. As we left the building, I turned around and saw my advisor at the fifth floor window of Philosophy Hall looking down at us with a very sad expression on his face. He must have known a bit how we felt right then, since he had gone through several divorces himself.

A father's attempt to escape responsibility

After the divorce my ex-husband simply disappeared. His family did not want to tell me where to find him until I was tipped off by a former colleague that he had signed up for Viet Nam where he was hoping to have plenty of opportunity to improve his surgical skills and at the same time get out of any financial obligations toward us. He was hoping to force me to leave the country and return to Europe. In a word, get rid of us. A treatment that reminded me of his Pakistani colleague in East Orange who sent his wife back to her brother because she caught him in bed with a student nurse. "How cruel and selfish men, fathers, can be," I thought. My father's only comment on my ex-husband's behavior was that he was "not a man." But I was able to track down my ex-husband in Texas, where he was for his basic training, and speak to his commanding officer who promised to take care of this. "The Army does not tolerate such behavior," he said. The child support payments I received were modest but at least started to arrive regularly since they were automatically withheld each month from my husband's Army pay. They helped me with the rent and utilities while I had to come up for food and everything else from our savings that were running out rapidly.

Budgeting

I have all my life managed to live within my means and make the most of the few dollars I had, while people sometimes told me that I looked like a millionaire. My husband's divorce attorney even made sly comments to this effect during our negotiations. "This Mr. Hirschfield was a man of low moral status," I told myself, and I was hoping he would someday have to pay for it.

8

Trying to Survive in the U.S.

My benefactors

In the fall semester, Columbia University saved our lives by appointing me research assistant to the chairman of the department. The position included free tuition and made it possible for me to continue my studies. My daughter's tuition for the following year had been advanced to me from our savings at the time of the divorce settlements, before my husband could disappear. Our survival was thus guaranteed for at least a year, even though on an extremely tight budget.

In the spring semester visiting professor Enid Starkie, from Oxford University in the U.K., hired me as her reader for a Symbolist course she taught to an overflow class of 70 students. I corrected midterm and final exams for her courses. It meant a bit more money for us, but the real and unexpected beauty of it was that she recommended to the chair of the Barnard College French Department to hire me the following year as an instructor. I was about to get an M.A degree and now I even had a dream job lined up without as much as having had to apply for it. There was a lucky star shining over us. I will forever be grateful to Enid Starkie and the wonderful chairman of the Barnard College French Department who offered me my first academic contract.

1968—My first year in teaching starts with a bang

Nineteen sixty-eight was the year of the international student and workers revolt both in Europe and the United States. In France, where the revolt turned quite violent, it became known as the "The Days of May '68." At Columbia University, where Bendit Cohn inflamed the student body and enticed the young faculty to follow him in his revolutionary fervor, several of my colleagues at Barnard joined in the unrest. My attitude was more reserved. After the many years of insecurity in my life, followed by a devastating divorce and struggle for survival, I felt very apprehensive that my newly gained position and relatively secure, even though still modest, income might be jeopardized and that I could not provide for my daughter. It felt hypocritical and selfish to me that some of the wealthiest faculty, who seemed to have everything they needed, family, status and financial security, would engage in creating this turmoil. As students gained more and more power over the circumstances, in the Spring Semester they asked me, as they probably asked all other instructors, to wear blue jeans and sit down in class instead of "throwing your weight about towering over us." That was fine with me, but then they also barred faculty from going to their offices and banded together to boycott final exams. Some of the most beautiful and previously elegant girls suddenly jumped up on the tables of the cafeteria and harangued their fellow students using the most vulgar language.

Toward a Ph.D. degree in the midst of the 1968 revolt

Fortunately, before all this happened, I had passed my qualifying exams and had defended my Master's essay, so my immediate future was somewhat secure, but in order to continue my academic employment, I needed to start working toward a Ph.D. degree and submit an original topic for my doctoral dissertation that had to be approved by the French graduate faculty. Changes were made in the curriculum but the older, tenured faculty remained the same for a while. I was much relieved when my topic received their approval.

New voices, new directions, at Columbia University

The campus quieted in the next year but attracted more and more visiting faculty from abroad that introduced new, often controversial theories and ideologies. They loved to come to the United States, and especially also to New York, to disseminate their views and catch good honoraria or visiting faculty salaries to supplement the one, generally much more modest, at their home institutions. A new order that broke with the old one had definitely gotten the upper hand on every level of academic life as it did at all other Ivy League and major universities of the country.

Feminists sprung up and following Simone de Beauvoir's "Bible," *The Second Sex,* published their own manifestos. When I attended a conference in Paris, female participants asked me: "Do American feminists really think that women have a creative imagination"?—how far have we come since those years! Several of my Barnard colleagues came "out of the closet" as lesbians and male homosexuals. They participated enthusiastically in the revolts, but I felt, since they did not have children, they did not understand why I remained more reserved. They all had support from family. One of them later inherited a million and stopped teaching altogether. Another, daughter of a distinguished mathematician, enjoyed vacations in their prestigious apartment near the Luxembourg gardens in Paris. Others had wealthy parents and husbands. My daughter and I depended on my salary for our living. Only one kind, sensitive colleague reached out to us, a very beautiful young woman with two children, who was also a fellow graduate student at Columbia University. She invited us several times to her weekend home and had us meet her parents. She seemed to understand my concerns as a single mother and sole provider after the difficult experience of my recent divorce. Unfortunately, she ended up divorcing as well and, despite several attempts in recent years, I have been unable to locate her whereabouts. I would have liked to tell her how much she had meant to us. The oldest female professor at Columbia also took us under her wings and assumed a bit the role of mother and grandmother when she learned of our being alone in the country in those turbulent times. Some of my Barnard colleagues seemed to resent her kindness toward us and let me know it after the professor died a few years later. The structure of departments at Columbia reflected the change brought about by the revolts. More Jewish faculty was hired and more easily tenured than in the past decades which had often given unfair advantage to Anglo-Saxon candidates. Nietzschean and Freudian philosophy led to new textual politics and focus on the body, sex, the Oedipal complex. With it came, from Marxist and Maoist left-wing politics, attacks on so-called "inauthentic, bourgeois values," "fetishism," "social myths," abuses of power and re-examinations of the system and role of language.

Cries for freedom

Everywhere, there were cries for freedom from various forms of oppression. I was shocked when I learned from the news and saw first hand on our trip south how Blacks were treated in this country and how women and older people were relegated to second class citizenship. The very existence of a violent, racist association such as the Ku Klux Klan, that seemed to take its inspiration from the Middle Ages and the Inquisition, seemed incredible in a modern country run by presidents such as John F. Kennedy. Also, I could not believe that wives and especially ex-wives in New York's wealthy suburbs such as Westchester voted against the Equal Rights Amendment because they feared they might be losing their hefty child support payments to which their ex-husbands were held by law. Dr. Martin Luther King's assassination, that had followed so closely the one of President Kennedy and his brother Bobby, showed how craziness, fanaticism, hatred and sheer evil can fell down the best of people not just in Hitler's Germany but also in an idealized country such as the United States that prided itself to be a refuge for the persecuted. We had come to America at a time when the war in Viet Nam, which Americans had foolishly taken over once the French had the good sense to pull out, became more and more shameful and upsetting, especially in view of the persecutions of those who tried not to be part of the massacre. "How could my daughter's father have volunteered to fight in such a war where entire villages of innocent people were exterminated?!" Decades later, a similarly immoral, foolish, warmongering president and even his female secretary of state, watched passively how an innocent population and its children were massacred by an aggressive, inhuman neighbor. And they did not believe in the benefit of diplomacy, just raw violence. My nature and upbringing have prevented me all my life from participating in street manifestations, which does not mean that I have refrained from expressing my views intellectually, in discussions or writing. The political events of the sixties and seventies and the atrocities of World War II have certainly influenced the choice and direction of my doctoral dissertation and my subsequent research and publications. All the while, in 1968, my own most pressing needs for liberation were freedom from poverty, loneliness, insecurity, abuse and discrimination, but I was determined to do all I could to overcome our problems.

Abuses of the revolutionary moment

Ironically, I felt most threatened in my relatively new existence in the United States by the very people who emitted the loudest cries for freedom while, compared to my daughter and me and millions of others, they seemed to live in opulence and have everything most of us could only dream about. Some of the wealthiest colleagues thought it chic to host Black Panthers for dinner while continuing to be chauffeured to work in Jaguars. Under the pretense of sympathizing with the underprivileged, they eagerly profited from the revolutionary moment, using the power of their wealth and the social status it provided, to help themselves to more fame and prestigious professional appointments not out of need but simply to kindle their egos. There were others who hid their personal greed behind the deplorable situation of Blacks in the United States or took advantage of even their slightest link to past political or historical events in Europe to help themselves to a better life. Some of the politically most astute still enjoy the fruit of their dubious ethics today but would never admit to the questionable means by which they obtained their privileges. Nevertheless, it was fascinating to live in the midst of this social, racial, sexual, ethnic and intellectual effervescence. It resulted in more freedom and opportunities, at least for the most aggressive.

Always a mother first

In 1968, which was not only the year of the student revolt but also the year my divorce became final, many doors opened to a new life, some fell gaping open, unexpectedly, frighteningly, others I pushed open deliberately, with all my energy and enthusiasm. In most instances, my guiding post was the happiness, welfare and future of my daughter. I know she suffered from the breakup of our marriage, but I wanted to make sure that she suffered less now than if we had stayed married.

A few years later, her teacher in English 100 at Wellesley College called me one evening, telling me that she wanted to share with me what

Suddenly, it was just the two of us but we tried to remain cheerful making short trips on weekends to parks and lakes near the City of New York.

my daughter, who was then 18 years old, had written in an essay about me. In a broken voice, she then red to me excerpts from that essay, dated October 11:

"Writing about my family should not be a hazardous venture. I could only go wrong once, since there would only be one person to describe . . . that is, if I chose to depict this person in her role of 'mother.' But what if I attempted a full-length portrait of her as the many faceted individual that she is? This is where the situation would complicate itself. Actually, I would have several 'people' to describe.

"My mother does not win first prize for having always kept all my school blouses ironed, or having had breakfast ready every morning to tempt me into having my 'most important meal of the day' (reference to the words of Dr. Spock, school, and every cereal commercial on TV). This is not because she was not capable of it or did not care, but because she followed a different set of priorities. Her goals as a mother, I think, were to make me independent, get me educated, and make sure I was never in doubt one second of her love for me. I know she reached the latter goal. She is still working on the first two.

"As a teacher, she knows that a very effective way to transmit something is to give an example. Her lifestyle for the last ten years has been just that: an example of how to be thrown out of a protected world and make it on your own. This brings me to image number two of my mother, that of the breadwinner, and it is basically characterized by a never ending need to . surpass herself. Amazingly enough, I have never felt left out in this stage. She has always managed to give me the impression that her victories were mine too. This is probably the best proof of our closeness. It also renders any argument against working mothers worthless.

"If you unwrapped this second box, you would find another one in which one last important side of my mother's personality, in relation to me, is revealed. She possesses the uncanny ability totally to rejuvenate herself and come down to any age level. Taking into account the fact that this sounds very corny, I must say that, as a child and even as a teenager, I often felt that she was my best friend. I do not think that my mother will ever be an old lady. She has too much youth and vitality in her, and I cannot see her blond hair going white nor her blue eyes disappearing in the middle of wrinkled pouches of skin. I am sure to grow old before she does.

"One of the principle reasons for the creation of a family is the perpetuation of people's beliefs, knowledge and physical traits. In my case, I can only hope that I have inherited my mother's qualities while keeping my own individuality, if one can speak of such a thing at the age of 18. Education has provided me with some of the former, I hope, but I still address many complaints to Mother Nature in her handling of my genes. For instance, why couldn't I have been made blond? I think I actually know the answer: because my mother always wanted a 'brownie.'"

Istill cannot reread this text without getting teary-eyed. How did I deserve this "grace"? I used to torment myself for leaving her alone early morning even before serving her breakfast, but for nearly five years I was scheduled to teach an 8 o'clock class at Douglass College in New Brunswick and had to leave our apartment in upper Manhattan before the sun came up.

In the decades that followed my divorce, my daughter hardly saw her father at all—he first went to Vietnam and then settled in California— but I tried to maintain in her some positive feelings toward him because I knew how important it was for a little girl to believe that her father loved her. I am sure he actually did, even though he did not show it, maybe did not know how to, or probably thought that he did not have to do anything to deserve her love.

I was more successful in protecting my daughter than was his second wife and the two children they had together, whom he completely abandoned after they divorced a few years later. Their mother called me one evening, shortly after I had moved back to the East Coast, to ask me how I did it. She told me that she admired me. However, a few years before that, only days after I began teaching in California where they lived as well, she urged my former husband to serve me with papers seeking authorization from the court of California to cease all support for us since I had become a college professor and should be able to make a living for the two of us. The wife's father, a well to do attorney, alerted her to the newly instituted law in California that favored abolishing child support payments in case both parents were gainfully employed, which I was, even though my salary was a small fraction of my former husband's earnings and the initial, very modest child support payments, that at the time of the divorce had been calculated on his pay as a medical resident and then his Army pay, had never been adjusted to conform to an escalation clause once his earnings rose considerably to many times mine. The uncharitable lady succeeded in having the payments eliminated, but her greedy and selfish action soon backfired and turned against her when her husband abandoned her and her children for his next flame.

Yet, once this second wife was out of the picture, I managed to appeal to my ex-husband's conscience and convince him that it may actually be to his own emotional benefit at his old age if he paid for our daughter's college tuition. After our daughter had graduated from college and law school, he even agreed to travel to New York for our daughter's wedding. He played his role as the father of the bride with a certain dignity but remarked to me that I "must be happy that she picked an intellectual," which revealed one of his insecurities. Indeed, I have been quite happy with my daughter's choice of an intelligent, cultured, responsible man. Her father, I am quite sure, would have preferred a more rugged sportsman like he is himself, but they have managed to get along during the rare encounters in the last two decades. Unfortunately, my daughter's relationship with her father has remained distant and at times emotionally strained. He never learned to show her his love and, to make things worse, adopted the youngest daughter of his most recent, third, wife, who is about the same age as our daughter, half of his own age. How lucky I am not to have had to endure such behavior for a life time.

At "thirty something," with an exciting new job and a little house in Montauk, I felt confident that we could survive in the U.S., and that my daughter would have the excellent education I hoped to provide for her.

9

A Single Mother with Child

I had to prove them wrong

After my divorce, I had become a "single mother," a "divorcee," with all the connotations these terms still tend to carry in society today, but I refused to feed into the established stereotypes. I knew that my daughter was more loved and better cared for than the children of the politicians, including the children of Presidents Reagan and Bush, who tended to portray and denigrate single mothers as one of the plights of society. They showed much sympathy to widows and their children, such as Jacqueline Kennedy, Caroline and John John, after President Kennedy's assassination. So did I. I thought they behaved admirably. At the same time, I knew that my daughter, living with her "single mother" was not less admirable in the way she handled her own distress and that she was not less loved and cared for. I was determined to show to those around us in society, at her school and my teaching institutions, that dignity did not depend on wealth and public status.

Also a young woman, barely thirty

I was still a young woman, barely thirty, when we divorced, and there were men, former acquaintances, who tried to approach me as soon as they found out about my being single again. I felt lonely and needy of affection and friendship but tried not to let such emotions interfere in my relationship with my daughter. She was always at the center of my life; her welfare and happiness were my guiding principles. I was so grateful to have her, and the more my religious feelings faded and ultimately disappeared, the more I looked at her as the only real manifestation of so called "grace" in my life, the only unfailingly positive experience that remained constant in the ups and downs we had to overcome together.

122

True friends

We owe much to a Swiss-American family we had befriended through the Lycée Français. Their young daughter became one of my daughter's best friends and still is. The whole family truly reached out to us when they noticed the emotional devastation we endured at the time of the divorce. We saw each other often. The mother, for years, became my best friend and tried to help me take care of my daughter when I needed to work. In many ways, she was "there" for me. We organized dinners and vacations and invited other friends to join us. Since my friend was a native European like I, we became very close and seemed to understand each other in many ways that would have been more difficult with the average American. I am glad we can still see each other once in a while even though our lives have followed different paths.

A true friend with a "big heart" whose friendship has been unique and precious to us.

I also befriended a fellow Ph.D. student at Columbia University who would become my most trusted friend for decades until he died a few years ago of an inoperable brain tumor. When we met, we were both in our first year of graduate school, foreigners and alone in this country, with our families living far away. We seemed to understand each other's needs and problems. He was always supportive and kind, and we both knew that we could count on each other and call each other anytime, anywhere, even when we lived thousands of miles away or separated by the Atlantic. He was Turkish, Moslem, an honorable, sensitive friend, a kind of brother to me and an "uncle" to my daughter. After finishing his degree, he held positions as a industrial engineer with several distinguished companies in New York, such as Elisabeth Arden. We never went on "dates" to restaurants, movies or drives in the country without including my daughter. He knew I would never leave her at home alone or even with a babysitter.

He brought her little presents for her birthday, and we spent many holidays together. His kind, cheerful presence created a nice atmosphere for all of us. But we also knew that a closer relationship or even marriage would not be good for either of us. After losing his father, leaving him as the sole male provider in the family, he was not ashamed to moonlight as "a cab driver with a Ph.D." so he could send money back home to his mother, three sisters and nieces. His family came to visit me during a summer vacation and we are still corresponding at least once a year for updates in the family. They are kind, warm and generous in their friendship like their brother was. I sometimes wonder now, since the two Bush presidents started their wars in the Middle East, whether the current political paranoia has put our friendship under surveillance.

Potential dates

There were other men who came into my life but I usually judged them for the way they treated my daughter. I made it clear from the day I met them that there were two of us and that I did not go on dates by myself. This no doubt helped me avoid some of the worst pitfalls in which I could have fallen while struggling not to give in to the obvious demands of my young, healthy body and the ever present temptations. I sensed that many men I met were more interested in conquest and adventure than a serious relationship. After the recent bitter experience with my husband which, I felt, had made me waste years on helping a man advance his career and putting my own professional interests on hold, marriage was the last thing on my agenda. I now wanted to establish myself professionally, earn enough money to offer my daughter the best possible education that would give her a chance at happiness and success in life. Like some women may dream about finding a husband, I dreamt about getting my Ph.D.

Occasional pitfalls

This focus on a secure future did not entirely prevent me from falling into a few traps in the course of my life but I always managed to divert any serious danger from my daughter. I never compromised when I became aware in a new acquaintance of even a hint at an immoral thought that I felt could hurt my daughter. Still, a vestige of my upbringing made me think at times that men who had acquired M.D. or other professional degrees would also have reached a higher moral standard. Not so. Two of the most immoral men with whom I became acquainted, fortunately once my daughter was off to college, were medical doctors, both of them born in Israel, a country where I thought high ethics and morals were cultivated. One of them, Uri, was working at a hospital at the North Shore of Long Island, the other, David, in San Francisco. Both seemed well educated and attractive when I met them but soon provoked disgust in me by the vulgarity of their speech and what seemed to me pedophilic fantasies, even slight allusions to my daughter. Uri even took delight in noticing my increasing apprehension. "You are getting scared for your daughter, aren't you," he remarked laughing after telling me of his adventures with under-age girls. That was the end of our "friendship." I am glad I never saw either of these men again after the first couple of dates and never invited them to my home. They were a disgrace to their country.

A long rocky relationship

There was a man I met at a colleague's party soon after starting to teach at Barnard. He did not immediately appeal to me physically because his face reminded me a bit of the attorney who had harassed me in Paris when I was a student at the Sorbonne, but he increasingly fascinated me by his intelligence, wit and gracious manners. He seemed charming, warm and kind. Tall and trim, he looked very professional in his dark business suite. When he asked me and my daughter later that Saturday to join him for a Sunday brunch in the country, I thought he was rushing it a bit, but since he also included my daughter, I did not see any other reason to refuse his invitation. We spent a very pleasant lunch and afternoon together, but after he dropped us off at our apartment he caused an accident by backing into a parked car. My daughter also seemed a bit uncomfortable having noticed my interest in this man. Years later she told me that she did not think him handsome enough for me, "why this man and not my father," she asked herself, and was also afraid he could come between us. On the next weekend, when we met him again, in spite of the accident that he attributed to his vivid emotions, he asked me to marry him. My daughter and I, he felt, were exactly what he needed for his happiness. Since he did not want children of his own, he liked "the ready made package." We would make a nice family. Naturally, he frightened me with his impulsive proposal. When I told him that I thought such a weighty decision needed much more time, he seemed disappointed and became defensive about my "rejection" of him and even a bit angry.

This was the beginning of a very rocky relationship that lasted, on and off, for nearly a decade, and sporadically, even much longer. I was impressed by the broad knowledge of this man who appeared so well integrated in society. He was a first generation American but had never been abroad. Still, I felt, that this relatively recent link to Europe brought us closer together. He was a bit "other," just as I felt I was. He had the advantage of having been born and grown up in this country. Very sharp and well educated, he also had the answers to many of my questions, and taught me much about life in the United States. It was he who convinced me to become a U.S. citizen at the earliest opportunity which, he felt, would help me professionally. In many ways, he helped me make helpful decisions in my daily life, and built my confidence with frequent compliments about my looks and intelligence. My self esteem had sorely suffered from my husband's unkind remarks toward the end of our marriage. Instead of discouraging me, he supported my determination to complete my Ph.D. degree. For the first time, I had a seemingly strong, protective, positive male presence in my life. His articulate, self assured voice over the phone so impressed my father when he called while we were visiting my parents, that even without being able to converse with him, my father, just hours before he passed away, made me promise to marry that friend. "He sounds like a man," he told me, which was exactly the contrary of what he said of my former husband at the time of our divorce. My father always worried about my being alone in America but also sensed, so close to his death, and rightly so, that I was not about to make a commitment.

I have precious memories of very happy moments we spent together with this man, especially "as a family." It was he who introduced us to Montauk that became such an important part of our lives when, with my father providing the ten percent down payment, about $3000, I was able to purchase my first modest house on a beautiful but little piece of land on U.S. soil, across from the Atlantic. My friend was also capable of being a very charming and interesting dinner partner, to the point where he provoked the jealousy of some of my female colleagues who had a hard time accepting the fact that a seemingly successful Wall Street attorney, whom they presumed to be of Jewish descent, would prefer me to "a nice Jewish girl" like themselves.

At the same time, while he often spoiled us with much too expensive presents and weekends at fancy hotels in the country or on the beeches of Long Island, my friend's beautiful large Tudor home was sometimes freezing cold in the middle of the winter because he had not paid his bills for the automatic fuel delivery. I became aware of his tendency to live above his means, his needing to be bailed out by his mother, and did not refrain from criticizing him for such irresponsible handling of his money even, and actually more so, when he continued to spend money on us, claiming that he just wanted to please us. Contrary to him, I am rather frugal. I tend to record all my expenses and am never late with my payments for mortgage, utilities or monthly credit card balances. So, even in our daily habits and responsibilities, it became very obvious that we were exact opposites and totally incompatible. But what bothered me even more, in addition to his lofty handling of money, were his unexpected tantrums and all kinds of emotional outbursts and even threats to his own life in the most embarrassing public places. I am glad I was strong enough to resist marrying this difficult man even though I also felt attracted to him. There was much good in him, warmth and even sweetness but, sadly, he was not made for a close relationship or even marriage. We finally broke up for good. He almost immediately rushed into marriage with a former girlfriend that lasted a few months.

10
The Last Years with My Daughter before College

Mother-daughter togetherness

Until my daughter was ready to go to college, the major consideration in my life was to avoid as much as I could situations that could jeopardize her happiness and future. I had heard so many horror stories involving step fathers that I was scared that a man I befriended would end up abusing my daughter once he moved in with us. Since my divorce, I have always insisted on maintaining my own separate home, and even on weekends during visits to a friend's house or occasional stays at hotels, I continued to share a room with my daughter rather than my friend.

All the while, my daughter grew up beautifully. We had just enough money to pay for our living expenses but to the world around us we appeared to manage much better and lived a happier life than our much wealthier friends and colleagues. My daughter did well at school, and together we worked on developing her talents, such as playing the piano, tennis, ice skating and skiing without being able to offer her lessons. On weekends, we would often drive out of New York City to catch some fresh air. We had bicycles and a sled. Bear Mountain was one of our favored places in the winter, where we could watch sky jumping, visit the animals in the small zoo, and have lunch on a hamburger, French fries and a coke. In the summer, we liked to go to Jones Beach, jump in the waves, swim when the waves became calmer in the late afternoon, build sand castles and collect beach glass.

*Our great trips into Canada and across beautiful,
awe-inspiring America*

The summer after my divorce, I decided to drive with my daughter up to Canada, the Province of Quebec and Nova Scotia. We stayed in youth hostels, even in Montreal, and Beds and Breakfasts if there were no hostels available. For food, we lived essentially on sandwiches, milk and fruit, except for one nice French meal in Montreal. The ten days on the road were enchanting. My daughter, who was already a good reader, revealed a talent in deciphering maps and took great pride in functioning as my navigator. Wherever we visited sites or stopped for the night, people could not have been kinder to us. They all seemed to enjoy being nice to my little girl who was indeed at an adorable age—we celebrated her eighth birthday during that trip—and full of enthusiasm about our adventurous trip. We felt like explorers of a new world that gave us a sense of freedom after the many unhappy months that we had just endured. We enjoyed our trip so much, that several years later, before my daughter left for college and I assumed a position at the West Coast, she joined me in driving across America in our new Pinto, acquired with a hefty car loan after my Beetle burned down on the New Jersey Turnpike. It was a memorable trip that acquainted us with the majestic sites of this vast, enchanting country and often left us in awe of its natural beauty, its endless fields, deserts and mountains. While I have always felt uneasy about the rockets and bombs exploding in the lyrics of the National Hymn, this trip created in me a deep fondness for other "Americana" songs, patriotic hymns, especially "America the Beautiful." My daughter and I bonded even more, if that was possible. This time, it was pure joy, a happy, rewarding time together before we started to live apart for the first time in our lives, she at a beautiful top women's college in Massachusetts and I at an excellent liberal arts college in Oregon.

Weekends in Montauk and around New York

In the years before this split occurred in our lives, we usually spent weekends in the off season in our little house in Montauk that was normally rented from Memorial Day to Labor Day to help us pay our bills. The rental income really saved us financially by helping us pay for my daughter's tuition which the French institution reduced by one half once I had become an instructor in French at Barnard College. We anxiously awaited "to get our house back" at the end of the summer and spend time in what then still was a small fishermen's village. I loved the somewhat rough, non-manicured vegetation, the Japanese pine trees and the Montauk daisies that seemed to grow unattended. Little Pony, one of the original Montauk Indians, still lived in the area with his family and we saw him a few times. In the spring, we boarded one of the local fishing vessels for the yearly "blessing of the fleet" and the subsequent, fun filled sailing out on the Atlantic Ocean. The restaurants, such as the Shagawangh in town and Gossman's out on the Bay, were still affordable and served wonderfully fresh fish from the catch of the day with delicious cole slaw, baked potatoes and warm bread. But to save money, we prepared most of our meals, usually fish and white corn purchased in local markets, on the grill in the back yard. The simplicity of the town that for a long time managed to keep its character despite its closeness to the fashionable Hamptons provided us with quiet, rest and closeness to nature. Our best friends had a magnificent house in East Hampton, so we also spent time with them, went to art exhibits, concerts and plays at Guild Hall or enjoyed a Saturday evening movie. Quite frequently, we invited one of my daughter's classmates to come along for the weekend. My daughter was always popular with her school mates and we both got along well with their parents. They trusted me, but I was at times fearful when in New York they took my daughter too deep into Central Park or drove to some amusement parks. I do not like roller coasters. Those were also the years, when there were many dangerous gangs in New York, and I sometimes had nightmares about having to rescue my daughter from their grip, even having to kill one of them to save her. After such nightmares, in view of the fact that I am also much opposed to capital punishment, and in favor of strong gun control laws, I used to wake up drenched and upset, jumping out of bed to make sure that my daughter was safely tucked in. Fortunately, we survived those perilous times in New York without major problems. HIV and heavy drugs posed no peril yet, even though marijuana had arrived, and became more and more prevalent at high schools during the Viet Nam war years. I am still grateful we escaped those dangers, as I am for every minute we had together, most often just the two of us, a single mother with child, alone in a foreign country, but rather happy, and on the way to realizing our goals.

My daughter's sweet voice and rhythmic strokes on the guitar charmed friends and family on both sides of the Atlantic.

My daughter (right) with her cousins from Germany enjoying Montauk and American ice cream.

In a boat at Montauk harbor during the yearly "blessing of the fleet."

PART THREE

Making a Life in Academia

11

<h1 style="text-align:center">*Will I Settle for a Life in Teaching?*</h1>

Searching for my place in life

It was by chance and circumstance, not by vocation or choice, that I became a teacher, but once I started life in Academia, I realized that it could be just as fulfilling, and maybe more so intellectually, than if I had managed to go to medical school, which has remained my unfulfilled dream ultimately curtailed by the consequences of a wrong marriage. As a teenager, in a youthful rebellion against the heavy presence of medical doctors in the family, I felt the need to explore other horizons and possibilities. My father, uncle, several cousins and then also my eight-years older sister, her husband and his father, all of them medical doctors, seemed to dominate the family discourse over dinners and at parties as if they belonged to an exclusive club from which I felt excluded, certainly on the basis of my young age but also because deep down, filled with youthful insecurities, I feared I could never qualify. It was not by design but may have been influenced by my subconscious that I later dated several medical students, ended up marrying one and after divorcing him still continued befriending several MDs, especially while living in California, without wanting to get attached to any one. At the same time, also in California, I began to look into the possibility of applying to medical school, which my husband had previously opposed for selfish reasons, I thought, maybe because he feared some competition in our household. To this day, he has not given me credit for any of my professional accomplishments. I began to take pre-med courses and completed a whole year of chemistry, with lab and all, got an "A," but then gave up. I was head of household with the obligation to support us with my full time teaching. Soon my dream became a mountain too formidable to climb without a scholarship that would pay both for tuition and our living expenses. Harvard Medical School, where

I inquired, for years sent me invitations to apply. They were searching for Ph.D.s from Ivy Leagues interested in pursuing a career in medicine because they felt the combination might enhance doctor-patient relationships and lead to superior care.

In the end, things turned out to be OK. Ever since I started studying foreign languages at high school, I fell in love with French and longed to visit France to learn more about the country and its distinguished history and civilization. After a semester of taking French and Italian at the School for Interpreters in Munich, Germany, I was eager to perfect my skills. Subsequent studies at the Sorbonne and working at various summer jobs in Paris soon allowed me to become fluent and comfortable in speaking, reading and writing the language. Having lost my home in Hungary, Paris also became, quickly and easily, the place where I enjoyed living. Later, my graduate studies at Columbia University and teaching French at several colleges and universities, made me ever more knowledgeable about France and at the same time strengthened my attachment and admiration for the country which made it possible for me to call it "home."

Student life in Paris and the U.S.—quelle différence!

Yet my student years at the Sorbonne had not prepared me in every way for my later studying and teaching at U.S. campuses. My life in Paris was much less organized and structured than it is for students at U.S. colleges and universities. I don't remember having an advisor. It was entirely up to me to make sure I lived up to written requirements and pursued the best way to prepare and pass my exams. I feel that at the Sorbonne there was more personal freedom but also more responsibility put on the individual student's shoulders. Another major difference consisted in the free tuition at universities, including law school and the faculty of medicine. Students received free medical and dental care, including operations and hospitalization, free pregnancy care and assisted birth at hospitals by doctors and midwives. Living expenses for students were extremely low. But while I benefited from a room at the Cité Universitaire, the facility was just a simple agglomeration of dormitories for thousands of students located in the fourteenth district of Paris, and I had to travel two métro stations to reach the Latin Quarter, in the Fifth and Sixth Arrondissements, where the Sorbonne was located and most of my courses took place. French students rarely held jobs during the school year. My father in those years was still supporting the studies of all three of us children outside the home and could give each of us only a relatively meager allowance, but I usually managed to live off it, even though frugally. On the other hand, I nearly always worked at least partially during the long summer vacations to be able to afford buying new clothes and have some extra cash for the school year.

In the United States, my graduate studies and teaching took me to truly wonderful campuses, both at the East and West Coast of the country, where the excellence of instruction came at a very high cost and was essentially reserved to benefit students with either wealthy parents or those lucky enough to have secured scholarships based on academic performance, talents in sports, music or the enforcement of equal rights. The system of scholarships was new to me. It would never have occurred to me to apply for public or institutional funds as long as I could find other means to survive. To a European student like me asking for funds was a bit shameful and warranted only in cases of extreme personal need. Scholarships did not add distinction to one's curriculum vitae as they seem to do in the U.S. and are therefore aggressively pursued by the richest of students. After my divorce, when I had very little money to support the two of us, I was able to pursue graduate studies at Columbia University only because I was fortunate to have secured a research assistantship and later a full-time teaching position at one of its affiliate schools which provided me with free tuition, but I always worked for what I got.

My teaching ethics—a love for the civilization of France

Before immigrating to the U.S., my life in Europe, and especially in Paris, had been like living my "Bildungsroman," my period of enlightenment, about which I felt both enthusiastic and grateful. Once I became a teacher, naturally, it was my duty to pass on my knowledge to my students, but what I tried to transmit more than anything else, in addition to the beautiful, sophisticated, musical French language, was the humanistic thought I appreciated in France's "men and women of letters" from the Middle Ages to the present. I was captivated by the wisdom and independent thinking of Montaigne and the eighteenth-century philosophical writers such as Montesquieu, Rousseau, Diderot and Voltaire. I appreciated the deep emotions and sensitivity that infused the imagination and metaphors of the poetry of a Ronsard, Beaudelaire and Rimbaud. I admired the discipline and talent that combined to create the enchanting rhymes and rhythm of seventeenth-century classical theatre of Corneil and Racine, and the chiseled prose, the rigorous ethics and sense of responsibility developed by many other writers, poets and philosophers such as Pascal and Flaubert. No wonder my students, in their year-end evaluations, frequently commented on my enthusiasm for my subject. I loved to receive their postcards from abroad in which they thanked me for what they had learned in my class.

Discipline

Naturally, I was most successful with those wonderful students who came to me already with a thirst for knowledge, and was fortunate throughout my teaching career to be offered positions at institutions that attracted some of the brightest in the country. I have deep respect and admiration for colleagues who sincerely devote themselves and succeed in transmitting knowledge even in the worst situations of violence and total lack of discipline. Fortunately, I never had to confront that challenge on a large scale, only occasionally, in individuals. I have had very ambitious students who argued quite aggressively that they deserved better grades than I had given them, even though I always did my best to be just and equally fair to all.

12

The Intellectual Attraction of Paris and New York

Political exile and intellectual forum

After World War II and the Existentialist period, especially from the revolutionary sixties, followed by the dynamic seventies, eighties, and nineties, began an era during which France influenced American scholarship with a constant influx of new critical theories and philosophies. It was an exciting time to be attached or at least be at a commuting distance to the French departments of the great East Coast universities such as Columbia, NYU, Yale, Princeton, Brown and Harvard, or have access to Berkeley and Stanford in the West, which provided our hungry minds with lots of ideas and "happenings." After 1968, the turnover of chairmen and the hiring of young, liberal minded faculty opened up the Humanities departments to a myriad of avant-garde intellectual and artistic movements. New York, I felt, had become the center of the intellectual arena, and the U.S. the place of a flourishing intellectual dissemination, even though it was not always the place of intellectual genius and creation. That was Paris.

Paris, intellectual exile par excellence

During the Cold War, many young, ambitious people with creative minds, who felt stifled by the politics and ideologies or even persecuted by the governments of their own countries in Eastern Europe or the former French colonies in North Africa, chose Paris as their intellectual exile par excellence and quickly and easily adopted it also as their second home. It was in Paris that they created and published their first important works. But once that was accomplished, America, and probably also the dollar, attracted them like a magnet. They came to American universities to disseminate their views and to reap the prestige and financial rewards for their talents and labor. Columbia and New York University sizzled with lecturers and conferences on the novel literary practices. I loved living, studying and teaching in New York where I could meet, watch or listen to those whose creative work was transforming the Humanities.

Fascination with critical theory and philosophy

As much as I liked to teach the French language and the diverse aspects of its civilization which I admired, I was definitely most intrigued by the challenging influx of the new critical theories and philosophies that had sprung up in the academic world. I red voraciously but had to buy most of the books because I wanted to be, as much as my teaching allowed me, close to my young daughter after she returned home from school. I could rarely check out a copy of these new publications from the library since they were usually snatched up immediately after they arrived in the stacks and before I could get to them.

Yearly travels across the Atlantic

Until my father's death, my parents usually provided us each summer with round trip tickets for my daughter and myself so we could visit them for a couple of weeks after I finished teaching summer school at Columbia University. Once my own research had helped build my credentials and get me invitations and travel grants to conferences in France and later also to Hungary, I was able to travel to Europe and personally survey the intellectual scene abroad. I bought books at the huge FNAC bookstore in Paris, talked and interviewed scholars in my field while my friends either invited me to stay with them or sometimes let me have their apartment in Paris during their vacation. After my best friend's untimely death from cancer, which I still have a hard time accepting in my mind, her family continued to embrace me as if I were one of their own. Since she had been an only child, her mother remained close to me. Her cousin, too, often lent me his beautiful apartment on the banks of the Seine, just opposite the Conciergerie where Marie Antoinette lived out her last days before climbing up to the guillotine. My friends thus made it possible for me to continue my visits to France until I was able to provide for my own lodging. Later on, my daughter and I tried to reciprocate by lending them her New York apartment and finding families who could welcome the youngest members of the family for a youth exchange.

A wonderful friend to me for decades, my late friend's cousin in Paris has been helping and supporting everyone in the family.

My "surrogate Hungarian mother" in Paris, who is nearing her one-hundredth birthday.

13
Hurdles on the Road to a Ph.D.

Lucien Goldmann

A major turning point in my life and growing academic career came after I had completed my M.A. degree in 1968 and had begun teaching at Barnard College. I had been admitted to the Ph.D. program at Columbia University and was beginning to study for my qualifying examinations. In the fall of 1969, I signed up for a seminar on Jean Paul Sartre, conducted by visiting professor Lucien Goldmann, chairman of the department of the Sociology of Literature at the Ecole des Hautes Etudes en Sciences Sociales at the Sorbonne. As it turned out, Goldmann dealt not so much with Sartre as he did with the theories of the Hungarian philosopher György Lukács who had inspired his own work, in particular *Le Dieu caché*, a critique of seventeenth-century French literature and society, the publication of which attracted considerable critical attention at that time. To underscore the scientificity and modern aspect of his work, he called the critical method of analysis which he developed on the basis of Lukács's theories "genetic structuralism."

Unlike other professors, Goldmann was always very relaxed in his teaching, taught in shirt sleeves, never wore a tie and was easily accessible to students. In talking to him about my recently completed M.A. essay, in which I had studied the "Immobility in Gustav Flaubert's novels," he congratulated me about the choice of my title but then led me to view "immobility" in Flaubert's work from an angle quite different from my own. He attributed the phenomenon I had discovered to the historico-social situation of mid and late nineteenth century bourgeois France and thus introduced me to a novel, socio-critical interpretation of literature.

The first encounter with György Lukács's work

I was intrigued by Goldmann's "genetic structuralism." On the other hand, Goldmann also became interested in me when he found out that I was Hungarian. Most of Lukács's work was written in his "language of exile," German, but some of his early studies, in particular his one-thousand-page doctoral dissertation on modern drama, was written in Hungarian and, with the exception of one chapter, had not been translated into a Western language that would have been accessible to Goldmann. Yet Goldmann was very interested in this text, since he took most of his inspiration for his own Marxist theories from Lukács's early, pre-Marxist works. When I told him that I was searching for a topic for my Ph.D. dissertation, he suggested that I translate Lukács's *Modern Drama* and simply add to it a critical introduction. I started to read Lukács but quickly decided that what interested me was not a lengthy, tedious translation of a one-thousand-page treaties but rather a critical interpretation of Lukács's theories and philosophy which increasingly fascinated me, in particular his seminal *Theory of the Novel*.

Lukács's concepts of the "problematic hero" of the novel, "nostalgia," "alienation," feelings of "homelessness," the phenomenon of "reification" in modern society, the "fetishism of the merchandise" in capitalist society, etc. became important to my own way of viewing the world. It did not take me long to decide that I wanted to devote my Ph.D. dissertation to the study of Lukács's philosophy and literary interpretations. It was with considerable enthusiasm that I submitted my proposal to the French Graduate Faculties of Columbia University in which I outlined a plan for a study of the theories of György Lukács. Lucien Goldmann encouraged me to work with him and go to work immediately. He was curious to see how I would approach my subject and also promised to advise me on my research and writing. He knew that Lukács would not be an easy topic for me since I had not studied the German Enlightenment philosophy, the *"Geisteswissenschaften"* of Hegel, Marx and Engels, which was at the basis of Lukács's work. The French Graduate Faculties accepted my proposal with the condition that I do not discuss Lukács's overall philosophy as he developed it with extensive references to the broader field of comparative literature and philosophy but rather concentrate on "Lukács as critique of French literature." Naturally, I agreed.

When I arrived in Paris to begin my work under Goldmann's direction, I was told that he had contracted a grave liver decease and succumbed to it within a few days. I was devastated by the news, especially since the facts of his sudden death were somewhat shrouded in mystery. It was also a terrible blow to my hopes and expectations to write my Ph.D. dissertation on the work of György Lukács. At that time, only a few professors in the department had heard and even fewer had read Lukács. I ended up being among the few to research his theories and attract attention to his work in this country. But I was not ready to give up and tried to pursue my project.

A non-Lukácsean advisor willing to help out

Goldmann's widow Annie, whom I had befriended when Goldmann taught at Columbia, remained a supportive friend, as did one of his disciples in Paris, Michael Löwy. Upon my return to Columbia University, confronted with my despair over the tragic reality of my having lost my advisor, the chairman of the French Graduate Faculties offered to become my advisor even though he admitted that he was not very familiar with Lukács's work and had little sympathy for his theories. I was nevertheless grateful for his willingness to help me since I had been his assistant and admired his brilliant mind and wit, but I did not realize at that time how difficult and even risky the arrangement would become. My advisor's input on my work ended up being essentially limited to often sarcastic comments on Lukács ("sharabia" was one of his favorite words) and to suggestions on how to improve my writing (English was my fifth language), with little direction to my research and the development of my ideas. Unbeknown to me, he asked a Barnard instructor whom he thought more familiar with Lukács's work to read my chapters and provide him with comments that he could pass on to me. In spite of all these complications, my advisor still preferred not to refer me to another professor in the department whose sympathies would have been closer to Lukács and Goldmann. This other professor, however, was chosen as my second reader which led to constant tension between the two men. It also placed me in a painfully vulnerable position between the two with which I had to cope to the end of my studies. Their disagreements delayed the completion of my dissertation by one year when the second reader insisted on major structural changes after my advisor had already approved the 400-page manuscript. This meant that I could not continue teaching at Barnard since the stipulated four years as an instructor had elapsed. Even though I was given a one year extension, a grace period, I could not be considered for promotion to assistant professor and was forced to apply for a teaching position at a different college.

A rewarding defense and finale

In the end, however, the two professors reached a compromise and accepted my slightly revised version in which I tried to accommodate both of them as much as I could without detracting from my views. As I learned later, such arbitrary bickering between doctoral advisors is more the rule than the exception. They are unfair to the student and should not be tolerated. Finally, the day of the two-hour defense was scheduled and went very well, without any apparent tension or the slightest nasty comment. All five readers present at the defense congratulated me on my work and complimented me on the way I had defended it that morning. Among them was a young assistant professor, a Hungarian native, invited to check my translations of Hungarian quotations. She later became a distinguished Harvard professor and also remained a friend. Some of the readers stressed the fact that I had tackled a particularly challenging topic, Lukács's theories, which had the reputation of being very difficult, and that in addition, Lukács's work had forced me to acquaint myself, on my own, with a large body of nineteenth and twentieth century philosophy, while my area of graduate study and expertise was French Literature. Several readers actually thanked me for introducing them to the work of György Lukács who, with the revolutionary movements in the sixties, had gained world wide reputation and influence on socio-critical theory.

A gracious endorsement from an advisor

Pulling me aside from the others, my advisor excused himself and said that I was fully entitled to claim exclusive credit for my good work and that he deserved none. This was most generous of him but also too kind. I knew all along that he would have preferred that I chose an "intertextual" topic for my dissertation, since it would have shown my admiration for his own teachings and theories. Instead, I chose György Lukács's sociocritique. But for whatever reason, after Lucien Goldmann's death, the professor was willing to accept the responsibility of becoming my advisor, even if it meant having to read at least what I wrote about Lukács in order to see me through to the completion of my Ph.D. dissertation. I appreciated his kind and generous words the day this goal had been accomplished.

Quite brilliant, but also just a "mensch"

My advisor was not a man known for his modesty. Quite to the contrary. While he was an inspiring and dedicated teacher, he also had acquired a reputation for an obvious need to prove to himself and to the world around him his "seductive" powers over female students. He tried to make the most of the aphrodisiac power derived from a brilliant mind and an ambitiously pursued academic position which culminated in his becoming university professor at Columbia University. Unfortunately, as I was told later, he was also known to boast to his friends about his sexual conquests even when they were simply imagined, maybe wishfully, in his mind and not supported by facts, to the point where a colleague at Barnard who had become my close friend warned me not to ask him to speak about me and my work. Today he would have to be more careful, since some women would be likely to resent some of his behavior and insinuations as harassment and would not allow him to get away with it. But besides this "male" weakness, he was also capable of being generous and supportive. I actually owe him for his words of encouragement and support at the time of my divorce which made a difference in my moments of discouragement. Furthermore, his choosing me as his research assistant allowed me to continue my studies when I suddenly found myself in deer financial need. He passed away in 2006, in his eighty-second year, having had to endure a painful surrender of his quite brilliant mind and finally also his body to Alzheimer's disease.

A supportive senior professor

My second reader, who was less able to display his wit, sensitivity and intelligence in public and in the class room, turned out to be one of my valued supporters. He was not flamboyant but rather serious, dedicated to his students, social causes, his wife and children. As senior professor, he also took his role of advisor to the more junior faculty seriously. Just prior to the defense of my dissertation, in the weeks when my manuscript was circulating among the assigned readers, I attended a lecture at Columbia's Maison Française given by a visiting professor from Paris who had been appointed to fill Lucien Goldmann's position at the Sorbonne. My second reader introduced me to the lecturer and recommended that he read my thesis since it addressed a topic which fell in the area of his expertise. This led to a long discussion and subsequent collaboration with the French professor on several projects. I read papers at conferences he organized and also published an interview with him in a prestigious journal.

Developing a reputation as a Lukács scholar

Almost immediately after the completion of my dissertation on Lukács, I also began to receive invitations to read papers at academic institutions and sessions at the yearly MLA convention. Word about my dissertation on Lukács got around. Not many scholars had yet dealt with his complete work, not just for the obvious linguistic predicament with Hungarian—even though most of Lukács's work had been written in German—but the philosophical basis of his critical theories posed difficulties for those not familiar with the German "Geisteswissenschaften," essentially the philosophy of Kant, Hegel, Marx, Engels and Nietzsche. At the same time, the revolutionary sixties had created much interest in Lukács's socio-critical theories in most humanistic disciplines. I organized and chaired the first ever session on György Lukács's work at the MLA and was slowly but surely developing a reputation as a "Lukács scholar" not just in the U.S. but also in Europe.

14

Teaching at Fine Colleges and Universities on the East and West Coasts of the U.S.

Barnard College, Columbia University, New York

It was quite a challenge when my sudden appointment as Instructor in French at Barnard College plunged me into an academic environment that I had not experienced as a student. Grateful to have been offered a prestigious teaching position with the help of Enid Starkie, and the free tuition at Columbia University that came with it and allowed me to continue my graduate studies, I tried hard to adjust to all the novelty in my life.

My first semester of teaching began in the fall of 1968, shortly after the student revolts in France that had spilled over to most American campuses. Under the instigation of Bendit Cohn, the uprising became particularly virulent at the Columbia University campus and its affiliate, Barnard College, where I was taking my first steps as an instructor in French. It was exciting to work with these bright, savvy, young women who had recently been "liberated," and rather emboldened by the revolts. My colleagues in the department, mostly women, were sophisticated, elegant New Yorkers and came from privileged families or had rich husbands. Both the student body and the faculty were, I thought, "classy" and inspiring. I enjoyed our monthly faculty lunches. For the first time since my divorce, I had a feeling of belonging to a kind of family that accepted both me and my daughter. I was the only "single mother," living on a very limited budget and did not belong to the dominant ethnic group, but most colleagues were kind and several even reached out to us with invitations to their homes, which I deeply appreciated. Only once in a while did a colleague make somewhat hurtful comments about my Arian looks, or tell pointed "dumb blond" jokes. I pretended not to have noticed. My

148

fluency in French helped me feel comfortable in the classroom, and I worked diligently at perfecting my teaching methods. I was eager to teach my students how to speak French, but I did not want to teach them just how to conjugate French verbs, practice little dialogues and read novels. I wanted to help them shape their future and build a better world, transmit what I had learned in France and from its Humanistic culture and that would benefit them most: a sense of responsibility, self-discipline, a striving for excellence, openness to other cultures and values that may help them grow into educated, skilled but also moral and ethical individuals who would contribute positively to human society. Ultimately, I think it was my enthusiasm and my deep commitment to imbue my students also with moral and ethical values found in French literature that won them over to me.

Distinguished visiting men and women of letters as "teaching aids"'

While teaching my very first literature course, at Barnard College, entitled "The French New Novel," I was extremely fortunate to have several of the most famous representatives of this genre visiting New York that year. I was able to meet Michel Butor, Alain Robbe-Grillet and Nathalie Sarraute and take my students to their lectures given at Columbia's Maison Française. It was a wonderful boost to the success of my chosen topic in my first course, and I was grateful for the fortuitous "teaching aid" and inspiring encounters. I adopted the authors' most famous novels for my syllabus. Among other aspects of the new genre, Butor's *Modification* illustrated for us the New Novelists' refusal to "conclude." We read Robbe-Grillet's *La Jalousie* as a mystery novel, characterized by its "chosisme," or "thingification," that subsumed characters into their physical environment and eluded precise identification. Nathalie Sarraute revealed in her work the importance of the non spoken part of a conversation, the "sous-conversations," or sub-conversations, and their revelatory function. Marguerite Duras was in town to present her film *Soleil,* (Sun) and in later years I included her famous novel, *Moderato Cantabile* in many of my courses on contemporary literature.

Second jobs

Since my salary as an instructor of French at Barnard College was quite low and covered only a ten months period, I was happy to teach courses during the summer for students from Columbia College and General Studies. My first course was in a basement room, without air conditioning, during the hottest summer months, but in later years I was assigned classrooms in the newly built law school with its cool modern amenities. For a few semesters I also taught evening courses at Fordham University's Lincoln Center campus, which provided an additional modest income even though it meant leaving my daughter alone in the evening for a few hours three times a week. Most of my students at Fordham were adults, including the lady featured in ads for the *New York Times*'s large-print edition for seniors. The atmosphere in these classes was usually very cordial, less competitive, since grades did not matter that much toward the students' careers or chances for scholarships. But the evening courses downtown at the Lincoln campus of Fordham University for me also meant rushing to cook dinner for my daughter before leaving and, after my courses, doing corrections and preparations for my courses next morning at Barnard, sometimes late into the night.

Douglass College at Rutgers University in New Jersey

I look at my five years at Barnard, Columbia and Fordham as the time when I trained myself to become a teacher. It is not enough to be a native speaker or acquire fluency in a language, it takes a skill to impart knowledge in your students. I taught French language, but also survey courses in literature and civilization and tried to do so better each year. Even though my contract with Barnard had been extended from four to five years, I still needed the following year to defend my dissertation which had been delayed due to the disaccord between my two advisors. As head of household my first and foremost priority was to allow my young daughter to continue her studies at the Lycée Français and earn a French "baccalauréat." So, I felt fortunate to be hired at Douglass College, an hour's commute from Manhattan, which allowed us to continue living in New York hopefully until my daughter was ready for college. Douglass was still another woman's college, at the New Brunswick Campus of Rutgers University. For various reasons, though, the five years I taught at Douglass were to become both physically and emotionally the most exhausting and painful of my thirty-three years of teaching. On the very first day that I was supposed to report to my new position at Douglass, my new VW burned down on the New Jersey Turnpike. Fortunately, I was not hurt and was reimbursed by my insurance for the deposit I had made on a long-term car loan, but emotionally I could not handle buying another car for quite a while. The commute by subway and bus was particularly difficult during the winter when I sometimes stood next to the road, without benefiting from a shelter, waiting for the bus that was often delayed because of snow, pouring rain or accidents. I caught several colds that winter but never missed a day of teaching. Even after I had bought another car, accidents or the days before holidays, for instance the Wednesday before Thanksgiving, kept me on the road up to three hours one way and then had me hunt for a parking place in our New York neighborhood sometimes for an hour. I could not possibly afford a garage. Besides these purely logistical difficulties, in the first years, I still struggled to finish my Ph.D. dissertation while having to overcome the tension between my advisor and first reader. The worst part, though, came from the animosity of my chairwoman who often made my life to hell with her nasty comments and unfair assignments. She had had a romantic interest in the professor at Columbia who was directing my theses but apparently was cruelly rebuffed by him. So she had a hard time dealing with the fact that he was relatively nice to me. Because of the venom with which this lady treated me, she constantly reminded me of the character of Madame Merteuil in *Les Liaisons dangereuses* by Laclos. She assigned me to teach four courses per semester, starting at eight in the morning and often until six in the evening, so that I had to rent a tiny room close to the college for two nights a week in order not to succumb to physical exhaustion. Meanwhile, I was forced to leave my young daughter alone in Manhattan on those two nights, prepare dinner for her the day before and ask my neighbor to look after her when I could not be with her. Fortunately, my daughter, even in her early teens, was very serious, brave and reliable and we survived those difficult semesters without major problems. After I had taken three days to attend my father's funeral in Europe and returned to my teaching physically and emotionally exhausted, the chairwoman got upset with me for wearing a black dress and showing my grief in front of her who had lost her father in a concentration camp. I felt sorry for her but did not expect, nor did I feel I deserved, such total insensitivity on her part. I liked my students at Douglass, both the women and also some of the men who came from other Rutgers campuses. Several kept up with me once they moved on to graduate school and came to the sessions of the MLA conventions where I was scheduled to chair a session or read a paper. I have kept many fond memories of parties we organized on campus, but most of the faculty were native French, including the nasty chairwoman, and in the all too frequent demonstrations of arrogance several of the colleagues tended to conform to the widespread negative stereotypes about the French which not only I but also some students did not appreciate. Because they had been born in France and I had not, some colleagues thought they had the right to relegate me to a position of second class citizen. They took it poorly when my teaching and research did not corroborate their views and, after the completion of my Ph.D. degree, allowed me to move up in national and soon also international recognition. The lady, who tortured me for five years, I was told, died of cancer a few years after I was lucky enough to move on to a wonderful college at the West Coast. My daughter gained admission into a prestigious and beautiful women's college in Massachusetts where, after only three years, she graduated with honors in Philosophy. With my dissertation on György Lukács completed and my Ph.D. degree in hand, I was invited for ten interviews at institutions across the country which resulted in several job offers. After the many years of struggle and uncertainty about our future, I felt extremely lucky, vindicated and even privileged. When Reed College offered me a position, I was told that I was, nationally, among all those who interviewed at the MLA convention, the top candidate in French. I savored Sam Danon's, my new chairman's, compliment.

Reed College, Portland, Oregon

Reed College was a choice intellectual oasis, a small, very liberal minded institution that attracted some of the best students in the country. In the midst of the Viet-Nam era and the rising drug culture, their tee shirts displayed provocative slogans about communism, atheism and free love. Even the smartest students sometimes fell prey to the seduction of marijuana and even more potent drugs such as heroine, and it happened a few times that students came to class under the influence and either fell asleep or behaved in a vulgar, rude manner. It actually happened, that a senior, quite politely, asked me at a graduation party whether I would care for a "joint." Yet I don't know of any who permanently ruined their lives with drugs. All seemed to have gone on to graduate school and acceded to highly distinguished positions in life. Most of the Reed students were indeed truly special, highly intelligent, talented and eager to learn. While they were still learning French grammar and vocabulary, they also wanted to know about French literary theory. There were no grades given but they spent hours at the library writing papers which subsequently were discussed, sometimes for hours, at the instructor's office. Both students and faculty loved to get together. The president gave me money so I could cook French dinners for my students. There was always much wit and fun generated at such events. Individualism and originality characterized the college atmosphere. Since it rained a lot during the year, students adopted a positive attitude to cope with the weather, wearing silk shirts and hats but no shoes to avoid ruining them. They also claimed that they needed the rain to be able to think and study. It was at times difficult not to be swept away by their charm and highly individualistic attitudes. Overall, I thoroughly enjoyed my year in the midst of this intellectually charged, exciting college family where much learning and excellence was achieved. Yet, since Reed had no tenure-track position for the near future, I decided to move on and accept another visiting position in the West.

The University of Washington, Seattle, Washington

There was much that was beautiful about my next home and institution, the University of Washington in Seattle. The imposing university buildings spread out over the hill like a fortress of science and learning. My apartment on Lake Washington was beautiful and quiet. I loved to visit the fish market, enjoyed the homey atmosphere of the restaurants and coffee houses filled with students bent over their books and notes, sipping coffee. The movie houses, many of which projected classical films, welcomed their patrons with cups of fragrant tea while they were waiting to be allowed into the theater. The inhabitants of Seattle seemed to be natural sportsmen and women, born with skis on their feet, which enhanced the young spirit of the town. The dynamic, friendly colleagues in the Department of Comparative Literature with its distinguished guest lecturers and visiting professors provided friendship and intellectual inspiration. I enjoyed having some serious, mature students in my graduate seminars on Denis Diderot and critical theory. They brought interesting points of view to our discussions and appreciated my own enthusiasm for many of the new approaches to textual interpretation. I grew to love Seattle and the majestic University of Washington on the hill and sometimes just stood there next to the water near my apartment or on a bridge, looking at the city that appeared bathed in an enchanting gray-blue light that reminded me of the colors of Paris.

Only my own French Department was rather disappointing. My colleagues were mostly middle-aged men, who had years ago comfortably settled into their tenured positions without much effort and academic distinction and chose their weekly poker games as their favorite setting for departmental decisions. The only female professor in a department of about twenty was the wife of another professor whose international reputation, a visiting editorial position at the University of Tübingen in Germany, assured him enough clout to have his wife promoted to tenure. Jacqueline was intelligent, hard working and kind to me, but she also warned me to be careful in dealing with my growing reputation as a scholar to avoid upsetting or threatening the quiet comfort of my male colleagues. I continued to attend conferences, read professional papers and publish articles and reviews, especially since I was encouraged to do so by René Wellek who at that time was visiting professor in Comparative Literature. I enjoyed the strong support of my students who, together with all colleagues in Comparative Literature, petitioned that my contract should be converted into a tenure-track position and linked with Comparative Literature, but when a male candidate, a husband with child, applied the following year, the French Department chose him over me because, as they said, he seemed to "fit perfectly amongst the rest of the colleagues." I left with some regret after the one year as visiting professor but felt a bit vindicated when a year or two later I was told that this "perfect candidate" was threatened with expulsion because he engaged in an illicit affair with one of his undergraduate students.

My visiting year at the University of Washington, 1979–80, was also marked by the deaths of French Existential philosopher Jean-Paul Sartre, whose work had great influence on my concept of responsibility, "engage-ment" (commitment), as it is called in French, and Roland Barthes, whom I had met at New York University after having read most of his theoretical work and whose influence on some of my conference presentations and this present "autobiographical fiction" is undeniable. Toward the end of my stay, I also had to cope with the sudden volcanic eruption of Mount Saint Helen, the day after having traveled to Spokane with a journalist friend, near the foot of the mountain that layered the town with a heavy downpour of ashes. One of my brightest students from Reed College was climbing Mount Adam, opposite Mount St. Helen, when the eruption occurred. He was able to take half a dozen pictures during the eruption, one every minute, which later appeared in National Geographic and brought him recognition and even some money. Years later, when he came to study at Saint John's College in Annapolis, he brought me a vial filled with ashes from the volcano as a souvenir.

Mills College, Oakland, California

Mills College in Oakland, California, had offered me a position the same year as had the University of Washington. Since they seemed still interested in me, I signed a three-year contract with Mills, my third woman's college, which was described to me as the "Radcliff of the West." I moved into the faculty village near the house where Darius Milhaud, the French musician and composer, had lived while teaching at the college.

I was assigned a very bright, comfortable and appealing town house built in colonial Spanish style, with a red-tiled roof and tall cathedral windows. It had previously been occupied by a French professor who apparently loved snails and bred them in his backyard which years later still made it impossible for me to keep my garden healthy and attractive. The bigger problem, though, was my neighbor whose curiosity about my private life became a real nuisance and even hurt me with my colleagues and the administration because of all kinds of insinuations dreamt up by his somewhat sickly fantasy. As much as I loved my home and the proximity to my students and classrooms, I finally decided to move across the Bay into an apartment on top of one of the Twin Peaks with a view of much of San Francisco. Before I signed the contract, the realtor felt he had to make a confession to safeguard his professional ethics: the man who lived in that apartment had been murdered. The perpetrator was a young boy whom the man had brought back from his vacation in Mexico, but who did not like the man's sexual advances, killed him and fled back to Mexico taking with him all the money he could find in the apartment. Since I could never imagine myself in a similar situation, I did not hesitate to move in.

My three years in California were unlike anything I had experienced before. I spent my first Christmas in a bikini taking in the sun on my balcony, admiring San Francisco stretched out at my feet. Since my daughter spent one of her few Christmases with her father who lived further south, close to Los Angeles, I had not bought a tree, just a small wreath to remind me of the holiday. I was lonely and would have loved to share all this beauty with my daughter, but after her short visit at the West Coast she had to return to her college in Massachusetts to resume classes in January.

I liked my students at Mills College and enjoyed teaching the courses assigned to me. We staged a French poetry reading which my students "acted out," and for which they dressed in appropriate self-fabricated costumes. I put together an international conference on Sartre, to which I invited well known Sartre scholars from France. René Wellek accepted my invitation to a conference in honor of his work and contributions to

I staged a dramatic reading of French poetry with my students at Mills College.

I was director and "disk jockey" for the show.

Comparative Literature. Both my students and the Mills administration seemed to appreciate these gatherings very much and joined me and my guests at the cocktail parties I offered after each event at my home in faculty village.

The proximity of Berkeley, only six miles away, was intellectually stimulating, especially when I could attend lectures and seminars by such visiting luminaries as the notorious French philosopher Michel Foucault. Stanford University was just a short drive away so I could easily attend lectures and conferences. I met René Girard, who was teaching there and had shown an interest in my work on György Lukács and especially Lukács's concept of "mimesis" which he himself had discussed in a book.

A friend I had met in Seattle came to visit whenever his journalistic activities allowed him to come to the Bay Area. There were also people I met in Oakland and San Francisco who tried to become friends but I felt that, even though two of them had medical degrees, there was an immaturity and self-centeredness about these men that soon discouraged me from continuing to see them. I felt the same way about several people I met in San Francisco and even about some of my colleagues. Maybe it was the homosexual culture so prevalent in the Bay area that prompted their different behavior.

The female students in my classes were very smart, similar to those at Barnard and Douglass, but they frequently tinted their hair green and purple and refused to share Mills dorms with Berkeley men because, they felt, "it would interfere with their privacy." I never noticed but was told that at least thirty percent of the students at Mills were lesbians. All this was new to me but fortunately made no difference in the class room and during extra curricular activities that I sometimes organized. Only one older woman one day handed me a note in which she was saying that she was in love with me and was looking forward to the three fifty-minute periods she could spend in my class each week since they were the only really happy moments in her life. I thanked her for what I accepted as a compliment but her confession also worried me and I believe she noticed. When soon after this embarrassment, I also declined her invitation to a picnic she must have had the maturity to realize that I did not share her emotions. She continued attending class and remained pleasant and hard working to the end of the school year when she graduated and we all left for the summer. I never saw her again but trust she found happiness at the next station in her life.

On the other hand, it seemed like a freak coincidence, that I met still another physician, of all places at a gas station in Oakland. The man seemed happily surprised to encounter someone with Seattle car plates since they reminded him of his alma mater, the University of Washington. He handed me his card and asked whether I would agree to have a cup of coffee with him. I found no reason to refuse his request. He was a neurosurgeon and, as I found out later, a very intelligent, cultured man, whose enormous responsibility on the operating table probably helped him become not only a skilled but also a serious and thoughtful individual. At home, his wife cared for an autistic son. Our friendship remained just that, a friendship, but it has endured for decades.

My West Coast experience

Looking back at my five years at the West Coast, they now definitely appear like an important part of my "Bildungsroman." Having completed my Ph.D. dissertation on György Lukács had provided me with a sort of union card and allowed me to take the first significant step up the professional ladder. Five years in three different states at the West Coast, filled with moments of happiness but also loneliness and struggle, taught me a great deal about life, America and myself. It also acquainted me with all the major West Coast universities, Stanford, Berkeley, UCLA, San Diego and Irvine where I attended conferences, read papers and organized some of the first sessions on literary theory at the yearly meetings of the PAPC (the Philological Association of the Pacific Coast) which alone brought me quite a bit of professional recognition. It allowed me to meet many very intelligent and interesting colleagues who were teaching at West Coast universities, but in the end I had no regrets about my decision to move back East.

15

At the United States Naval Academy

Moving back east

After three years at Mills College in California, I started to interview for a new position. I was invited for an interview to Dartmouth College but they ended up keeping their in-house candidate. Other possibilities seemed less attractive. Rather than accepting to move to a large university in the middle of the country, I accepted a three-year contract offered to me as assistant professor of French and German at the Naval Academy in Annapolis. It allowed me to move back east, closer to my daughter who was studying at a beautiful college in Massachusetts. It was also a shorter flight to Europe.

Driving by myself across America in a U-Haul filled with everything I owned; arrival in Annapolis

I moved back to the East Coast just in time to attend my daughter's graduation from Wellesley College with honors in Philosophy.

It was August 1st when after driving all by myself across the country with its deserts and about three thousand miles of seemingly straight highways, I edged my U-Haul packed with my piano, books and other belongings into Annapolis, Maryland, the sixths state of the United States in which I was going to live and make my new home. I remember slipping into a clean pink tea shirt before arriving at the rather modest apartment complex where I had rented a one bedroom apartment during my

160

My daughter and her future husband after their graduation from Law School at Columbia University.

My daughter's wedding celebration at the Plaza in Manhattan.

previous visit to Annapolis, right after my interview, when I was told that I had on the same day been accepted for a teaching position at the Naval Academy. To me the temperature on that day seemed terribly hot, humid and almost unbearable, even though my colleagues who welcomed me told me that the temperature was actually moderate, relatively low in

My sister and her husband joined me at the wedding party. They had flown in from Germany with their daughter.

humidity and "only" 85 degrees Fahrenheit. After California, even this so-called moderate humidity hit me as if I had moved into a hothouse. But I appreciated the warmth of the welcome and all the help in unloading I received from my colleagues. Only later was I told that, in a somewhat military fashion, they had been asked by the chairman to rush over and help me. In the evening, my new very gentlemanly and charming chairman, accompanied by his beautiful wife who looked like a delicate porcelain figure, invited me for dinner in a fine restaurant near the water. It was a marvelous beginning. My ground floor apartment was roomy enough and looked fine after a few days of unpacking and arranging things. I planted mums and azaleas next to the entrance door. The only problem was the air conditioner that broke down periodically and left me exhausted in the humid weather. On those days, even before classes started, I took refuge at my new office at the Naval Academy where I met some of my future students wearing white, starched and perfectly pressed uniforms who called me ma'm. I tried not to let any of this new environment intimidate me and went to work assembling the books I would need for my classes, composing my syllabi and establishing my first course outlines.

Teaching at a military institution

I had never been a militarist and felt a bit ambiguous about accepting a position at a military institution. Once classes started and, coached by the chairman and my colleagues, I had understood the routine and responsibilities, I actually no longer noticed the uniforms, and thought that my new students were quite like my previous ones, intelligent, bright, ambitious and at times aggressive, above all eager to make good grades. A bright, charming red head, who must not have had a course in logic yet, came to my office one day and asked me: "Why did you not give me an 'A'? I really liked you." Besides a few paramilitary formalities at the beginning and end of classes, it was really just teaching and learning as usual, not very different from the other institutions where I had taught. But these midshipmen were also physically attractive, some even very handsome, with chiseled features, clean haircuts and healthy-looking, trained bodies. There was also a lot of wit and laughter in class and sometimes they stretched their wit to see how far they could go. In one of my first classes, at a time when there were still very few female faculty teaching at the Academy, I caught a male student whispering to his classmates, but loud enough for me to hear, that he "just loved" my blouse. When on a winter day I wore boots and a leather jacket to class, one joker couldn't refrain from greeting me with: "Madame, have you parked your Harley close enough to the window so we could see it?" Mostly harmless comments and events without consequence. The only problem that I soon noticed was that a few midshipmen seemed often very tired but was told that this was "normal" at this place where upper classmen tended to be quite harsh with plebes, midshipmen in their first year, keeping them up for much of the night assigning them chores or exercises. As years went by, more women joined the ranks of student and faculty. In their military training, midshipmen were also instructed in proper behavior and the protocol in dealing with women even though some found it difficult to live up to the rules.

Challenging moments

Among my most challenging moments came when I became faculty representative and was one of the very few women, sometimes the only civilian, in a meeting with about thirty high ranking officers who wore lots of gold on their sleeves and shoulders and were sometimes even decorated by as many as four stars. They looked like men in "shining armor," impeccably dressed in their whites or Navy blues. Fortunately, and that was the real beauty of it, most of these officers were also true gentlemen, respectful of my faculty status and academic titles and accomplishments. At least they pretended to be! The superintendents and commandants of midshipmen I experienced in my seventeen years at the

Midshipmen admiring Dali's "Last Supper" during the once-a-semester field trip I organized for my students to the National Gallery in Washington, D.C.

Midshipmen posing in front of a Picasso. These women were not only highly intelligent, physically in top condition, and morally committed but had already demonstrated leadership qualities comparable to the ones of their male counterparts.

Academy were most impressive individuals and, in my mind, I did not associate them with the cruelties and violence of war. The same was true of my students. Some of the midshipmen in my class wrote poetry, had insightful questions about literature and philosophy, were devoted to rigorous morals and high ideals of service, but also showed enthusiasm for painting, sculpture and architecture when I took them to visit galleries in Washington D.C.

After the visit to museums, we usually stopped at a French bistro in D.C. before the trip back to the Naval Academy. I am at the head of the table in the back.

Midshipmen enjoying the once-a-semester French dinner I used to prepare for them in my home in Annapolis.

1985 and 1987 study tours with midshipmen to Germany and France

In 1985, I was faculty escort on a five-week study tour to Germany during the summer recess, visiting the German Marineschule in Flensburg (the German Naval School), off the Baltic Sea, and also the divided city of Berlin, passing through Check Point Charlie into Soviet occupied East Berlin, later being received by Chancellor Kohl at his office in Bonn, then traveling south to Munich and touring some spectacular Baroque churches and castles in Bavaria. Inspired by the experience, two years later, I was allowed to organize a similar tour to France where our group of ten top midshipmen, a French exchange officer, the Academic Vice-Dean and myself were received with much generosity but also pomp and circumstance by the Admirals running the French Ecole Navale (Naval School) on the coast of Brittany. In a special small Navy plane, we were flown down to the South of France and had lunch in the frigate "Duquesnes" moored in the Mediterranean, close to Toulon. We climbed down into a submarine. Since I wore a skirt, the gallant Navy officers allowed me to be first to climb down the narrow ladder and then the last coming back up again! It was the day of the famous French Air Show, so on our flight back up to Paris the pilot showed us that he could rival the other performers and plunged us almost vertically down near the grounds before lifting us up to safety seconds before we would have crashed. The emotion was nearly heart stopping. In Paris, we were hosted by the Chief of Naval Operations at the Maison de la Marine, Place de la Concorde, who took pleasure in recounting the time of the 1789 French Revolution and Robespierre when their predecessors could watch executions by the guillotine from inside their headquarters since they took place at the Place de la Concorde, just outside their windows. We also toured the Loire castles in a huge bus provided by the French Navy and everywhere during our tour in France enjoyed the most delicious meals and the ever popular baguettes. The extraordinary reception we received everywhere in France and Germany was really a once in a life time experience. We made headlines in several papers and the midshipmen's "after action reports" were glowing.

I was faculty escort on a five-week study tour to Germany organized for midshipmen studying German. After observing a session at the "Bundestag," our group was received by Chancellor Kohl at his offices in Bonn.

At Check Point Charlie, crossing over into East Berlin. The midshipmen in their uniforms provoked curiosity but no hostility from the crowd.

Accompanied by the French Exchange Officer, the Vice Dean of the Naval Academy, and ten top midshipmen from my French courses, I was the organizer of a five-week study tour through France hosted by the French Navy.

High spirits—special events

Because of their high spirits and agile minds midshipmen invariably generate a great deal of fun wherever they happen to be, even during class time. Our routine was occasionally spiced up by special events. One day, my class had a surprise visit from Joan Lunden and her crew from "Good Morning America," which resulted, to our disappointment, in a mere two-minute report next morning on "midshipmen studying French at a distinguished military academy." On another occasion, the mayor of Annapolis, Mr. Hopkins, invited himself to my class because he had "always wanted to be a midshipman" and would also have liked to study French. We showed him that he would have to work hard if he wished to qualify.

With my colleagues in the Department of Language Studies at the U.S. Naval Academy where I was Professor of French and German for seventeen years.

The mayor of Annapolis had asked to visit my French language class and revealed to us his youthful dream of becoming a midshipman and also learning French.

I walk in the faculty procession for a USNA Commencement exercise at the Navy-Marine Corps Memorial Stadium in Annapolis. Every third year, the President of the United States delivered the Commencement Address to the graduating class. President Reagan made a point of shaking hands with all of the nearly one thousand graduating midshipmen.

Looking back at the 17 years at the U.S.N.A.

The seventeen years at the Naval Academy were no doubt among the happiest of my teaching career. Once I received tenure and decided to acquire a large, colonial-style house which I truly loved, I felt that at long last I had found a home in the U.S. as well, even though it did not diminish my attachment to Paris. I did not see why it should, but I know that some people did not realize how much my years in Annapolis and the kindness of the people around me meant to me.

Similar to other teaching institutions, the Naval Academy scheduled student evaluations at the end of each semester. Typically, some reflected the frustration with bad grades, and could be angry and even vengeful, while others expressed enthusiasm for what professors had tried to accomplish. There were year-end evaluations by the chair, periodic evaluations for tenure and promotion, which often stressed, on whatever level of instruction, my insistence on the importance of some philosophical thought that encouraged responsibility, moral action, integrity and ethics. I think that this personal humanistic mission in the midst of the military environment helped me remain an enthusiastic teacher and survive my professional evaluations with relatively little hardship.

Promotions all the way to full professor

Since I always tried to be well informed and was a devoted, enthusiastic teacher, loved to engage in research, writing, presenting papers at conferences, and also organized professional meetings, became several times regional delegate to the Modern Language Association, member of some of its executive committees, and also sat on numerous institutional committees at the Naval Academy, I was able to move up the academic ladder without interruption and receive promotion from assistant to associate and finally to full professor within the normally prescribed number of years.

In my first year as instructor of French at Barnard College and, some years later, on the day I made it to "full professor."

Receiving the "Excellence in Research" and the "Meritorious Civilian Service" Awards from the Superintendent, the Director of the Alumni Association and the Academic Dean of the United States Naval Academy in Annapolis.

My first book: György Lukács and the Literary Pretext (1987)

Soon after completing my Ph.D. dissertation, I started to think about a book length project in which to discuss Lukács's theories, but this time not limited to his views on French literature, as I had been asked to do for my dissertation, but rather approaching Lukács's work in its broad philosophical significance from his early interest in the German Geisteswissenschaften to what was later described as the first systematic elaboration of a Marxist critique of literary theory and philosophy. For years, I continued to discuss Lukács's theories in conference presentations, book reviews and articles.

Not surprisingly, the pleasant, secure and quiet environment of Annapolis also allowed me to devote myself more seriously to writing my first book. When at the MLA convention I mentioned to the chief editor of Peter Lang that I had just completed a book length manuscript on György Lukács, he took only a few minutes before asking me to submit my manuscript and shortly thereafter offered me a publishing contract. The Academy, upon the recommendation of the department, was always very generous in supporting my research by providing me with travel grants to conferences and scholarships for the summer. With my publishing contract in hand, I was thus able to devote the following summer to the writing of a lengthy introduction to my book.

Mementoes from ceremonies of my promotion to full professor and other academic awards presented to me by the Admirals, who at that time were the Superintendents, and the Academic Deans of the Naval Academy.

A publication contract and quick publication

The signed contract for my book brought enormous relief on my way to obtaining tenure. I was happy that the publisher even allowed me to design my own cover and be essentially my own and only editor. Peter Lang advised me more on form than content, and when the book appeared within a year, in 1987, it provided me with a sense of accomplishment and brought me quite a bit of recognition both in the United States and abroad. I could not have asked for more.

Colleagues at the USNA

The relationship between colleagues in the Language Studies Department was generally cordial, more so than in most other departments where I had taught but, like everywhere else, it was human, not perfect. There was jealousy and unfair treatment in certain cases, like at most work places, but I had also made many very good friends with colleagues in other departments and staff all across the Academy. We exchanged visits at our homes and organized dinners and parties.

Pomp and circumstance around distinguished visitors

There were receptions in the rose garden and inside the beautiful home of the Superintendent, academic processions at commencement exercises in the Navy stadium, hand shakes from the podium for faculty with presidential speakers such as Ronald Reagan, Bush the Elder, and Bill Clinton while Secret Service men kept a close eye on them and, in the case of Bill Clinton, held the president back so he would not accidentally be pulled down from the podium by enthusiastic supporters. The visits of famous political or artistic figures such as Mrs. Thatcher, Colin Powell, John McCain, Steven Spielberg, Bob Hope and many others were usually accompanied by much pomp and circumstance at the huge Alumni Hall. I enjoyed participating in these events.

Midshipmen performances

Throughout the year, there were numerous artistic and military performances by midshipmen such as concerts in Alumni Hall when they lent their beautiful voices to the singing of the typical "Americana" hymns, "America the Beautiful," but also the more macho "Barber Quartets." At Chapel I always enjoyed listening to their emotional plea, "Eternal Father strong to save." I rarely missed their theater performances such as *The Mikado, Man of La Mancha* or *South Pacific*. It was impressive to watch the four thousand midshipmen parade on the manicured grounds of the

USNA in perfect unison, presenting colors. Occasionally, I even sat through a football game, which I never learned to understand, but during which I was able to identify my own students by the number on the back of their jerseys. I watched the basket ball game at which David Robinson, nicknamed "The Admiral," placed the winning ball into the basket at the very last moment of a Patriot Game.

Stress on my health—not acknowledged by the chairperson

The four courses I was usually asked to teach per semester often wore me out, and the many hours of standing in front of the class put tremendous stress on my weak arteries in my polio-affected leg, even leading to mild phlebitis, increasing my blood pressure and causing me to suffer from frequent sleepless nights due to painful headaches, but I did not know the precise origin of these health problems before my retirement because I usually did not go for check ups. It was also completely brushed aside when I mentioned some such symptoms to my then chairperson.

A beautiful home

Overall, I was happy with my life at the Academy and in my nearby beautiful home that I was able to enjoy in the last ten years, while putting the largest portion of my salary into huge mortgage payments and struggling to keep up with maintenance and gardening—oh those tons of leafs in the fall in my enchanting park like grounds! Despite the toll on my budget, my home brought me tremendous pleasure and provided me with feelings of privilege, reward and satisfaction. I had never in my life lived in one place as long as I did in Annapolis, seventeen years, so I will always remain attached to my years around the Naval Academy and the people of Annapolis which came closest to providing me with the feeling or at least the illusion of having found a "home" in the United States.

Good people

It was also at the Academy and in Annapolis where I believe to have encountered the greatest number of truly "good" people in the United States. I have hated war since World War II, but I nevertheless admired and appreciated many of the officers I met at the Naval Academy. I am sorry some of them and several of my former students were drawn into bad wars and had to give their lives in tragic events that should never have happened. It makes me sad that millions of Americans allowed themselves to be misled by an evil and incompetent government.

I loved my house on Pendennis Mount in Annapolis, just across the Naval Academy, with a view of the Severn River, and its expansive, park-like grounds and old trees. It came closest to being a true home for me after I lost my original one in Hungary. The large colonial-style house was perfect for quiet, restful moments but also joyful gatherings of family and friends.

16

At Her Majesty's Service

Britannia Royal Naval College, Dartmouth, Devon,
United Kingdom

Among the highlights of my association with the Naval Academy was a faculty exchange that allowed me to benefit from a year of teaching at the Britannia Royal Naval College in Dartmouth, Devon. It turned out to be one of the most interesting experiences in my teaching career, and I am grateful to the Academy for having selected me for the position.

My house on Kent Island

In those years, I still lived on Kent Island, across the Chesapeake Bay from Annapolis, about ten miles from the Academy, in a modest home but on a wide expanse of land facing the beautiful Chesapeake Bay. It was the first house I could afford in Annapolis with a low down payment and a special mortgage based on my modest income. I loved my house but the visiting professor from Dartmouth and especially his wife would have preferred to live in Annapolis with its shops and entertainment without having to cross the Chesapeake Bay Bridge to get to the Academy. I usually loved to drive to work over the bridge, but for my British colleague's wife, living on Kent Island meant isolation and apparently loneliness since she did not work and had no car for herself. I, to the contrary, had the privilege of occupying their attractive cottage in Dartmouth in walking distance to the Britannia Royal Naval College and enjoyed using their car even though the latter caused me quite a bit of trouble as well.

At Her Majesty's Service

What an honor it was teaching French and German "at Her Majesty's service." Most of my students, called OUT's, "Officers under Training," had been to Europe which helped in teaching them not just the language but also the culture. The languages were less "foreign" to them than to American students and more easily acquired. My colleagues, typical Englishmen, were very charming and witty. I loved our lunches in the faculty dining room and tea and biskets at the wardroom where everyone gathered in mid morning.

Lunch with the Queen, chat with the Duke of Edinburgh

Since I was only the second woman and the only visiting female faculty at the College, I was treated with much kindness and charm. The day Queen Elizabeth and the Duke of Edinburgh came for the "Passing Out Parade," their commencement exercises at the end of the year, I was invited to have lunch "with" the Queen and about forty faculty and administrators. I felt privileged sitting across the table of her Majesty's press secretary who said he would mention me and our conversation to the Queen. After the parade, as the royal couple descended the large steps to their waiting cars, the Duke spotted me and stopped to talk for a few minutes. Since I wore my academic gown from Columbia University that bears the insignia of the crown of the original King's College, he asked me about it and chatted with me for a while, which my witty colleagues later exploited in some jokes, saying that the Queen had become impatient waiting for her husband, had come back up the stairs to take him by the hand, saying "that's enough." The Duke had the reputation of noticing women, but one of the colleagues thought the spirited joke was "out of order." One never makes a joke about the Queen, I guess similar to Moslems who do not tolerate any jokes about their prophet Mohammed.

The wit and charm of colleagues, mess dinners, plush invitations to the Captain's house

During my year long stay, I actually enjoyed besides the wit, charm, kindness and fun also much of the pomp and circumstance to which I was exposed even though it meant that I had to purchase some "fancy frocks" to live up to the occasions. There were the numerous and lengthy mess dinners during which one could not leave even to go to the bathroom before the Port and Madeira had been served and consumed and the Captain had concluded the event. The small, "black tie" dinners at the Captain's house were equally impressive, very elegant, very formal, and I feared not to know how to behave properly according to protocol. I found it a bit amusing when after the dessert, the captain's wife led us upstairs to the couple's bedroom where we could use their bathroom to powder our noses before descending for coffee with the men who in the interim had smoked a cigar. All this, apparently, is according to established customs.

With my colleagues at the Britannia Royal Naval College in Dartmouth, Devon. I am the only female faculty, seated in the front row, wearing my doctoral gown and cap from Columbia University.

Her Majesty's Yacht Britannia just outside the entrance to Dartmouth harbor after the Queen's visit to the Royal Naval College.

On a small boat with friends sailing past the Royal Yacht Britannia to honor Her Majesty the Queen

A privileged life around the College and in Dartmouth with emotional twists

Dartmouth was an enchanting small town on the River Dart. During my entire stay, I was extremely spoiled by the captain of the yacht club who was at the same time president of the local Rotary club and invited me to many functions as "his lady." Things were a bit complicated for me since I had developed an attachment to a faculty member who had visited us for a year in Annapolis. Typical of several of the men in my life, the colleague was quite brilliant and seductive but just as complicated and capricious and sent me on an often unpleasant emotional roller coaster. My other friend, on the contrary, was much more stable and did not easily give up. He invited me to Paris in a small plane from Exeter that flew very low and thus allowed us to admire the small islands and graceful coast of the Channel. We stopped on the way at Guernsey to shop a bit. It was all pretty enchanting for me, as was his gracious company in Paris. I just could not sincerely attach myself to him as much as he hoped which caused some unpleasant moments between me, my gracious host and my other "friend." It made for a painful threesome that did not end happily even though it had its moments of happiness as long as it lasted, including more trips to Paris, London, museums and theaters. I guess I had to pay for all the enchantment of the place and its people that I experienced. After forty years, it was the first time I spent a year in Europe, or at least near it, on the British Islands, and I had a hard time tearing myself away from it.

Jealous colleagues back home

Back home, some colleagues envied me and made fun of my accent that had become again more pronounced since British English was the one I had learned in Europe before immigrating to the United States. I caught one young colleague making fun of my accent, trying to imitate me in a gathering, not knowing that I was nearby. I realized how lucky I had been to have benefited from this exchange with BRNC. While I had not appreciated England much during my first visit there, the year before I married my future husband soon after my return to Paris, this time, about thirty years later, I returned with a sincere attachment for the country and its people. I appreciated the countryside, the gardens, the mansions and the classy, witty, a bit formal people among whom I truly felt more at home than among some of my American colleagues.

Professional success in the U.K.

Professionally, too, my year in England opened many doors for me. I had just published my first book and received invitations to lecture on

Lukács's theories at several of the most prestigious universities of the U.K., including Oxford, Cambridge, Leeds, Essex, St. Mary's in London and Exeter. I shall never forget my talk at the Taylor Institute of Oxford University, or the night before which I spent in a guest room at Christ College. The invitation to lecture at the University of Edinborough was another unforgettable experience. There was not much more I could hope for, and my institution back home was very pleased with my accomplishments during my exchange with BRNC.

The visit of Admiral Larson—the "John Wayne" of the Navy

When the USNA Superintendent Admiral Larson, a four-star admiral, visited the Britannia Royal Naval College during my exchange, I was allowed to dine at the head table, seated opposite the Admiral, and benefited from lots of compliments for my work from my employers at both sides of the Atlantic. My British colleagues were very impressed by the admiral and referred to him as "the John Wayne of the Navy," which I unfortunately reported to him and his wife at a reception back home in Annapolis. It was thoughtless of me and definitely a mistake. The lady considerably cooled toward me after that, and I don't blame her.

PART FOUR

The High Time of Theory

17

In Awesome Intellectual Company:

The privilege of meeting some of the most distinguished scholars

The advantage I had while teaching at both the West and the East Coast was the proximity to many intellectual happenings. There was never a shortage of visiting critics, writers and artists. At first, in the late '60s and '70s, it was the newly developed, language based theories and methodologies that occupied center stage. Inspired by Ferdinand de Saussure's *Cours de linguistique générale,* published in the early twentieth century, scholars stressed the function of language as a mere system, based on arbitrary signs that had no intrinsic, direct connection to the human experience. This systemic, para-scientific approach to language led to the very influential movement, called Structuralism, that gained a plethora of followers but never quite satisfied me.

Claude Lévi-Strauss

I was still teaching at Barnard College when the distinguished anthropologist Claude Lévi-Strauss joined us for a discussion at the faculty room. Lévi-Strauss became famous for works such as *Tristes tropiques, The Raw and the Cooked, Totemism,* and *Structural Anthropology,* based on research accomplished during his expeditions to the Nambikwara and Tupi-Kawahib Indians in central Brazil's Amazon region. These were soon regarded authoritative models for a "structural anthropology" and con-secrated their author "Father of Structuralism."

The purpose of structuralism, which attracted so much attention, was to replace the traditional, subjective ways of interpretation with a more scientific, "structural," and therefore more valid approach to the analysis of civilization and its creative products. The movement spread like wildfire through the academic world. It had tremendous appeal to most of us young scholars eager to discover new directions in our discipline. In line with his structural and "analogous" approach to knowledge, I asked Lévi-Strauss whether there existed a generation gap in the tribes he visited similar to the one in our civilization. He responded affirmatively to my question by providing a "Structuralist" comparison between socio-political realities in the so called civilized world and the role of elders in primitive societies.

In March 2007, during a debate on French television, I saw a segment of one of the most recent interviews with Lévi-Straus in which he confessed: "the world in which I am finishing my existence is not a world I like" (le monde dans lequel je finis mon existence n'est pas un monde que j'aime). I am thinking of his statement a lot these days now that America has been waging nasty wars in the East and that current presidential election campaigns and results on both sides of the Atlantic may lead to similar tragedies in the future. I wonder whether there will ever be a better world. I probably believe that there at least could be one, why else would I invest so much of my thought, time and energy to participate in political debates, at times experience sleepless nights and give so much of my rather modest income to charity and even to a political candidate I would like to support. Deep down, I may be a hopeless dreamer, but I believe we need dreams to realize ourselves and participate constructively in human society.

Roland Barthes

While I was teaching at Barnard College, among the famous visitors from abroad was Roland Barthes whom I had a chance to meet but only very briefly at New York University. He gave me a big smile and a long glance with his dark brown eyes, but I knew that he really rather talk to the young male students rushing him after his seductive lecture. In his publications, Barthes demonstrated his own "Structuralist" approach in intriguing and highly successful treatises, such as *The Zero Degree of Literature, Elements of Semiology, Mythologies* and his so-called autobiography, *Roland Barthes by Roland Barthes*, that was really an anti-autobiography, filled with photographs and short excerpts from his theoretical texts, to underscore Barthes's point that it was impossible to use language "to write the truth about oneself." It was this latter work that led me to approach my current writing with a certain modesty, caution and even a priory skepticism about my own "truth." But while I wanted to acquaint myself with the various Structuralist practices, especially those concerning the arbitrary, systemic function of language, I remained attached to the value and use of language as a means of communication. Imperfect as I admitted it to be, it was still the most effective one we had at our disposal.

Tzvetan Todorov and Hélène Cixous

Another "star" among the young theoreticians, originally from Bulgaria but living in France, was Tzvetan Todorov who dazzled us with his lectures at the Maison Française of Columbia University. Editor of *Tel Quel,* the most fashionable literary journal of the 1970s in Paris, he also introduced still another theory, "Russian Formalism," to the West. His theoretical treatise, *The Fantastic,* inspired me to analyze Hélène Cixous's feminist novel *La* using some of his views. It led to one of my first articles published in a graduate student journal at the University of Washington in Seattle while I was visiting professor there for a year. Cixous must have appreciated it since she immediately recognized my name when I met her at a conference in California. She has also included my article in her official list of critical publications on her work, *cached* by Google and included among the entries under my name. At a recent conference in Paris, I was able to thank Todorov for the inspiration his work provided for my rooky publication. More recently, in March 2007, Todorov took on the new French president's political slogans in an article published in *Le Monde.* Again, I thought, he was brilliant and convincing.

Michael Bakhtin

Another importation from the East, this time Russia, was the work of Michael Bakhtin banned under the Russian Stalinist regime but exported after the war to the West. Bakhtin's "dialogic," linguistically based approach to interpretation, as opposed to Hegel's dialectics, prompted numerous debates in which I involved myself with a comparison between the Lukácsean and Bakhtinian approach to the analysis of the form of the novel. My article was published in the *Ottawa Quarterly,* and to judge from the feedback I received, met with interest, especially among Bakhtin scholars. Google is also listing it to this day.

Structuralism and psychoanalysis

One of the newly hired young professors at Columbia in the 1960s, Sylvère Lotringer, invited provocative lecturers and organized daring happenings around the Columbia campus. We witnessed how para-scientific Structuralism combined with post-Freudian psychoanalysis, explorations of schizophrenia, Nietzschean body politics, feminism, homosexual rejections of conservative interpretations and the Viet Nam era drug culture. I read Félix Guattari's *Anti Oedipus,* plowed through Gilles Deleuze's theory of the "rhizôme," "chaos" theories, Jean Baudrillard's critique of capitalism and technology (Baudrillard died March 6, 2007, at age 77), and Jean-François Lyotard's and Sylvère Lotringer's writings in the new journal called *Sémiotexte(e).* I was less intrigued by Luce Irigaray's feminist analyses and, as junior faculty, was not admitted to Jacques Lacan's (the so-called French Freud's) lectures at Yale who accepted, quite arrogantly I thought, to address only "full professors." I nevertheless read several of Lacan's major works but found his terminology, laden with meaning from a special field, a bit too much of a particular jargon with which I was not familiar.

Julia Kristeva

Ever since I met her, I admired Julia Kristeva, who became a yearly visiting professor at Columbia University. Her intelligence was phenomenal, and I tried to read her fascinating publications as soon as I could get hold of them about topics such as the life of Chinese women, the function of her concept of the "chora," and what it meant to be a "foreigner." Unlike some of the women who gained renown in theory, but also became practicing lesbians, Kristeva was not only a uniquely talented intellectual but also wife, mother and an attractive, elegant woman, one of the few truly brilliant mentors we had as young females in academia. I always felt fortunate to be in her inspiring presence and grateful for her friendship. She was married to a quite brilliant, witty critic and writer, Philippe Sollers, who became famous in the literary world of France as editor of one of the influential literary journals but, unfortunately, later, also for his often sensationalist, and I thought, superficial, sarcastic portraits, snappy comments and "badinage" about women, politicians and whoever was "in" or had some charisma or power. He never reached Kristeva's level of intellectual brilliance and influential creative talent as serious theoretician and philosopher. Sollers remained somewhat a populist intellectual quite well known in France for his editorial columns in French papers which consisted most of the time of witty political commentary.

Michel Foucault

I read most of Michel Foucault's major publications concerning the power of discourse in various social systems such as prisons, medicine and sexuality. I discussed his theories with my students in my courses on literary theory. While teaching at Mills College, I attended his seminars at Berkeley, mostly devoted to an analysis of Saint Augustine' writings, including his quite negative pronouncements on women, and even dared confront Foucault on his own discourse by which he seemed to reinforce Saint Augustine's deplorable views. He paused for a few seconds before responding to my comment and then invited us women to now analyze his own discourse as he had done with Saint Augustine's. At a conference organized in his honor at the University of Southern California, I read a paper in which I addressed Foucault's theory on the alleged "aphasia of intellectuals." In those days, Foucault had such star power, especially at the West Coast and among his homosexual contingency, that it was not easily tolerated by some faculty to voice even the slightest critique of his work. But Foucault himself was very accessible to students and faculty and chatted with us at the student cafeteria. Yet, there was also another, selfish side to him. After my application for a Mellon scholarship had been accepted by the committee at USC, Foucault used the power of his own discourse to make them replace me by his young blond male companion during his visiting year. I was hoping to devote a year at U.S.C to writing a book, so Foucault's arbitrary imposition clearly impacted the course of my career path.

René Wellek

While teaching at the University of Washington in Seattle, I met René Wellek, who had created the first Department of Comparative Literature at Yale University and for many years functioned as its illustrious chairman. Among numerous other publications, Wellek was also the author of the famous *Theory of Literature,* which for years was mandatory reading, a sort of "Bible" for all college students of literature. Since meeting him in Seattle, and until his death, Wellek occupied a special position in my life. He frequently talked to me at departmental gatherings about his first academic prominence back home in Czechoslovakia, in the company of other famous linguists. Occasionally, he also invited me for a talk over dinner, such as the one at Seattle's Tastevin. My having been born in Hungary may have given him the feeling that in my company he could more openly indulge in a certain nostalgia for his home country than he would have allowed himself otherwise. There was a similar, somewhat nostalgic "East European" link I shared with his wife Nona, who was Russian. After the year in Seattle, in the 1980s, I saw Wellek at several professional conferences and also organized a special day at Mills College in his honor while I was teaching there. He became a sort of mentor to me in professional matters and also a supportive friend. Despite all this, I never became his "disciple," since he was quite opposed to left oriented criticism and to most of the theoretically based trends in literary inter-pretation which he rejected but that interested me. In my review of his *Four Critics,* I felt that I had to maintain my own integrity and express my disagreement with his views of Lukács. At first, he resented my "betrayal" but then forgave. When Yale University Press published several large vol-umes of his enormous oeuvre, I was asked by the publishers to review the last two in the journal *Philosophy and Literature.* By then, Wellek had changed his approach to Lukács, provided prominent reference to my research, and chose a photograph I had taken of him on the Bay Bridge during his visit to Mills College for the jackets of these last two volumes.

René Wellek, in whose honor I organized a colloquium at Mills College. He submitted the picture I took of him that day, near San Francisco Bay, for the dust jackets of his last two volumes on Literary Criticism published by Yale University Press.

Yale University Press later acknowledged my photographic contribution which, I thought, was most generous. René Wellek's enormous erudition was, I believe, unique, and so was his witty, "old school," gentlemanly charm and gracious company which I had the privilege to enjoy many times including a visit to Lukács's Archives in Budapest, at the time of an International Conference on Comparative Literature, when Wellek asked me to accompany him since he did not speak Hungarian. The many thick volumes of comparative literary criticism Mr. Wellek left us remain a monument to the intellectual world of his time and his own enormous erudition.

Umberto Eco

There were numerous other critics and theoreticians who crossed my path and who would play a more or less influential role in my academic career. I red Umberto Eco's works and met him not just at lectures on his semiotic theories but on a much more banal level, when he rented my apartment while he was visiting professor at Columbia University and I had taken a position at the West Coast. This happened a couple of years before he published *Le Roman de la rose,* which would bring him international fame and considerable fortune as a novelist. I don't think to be mistaken in my belief that he was working on his "chef d'oeuvre" while living in my place on East 87th Street. After he moved back to Italy, besides a kind letter, the only signs of his presence, his "semiotics," left in my apartment were a few splashes of olive oil on the walls of my kitchen. This literary giant apparently also likes to spend time cooking Italian pasta!

With Umberto Eco at the Maison Française of Columbia University after the "Debate on the Humanities: Où en sommes-nous?"

Edward Said

Edward Said and his first wife Maire Jaanus were early sympathizers of György Lukács's theories around Columbia University. Both became friends and remained so even after their divorce. It was a pleasure having Said as one of the inspiring faculty at the School of Criticism and Theory which I attended at Irvine in 1977. Said was a very good looking, witty man, quite talented in sports, and an accomplished pianist in addition to being a brilliant intellectual, inspiring teacher and a kind friend and colleague. Because of these appealing qualities but also his pro-Palestinian politics, I felt, he was often treated unfairly by faculty who were obviously jealous of his personal and professional achievements and resentful of his political tendencies that crossed their own. I know he was disappointed when I did not write a review of his *Orientalism* that meant so much to him. As much as I admired his work, I would have had to be slightly critical of its Foucauldian aspect. He, on his part, turned down my request for an interview on the Lukácsean influence on his thought, even though Said and his first wife Maire were among the few scholars around Columbia University who had at least read Lukács by the time I began writing my dissertation. Said's premature death due to leukemia was a real loss to socio-critical thought but also put an end to his despair over the Middle Eastern crisis.

Stanley Fish

I am grateful to Stanley Fish, another brilliant, generous critic and friend of Said whom I also met at the School of Criticism and Theory at Irvine, and at many other events thereafter. I still feel humbled by his unfailing kindness and support for my work. Even though he never openly endorsed Lukács' theories he expressed encouragement and even admiration for my Lukácsean research and writing. At Irvine, I hesitated to sign up for his course because I felt intimidated by his impeccable rhetorical skills, so unlike my own, and feared to disappoint him. I admired his professional ethics, his devotion to his students and his somewhat self-deprecating, witty remarks and seemingly flippant comments, by which he brought some of the starchy, conceited theories of other philosophers and critics down to earth. In recent years, he has become a true "public intellectual" who has been publishing leading articles in the *New York Times* and other papers and journals in response to current events. As co-editor with Fredric Jameson at Duke University Press, he was instrumental in recommending my book on Lukács for publication. I also remember the short but unquestionably effective recommendation he provided in support of one of my job applications. A generous, brilliant man. I was fortunate to have him believe in me.

Annie Goldmann, smiling as I was taking her picture, at a conference at Cerisy la Salle in Normandy, France. The meeting was organized in honor of her late husband Lucien Goldmann whose sudden death cut short his directing my Ph.D. dissertation on György Lukács.

Fredric Jameson

Ever since I began my quite lonely work on Lukács, after Goldmann's passing, Fredric Jameson became my major inspiration and intellectual "rock." He had read most of Lukács's major works and had written about them in several incisive articles. He, too, was a friend of Stanley Fish and I had much admiration for his views and brilliance. These critics, I thought, were among the best informed scholars I had met. I particularly appreciated the integrity of their thought and the absence of arrogance in dealing with students and colleagues. Jameson has written some groundbreaking works that helped me reach my own socio-critical conclusions. Once I had established myself as a Lukács scholar, Jameson agreed to participate in what became the most successful session I organized and moderated at an MLA convention, dealing with a comparison between György Lukács's and Jacques Derrida's major concepts. Once the ballroom was filled to capacity,

Edward Saïd and Stanley Fish at the final banquet of The School of Criticism and Theory at Irvine in which I was a participant. Both expressed much support for my work on György Lukács. Stanley Fish, together with Fredric Jameson, later recommended my second book on Lukács for publication within their series "Post–Contemporary Interventions" at Duke University Press.

the large audience spilled out through the open doors into the hall. Even years later, some MLA members talked to me about the interest and success of that uniquely rewarding event. When I began work on my second book on Lukács, Fredric Jameson was among the first to agree to an interview. Coeditor with Stanley Fish, they unanimously recommended my manuscript "Lukács after Communism: Interviews with Contemporary Intellectuals," for publication in their series, called "Post–Contemporary Interventions" by Duke University Press.

Jacques Derrida

Jacques Derrida was certainly the most flamboyant and most influential critic and philosopher I experienced during the more than three decades of my academic activities. His "Deconstructive" theory displaced Structuralism in fame and influence. His highly imaginative, provocative and often obscure writings, his notorious theory established on an enigmatic interpretation of différance," with an "a," circulated like fresh adrenaline in his disciples who flocked to his writings as if they were, paradoxically, the revelation of absolute truth, even though Derrida actually contested the possibility of establishing "truth" by means of a linguistic procedure. Derrida became particularly successful in the United States after Gayatry Spivak, an unusually intelligent and talented Yale student and now a noted critic of post-colonialism, wrote a brilliant introduction to Derrida's first major publication in English. Derrida soon became known all around the world as the "Father of Deconstruction."

I met Derrida several times at conferences on both the East and West Coast of the U.S., at his yearly October seminars at NYU, and at the Collège de France in Paris. I was also in Paris when he died on October 9, 2004, on the day that would have been my late father's birthday and when I also met a French artist who has since become one of my closest friends, so the date will probably stick to my mind. Over the years, I read most of Derrida's major, always provocative works, and also critiqued his work in several of my publications. When I spoke to him after one of his lectures in California, Derrida agreed to an interview on his "left" politics, but when, as agreed upon, I arrived at his office at NYU, he said he was tired and felt that he was not up to the rigor and stress of a taped, formal interview. Instead, he referred me to a publication that was about to appear and was likely to provide answers to most of my questions about his attitude toward left-wing critical theories. He had no objection to discuss his views with me as long as I did not record the discussion. I did not know at that time, that he was already suffering from ill health.

When soon after our meeting I was asked by an editor to review the book Derrida had mentioned to me, I was not overly surprised by Derrida's comments on left-wing critics expressed in *Ghostly Demarcations*. They were rather predictable, with the exception that, for whatever reason, Derrida also felt he had to knock Gayatry Spivak, even though her text was not even included in the volume to which he responded. Derrida's outrageous denigrations of her mind and character, I thought, were not just unfair but also in poor taste—and still inexplicable to me—so I could not refrain from pointing them out in the review I turned in to *Philosophy and Literature*. I know that my comments did not just catch Gayatry Spivak's grateful attention. At the MLA congress that year, several colleagues congratulated me for my "courage." Ever since my review appeared, Google has also features it on the top of their list of entries under my name. I don't know whether it was "googled" there for my discussion of Derrida's left-wing critique or his misogynist attack against a brilliant female scholar to whom he owed so much. Derrida usually appeared to me as the perfect gentleman.

My second book: Lukács After Communism: Interviews with Contemporary Intellectuals, Duke UP, 1997

In the early 1990s, I was ready for my second book in which I was determined to show what I could really do, that I was not just a "Lukácsean" as some, probably envious, colleagues remarked. Yes, I had acquired a thorough knowledge and understanding of the work of György Lukács that brought me some international recognition for what I had accomplished, but I had also kept my eyes and my mind open to other theoreticians, philosophers, writers and critics that gained importance on the intellectual forum. I was fascinated by some of their views, read their works and tried to listen and talk to them, confront them at professional meetings and in articles and reviews. While acquiring knowledge and understanding of the various trends and intellectual currents, I also gained the confidence I needed to pursue my project.

I set out to conduct interviews with ten famous critics and philosophers in various countries who, at the outset of their careers, had been influenced by Lukács's theories and, building on that basis, went on to expand and develop their own views and influential theories. Over a period of about two and a half years, drawing on my knowledge of four languages—even though, in Brazil, I could not understand the spoken Brazilian and had to resort to other European languages—I was fortunate to have ten of the most famous intellectuals at some of the most distinguished universities in five different countries agree to several hours each of recorded interviews: Etienne Balibar, Professor of Philosophy at the University of Paris I (14 November 1992, University of Massachusetts, Amherst); Peter Bürger, Professor of French and Comparative Literature at the University of Bremen (27 December 1991, Bremen); Terry Eagleton, Warton Professor of English Literature at St. Catherine's College, Oxford (9 March 1993, Oxford); Fredric Jameson, William A. Lane Professor of Comparative Literature and Director of the Graduate Program in Literature and the Duke Center for Critical Theory (11 March 1992, Duke University); Jacques Leenhardt, Director of the Sociology of Literature at the Ecole des Hautes Etudes en Sciences Sociales, Sorbonne, France (18 May 1991, Paris); Michael Löwy, Senior Researcher at the Centre National de la Recherche Scientifique, Paris, France (20 May 1991, Paris); Roberto Schwarz, Professor of Literary Theory at the University of Campinas, Sao Paulo, Brazil (15 August 1994, Sao Paolo); George Steiner, Extraordinary Fellow at Churchill College, Cambridge (30 December 1991, Cambridge); Susan R. Suleiman, Professor of Romance and Comparative Literature at Harvard University (31 July 1992, Princeton); Cornel West, Professor of Afro-American Studies and the Philosophy of Religion at Harvard University (25 March 1992, Princeton University).

Each interview was a true event for me. I had carefully prepared by reading all the major works of my interviewees with which I was not yet familiar, established a few points I wanted to highlight but at the time of the interview gave free flow to our discussion which, I believe, allowed for a natural, spontaneous exchange of ideas. The results revealed the rich seminal nature of Lukács's theories in a variety of disciplines. It was gratifying to be with these scholars who were all seriously interested in improving human society.

Because of my teaching commitments—I usually taught four courses per semester—it took me several years to travel to the places where these intellectuals taught or were visiting in the U.S., Europe and Brazil. Sure, I was a bit apprehensive, but not once did I encounter any negative attitude toward me or my project. My interlocutors received me all very graciously, even during their vacation time, or shortly after an operation, and seemed as enthusiastic about what I was trying to accomplish as I was myself. It was probably the most exciting time in my professional life.

Preparing the manuscript for publication

The big job came when the interviews that I had recorded had to be transcribed, referenced, edited and some of them translated from French or German into English. I also had to write a solid, detailed introduction to Lukács's work in order to satisfy the demands of the senior editor of Duke University Press, who had shown interest in publishing the volume. I had no secretarial help and did all of the transcribing, typing and even much of the translation work myself. But I owe much to my editor at Duke University Press for his strong support and guidance. He even allowed me to supply the cover picture, a photograph I had taken of the Berlin Wall when I accompanied ten top midshipmen from the Naval Academy on a five-week study tour through Germany. When we arrived at Check Point Charlie, and then crossed into East Berlin, the Cold War was still in full swing and the midshipmen in their U.S. Navy uniforms attracted much attention. The picture I took of the Berlin Wall at that time, a few years before the wall came crashing down, now graces the cover of my book. It will remain a reminder of our unique experience looking at the ominous wall and then crossing into Soviet occupied East Berlin. Each time I look at my book, I also remember World War II and its consequences on my family, and the effect Lukács's theories had on not only my own research but also on the theories of the ten distinguished philosophers and theoreticians I interviewed to assess Lukács's intellectual legacy after the fall of the communist regime.

Unlike the production of my first book by Peter Lang ten years earlier, which had been inspired by my Ph.D. dissertation and was published nearly in the form in which I had submitted the text, this time, Duke University Press provided excellent readers and editors whose comments I appreciated and tried to use in completing my manuscript. Once the laudatory comments of the readers arrived at Duke UP and Fredric Jameson and Stanley Fish had decided to accept my 400 page manuscript for publication in their series, "Post-Contemporary Interventions," I felt overwhelmed with joy. But not until months later, when I received the first printed copy with warm words of congratulations from the senior editor, did I allow myself to believe that my project was really done, like a dream come true. It is a very good feeling to be invited with a few other authors to a party organized in your honor at the book exhibit of the MLA convention, with a large poster of your book's front cover hanging there for all visitors to see. A chapter of my life was written then. It led to more exciting activities and rewards. I was invited to speak at even more professional conferences than before. Scholars that in the past I had just quietly admired at a distance treated me as if I were one of them. I had to get used to admitting to myself that, at least to a certain extent, I had earned a place among them.

18

Novelists with a Difference

A literary affinity

I felt particularly attracted to a certain kind of mostly contemporary novelists "with a difference." Lukács's theory of the novel that I had discussed from many points of view in various papers and publications, continued to be in the back of my mind when I read novels that dealt with problems such as exile, alienation, feminism, racial discrimination, and homelessness. I became particularly interested in francophone novelists, who wrote in French but were born in other countries, within other cultures. Maybe because of my own background and experiences, I often felt close to them. These writers were not typically French, many of them not even French citizens. Francophone and francophile but not French, they also had another side, marked by an ethnic, religious, gender, or national difference. They were in some ways exiles as I felt I was, and therefore "spoke" to me more directly than the average French writer would have. They all grew up with an admiration for French culture, as I did, reading and internalizing the works of Montaigne and Pascal, the problematic of great classical theatre, the grave beauty of the tragedies and the enchantment of poetry, searching answers from the French philosophers Descartes, Sartre and in the philosophical texts of Montesquieu, J.-J. Rousseau, Diderot and Voltaire, identifying with the socio critical preoccupations of nineteenth-century novelists Victor Hugo, Gustav Flaubert and Emil Zola, but all of them first had to gain entrance into the French language and the French culture before they could embrace it and most often make it their own. They then were ready to develop their own views and imprint their works with the specificity of their own experiences.

201

Maurice Roche

After the "new novelists," Michel Butor, Alain Robbe-Grillet, Marguerite Duras and Nathalie Sarraute, whom I had met and whose works I had discussed in my courses at Barnard College, I was introduced to Maurice Roche who agreed to discuss with me his own "theory of the novel" which was indeed quite different from Lukács's. I visited him in his Paris apartment, rue Berthollet, and met his strikingly exotic female companion. Maurice Roche was French but nevertheless a novelist "on the margins," whose novels revealed the rupture that had occurred in the contemporary novel not just on the linguistic level, but also in its content. Roche incorporated other artistic expressions such as music and painting within his text which prompted me to characterize his "theory of the novel" in a subsequent publication as "fictional theory." Published in the *French Review,* it was among the first critical evaluations of the revolutionary novelist's work and became recommended reading for Columbia's graduate students in contemporary French literature. The direct contact and lengthy discussions I had with this "marginal" novelist allowed me to really dig into his thoughts even though I tried to keep a critical distance of the author's own perceptions to let the work stand on its own.

Tahar BenJelloun and Other Maghrebian writers

The end of the Algerian war and the social transformations of the 1960s brought a new focus on francophone literature produced in the former French colonies in North and Central Africa. Among the Maghrebian writers, the novels of Tahar BenJelloun, such as *L'Enfant de sable,* were soon recognized by prestigious literary prizes. I was again fortunate that the author agreed to grant me an interview in his office at the Rue Jacob before I published a comparative article on his and two other Maghrebian writers' treatment of the role of the father. Once more, I was among the first in the U.S. to publish in the *French Review* a study of Tahar BenJelloun, a writer's work that had just recently attracted the attention of the literary world. My students, too, seemed quite interested in reading this very contemporary francophone work in my course on the French Novel of the 20th Century. Even though BenJelloun lived and wrote in France, his subject matter took its inspiration from his native mythology and provided a glimpse into his Moroccan culture. I was fascinated by the bi-cultural aspect of BenJelloun's subject matter and his unusual metaphoric prose that distinguished new francophone literature from the one written by native French writers.

Andreï Makine

Among the most successful writers from the East who sought exile in France during the Cold War was the young Russian writer Andreï Makine whose astonishing linguistic talent allowed him to produce a first novel in French, *Le Testament français,* hailed for its "Proustian" quality that charmed the editors and members of literary juries who rushed to award him two of the most prestigious literary prizes, the Prix Goncourt and the Prix Médicis. This assured him a place on the best seller list of French novels around the world. Some critics could not deal with the Apollonian physique of the novelist whom I heard a beautiful young female student at Harvard describe as a "young god." By chance, not really by design, I was able to attend several of his lectures given in Washington,

Andreï Makine after his lecture in Washington, D.C. His work inspired me to write my own "autobiographical fiction."

New York, Cambridge, Mass., and Paris. I also ran into him again at the "Ancienne Comédie," a historical coffee house on Boulevarad Saint Germain, where I had the pleasure of noticing that he remembered my name. It was flattering coming from a young man of considerable physical charm who, I know, is not lacking in female admirers. I probably owe this pleasant surprise to a young "Magyar" who, as he told me, left him favorably inclined toward Hungarian women. I usually participated in the discussions following his lecture. What really interested me most in his work was that he seemed to speak for me and echo my sensitivities as exile and writer in a language that was not his or my own. Decades ago, I had already adopted French as my "lingua franca" into which I liked to escape. Even though I wrote most of my papers and publications in English, in my private moments I continued to "feel" in French. Makine seemed to speak of my own struggles to find myself, my "home," and integrate linguistically and socially in the various cultures that I experienced but none of which was my own by birth, so that I felt constantly reminded, wherever I found myself, that I was "other."

I have just read Andreï Makine's recent *L'Amour humain*, of 2006, an extremely devastating tale of the world that unfolds mostly in Africa. Having gotten to know the author a bit provided an added dimension to the experience of reading his novel. The link between the text I was reading and his physical persona surprised me constantly. His incredible under-standing of human nature, his sensitivity for the plight of women and children, his absolute honesty in evoking the lowest levels of humanity, his disappointments with revolutionaries and ideologies made the text deeply moving and the author even more appealing by the depth of his thought and the maturity of his views. It was almost embarrassing to read how much this author knew of the experiences of a woman. It's less the stories he relates than the poetry of his scenes, in both cruelty and love, that are the most amazing. The structure of his tale was at times misleading me because I did not read with enough attention to detail which may be simply a sign of my weakening memory. But the inspiration for reflection was powerful, no doubt enhanced by the fact that I knew the author.

PART FIVE

Travels

19

Journeys East and West

A Love for travel?

People sometimes get the impression that I like to travel, which is misleading. I do not like to spend hours in an airplane or a train, unless these travels become journeys that are also enriching, conveyors to the realization of a desire, an interest, a dream. Yet, that was not always the case.

While my travels after our immigration to the United States consisted essentially of a tiresome shuttle between Europe and the East and West Coasts of the United States, I was also able to crisscross the U.S. many times to attend professional activities such as the yearly convention of the Modern Language Association, to read papers at special conferences, to interview for a job and even to drive a U-Haul filled with my belongings, including my old piano, to a new teaching appointment at the opposite coast of the United States.

One of the only times during my academic career that I engaged in the luxury of a gratuitous vacation was the week I spent on the beach of the Island of Saint Martin which my daughter offered me for my birthday—I still dream of the warm waters and gentle waves of the Caribbean in which I loved to swim. The other vacation travel was my participation in a cruise to the Western Caribbean that also functioned as the yearly Convention of the Rotary District to which I belonged. I found it a bit confining and even boring to spend days on that ship and nights in my windowless cabin, the least expensive on the ship. I would have preferred lying quietly on a sandy beach, surrounded by nature, not just the rocking waves of the ocean. And then there was my travel to Sao Paolo, in Brazil, to interview Roberto Schwarz for my book, to which I added a few days in Rio de Janeiro—truly a dream-like experience that I would love to repeat. Most importantly, there were the journeys back to Hungary on which I was able to combine professional interest with often highly emotional, sheer personal enjoyment.

I traveled to Sao Paolo, Brazil, to interview the noted literary critic Roberto Schwarz for my book on György Lukács.

A first, professionally protected, visit "back home"

My first significant travel back home to Hungary took me on a somewhat lonely and perilous but nevertheless determined journey to my lost native country where I was hoping to discover valuable information in my research on the work of György Lukács and, with slight trepidation, also visit a few uncles, cousins and places that hid the centuries old roots, painfully buried, of our family. It was my first return "home" after thirty years when we left precipitously one cold December night leaving everything behind just to escape the threatening devastations of World War II.

A conference on contemporary literature held in Budapest provided the framework and welcome protection from exposure to what had become a somewhat frightening unknown but was still a vivid memory of what I had experienced as a small child. The country continued to be under Soviet rule, and I was apprehensive of what might happen. My parents never again returned home. All they had owned had been taken by the state.

My having become a U.S. citizen was not the best letter of recommendation while the Cold War was in full swing.

On my way to Hungary, my first frightening experience occurred already in the train, the Orient Express, when we stopped for passport control at Hegyeshalom, the border town between Austria and Hungary, and the authorities found out that I did not have a visa. My friends had told me that I could obtain a visa right in the train. Not so. I suddenly found myself surrounded by half a dozen soldiers with rifles on their shoulders who were very upset by my negligence and also wanted to know why I did address them in German and not in Hungarian even though I was a native of the country. Unable to convince them of my innocence, they drove me off the train while the rest of the passengers were hanging out the window to watch me being escorted like a common criminal back to the control office at the train station. I was forced to take a $70 taxi back to Vienna and obtain a visa before I could board another train and resume my journey to Budapest. It was a nightmare, but in the end, I was nevertheless happy to have made the journey.

Two of Lukács's original disciples, Agnes Heller and her second husband, Ferenc Fehér received me in their home and answered some of my questions. Both also seemed eager to find academic appointments in the West but, as a junior instructor myself, I was in no position to assist them which, I know, they found very disappointing. Agnes Heller's first husband, István Herrmann, a Lukács scholar, would have liked to entrust his manuscript to me for publication in the West. Yet it was against the law to export creative works, such as manuscripts, paintings or any other Hungarian "treasures," so I could not accept. It would have been too risky, especially after my nightmare on the Orient Express. Soon thereafter I noticed that Ferenc and Agnes managed to get positions in Australia and then in the United States. Ferenc Fehér died unexpectedly a few years ago, but Agnes seems to live a comfortable life between New York and Budapest. I had hoped to interview her for my book on Lukács but she was unavailable. When I met her recently at several Hungarian related events in New York, she had first tinted her hair flaming red and then later changed to a dark brown, twisted in a bun, wore ankle long skirts and looked considerably aged. She seemed to have opted for a "gypsy" look. I found it somewhat surprising that she had no recollection of my visit with them in Budapest, which was followed by several contacts by mail, and our encounter at Cerisy la Salle, at a meeting in a castle in Normandy devoted to the work of Lucien Goldmann and Lukács. She also preferred to ignore that I had published two books on Lukács. Strange, I thought, of a former Lukács disciple.

One of the definite highlights of my first return to Budapest during the Cold War was my visit to the "hallowed grounds" of the Lukács Archives on Belgrád Rackpart, in his former apartment located on the banks of the Danube, where I was allowed to browse through his annotated books and correspondence with such people as Merleau-Ponty. The custodian promised to send me Xerox copies of the letters that seemed most valuable to my own study, but they never arrived. I extended my stay by two days after the conference and thus had the immense pleasure of reunions with a few members of my family, among them my revered aunt, Mancinéni, who had visited Lukács to talk to him about my study a few years before he passed away in 1971. He was very gracious to her and said, modestly, that he was not aware of his influence on French literary theory except on Lucien Goldmann who, he felt, would have preferred him "to drop dead after having written his initial pre-Marxist works," since, ironically, Goldmann built his own Marxist theory on Lukács's pre-Marxist writings. Altogether, my first visit back home was uniquely rewarding but also highly emotional for me.

More visits to Hungary followed, usually connected with professional conferences, and not without unusual events but with less threatening situations. On my next trip, a journalist came to "interview" me, he said, for "Rádio Budapest" since I wrote my Ph.D. Dissertation on the Hungarian Marxist philosopher György Lukács. He was very interested in the reception of my work in the United States and apparently surprised about the freedom I had in pursuing my work at the Naval Academy. The conference provided to the participants a block of relatively inexpensive rooms at the Hilton Hotel on the hills of Buda, but I was surprised about the top quality room I was assigned, overlooking the city. Somebody whispered to me that the room was likely to be bugged. That was OK. I had nothing to hide. The country was still very poor. The building of my aunt in downtown Budapest still bore the marks of gunshots from the fighting in World War II. The stores displayed eerily empty shelves. People asked whether I had some Nescafe or blue jeans I wanted to sell. Second hand stores and galleries had amazing treasures but I was afraid to buy some and take them back home. In the train taking me back to Paris, the controller asked me whether I had spent much money in Hungary and I fearfully admitted that I had spent some, but to my surprise he responded: "good, we want to have your dollars." During another attendance of a comparative literature conference in Budapest René Wellek asked me to accompany him to the Lukács Archives since he did not speak Hungarian. Even though Wellek was usually very critical of Lukács, the directors of the Archives were quite pleased with his visit. It was really an eventless visit, just to satisfy Wellek's curiosity, I guess, and leave behind an imprint of his name.

After the fall of the Berlin Wall and the end of the Soviet occupation of Hungary, I went back to Budapest several times and, during one of my visits, was happy to stay at the Gellért Hotel with its exciting wave pools and warm spas where, as a child, I used to frolic with my little friend Jóska on our frequent family outings to the baths. During each of my visits, I also made a point to visit my family and get to know the younger generation. One girl had been named after me, Livia, the same name I had given my daughter and as a middle name to my grand-daughter, in remembrance of the wife of my father's best friend who, with her husband, had perished in the war, probably in Auschwitz. After more frequent visits home to the place where I was born, my attachment to Hungary became quite strong again, and I even considered moving back but I needed a job. I inquired about an opening at the Technical University and talked to realtors, but it remained only a dream. A teaching position at the university at that time would have paid me about $300 a month.

My charming young nieces in Solymár, my father's birth place, who welcomed me at my first visit "back home."

Decision to stay in U.S.

Upon my return, I opted for the security of my tenured position I already enjoyed in the United States and also, most of all, for the presence of my daughter and her growing family. I loved my daughter more than anyone else in the world and developed a similar attachment to each of my grandchildren. Among my most cherished souvenirs will remain my daughter's and her family's visits to my home in Annapolis, when the little girls would improvise on the piano, check whether the red tulips on my park-like grounds were in bloom, my oldest granddaughter enthusiastically sing "Gloooooooooooria" for half an hour at our Christmas celebration, dance on their "tippy toes" in their Halloween costumes as princesses or ballerinas, compete with a hundred other children for Easter eggs spread out on the huge lawn of the Naval Academy. Once my grandson was born, he enjoyed to splash in the waves at the beaches of Montauk, a few years later he would play the piano, with much gusto, especially his Jazz piece which I love. I have thousands of such joyful memories that will remain forever. How could I possibly leave behind this sweet bunch of people, who have become one of my strongest "raison d'être"!? The emotional pull of Europe remained, though. Both Budapest and Paris I have considered "home" and have loved for their beauty and the many emotional ties I have developed during my life time.

"Thank God for little girls." My granddaughters often reminded me of Maurice Chevalier's famous song.

I love to listen to my grandson playing Jazz on the piano.

My daughter with her three children at the Montauk lighthouse which was built with the approval of first U.S. President George Washington.

Enjoying the summer with my fun bunch of grandchildren on the rocks of Long Island Sound in Montauk near Gossmann's, our favorite family restaurant.

PART SIX

Unique Life Choices

20

Paris

I have always loved Paris . . .

The significance of Paris in my life easily outweighs and outshines the one of all other big cities in which I have lived, and these include, besides Budapest, Munich, London, New York, Boston, San Francisco and Seattle. They have all charmed me in one way or another but I have always had the need to return to Paris, the only city that never failed to make me feel at home, at least until now. I prefer to say in French: "J'ai toujours aimé Paris," rather than in English, "I have always loved Paris," because in French, it seems to evoke more the music and poetry of my life in that city. In English, it merely states a fact. It is prose. Saying it in English, I probably offend people in America or in England, since I prefer "another" to them. They take it personally. People like to be loved not just for their own self but everything that surrounds them, their city and their country, but I have always loved Paris, just as I felt attracted and may have "loved" men—one man?—who possessed not only wit but also mystery, history, uniqueness, in addition to style, distinction, physical, professional and intellectual brilliance, like France in its centuries of an illustrious civilization.

A romantic attempt at putting down roots in Paris

In 1980, when the dollar was extremely strong, I bought a small studio walk up in the Marais, rue de Lesdiguières. It seemed ideal, even though tiny. I had a shower, toilet, kitchenette and a good size window overlooking the yard. It turned out to be a big mistake. I furnished it lovingly with pink velvet curtains, a comfortable mattress and even a TV. But late night, one of the first I spent there, a couple started to yell at each other in a language that I did not understand and soon I heard the woman scream as if she feared for her life. Heads appeared on windows around the yard until finally someone must have called the police and it was suddenly quiet. My daughter and her husband, on his first trip ever to Paris, were ready to fall asleep in my studio when someone rammed the door, trying to break in. My Pakistani neighbor later told me that he was able to intervene and tell his fellow Pakistani to stop, but the young couple was in panic and rushed to call my friend who picked them up and took them in for the night. A few months later, the police was alerted that four Algerians, a pregnant woman and a dog had broken into the place and lived there in horrendous circumstances. It took my poor friend weeks to have them evicted, because I was teaching in the U.S. and could not rush to Paris to help her with the police. The place was finally sold. My friend and her family told me I should have consulted with them before buying instead of committing myself to a romantic purchase. The building apparently was occupied mostly by single men from foreign countries, who had caused much unrest and had engaged in various crimes such as break-ins, thefts and even armed robberies with knives. All this, steps away from the Bastille and some very nice buildings in the same street.

A charming pied-à-terre in the Marais

After my retirement, when I had sold my beautiful large home in Annapolis, just across the Severn River from the Naval Academy, I settled for a small and inexpensive but still beautiful place on the Hudson so that I could again acquire a place in Paris. This time I found a just slightly larger but much more secure studio apartment in a well cared for building and, after having obtained the approval of my friends, rushed to buy it. I felt distressed by the election of George W. Bush to president of the U.S. and yearned to escape for at least a few months a year into a more humanistically oriented country. I now have a charming "pied à terre" in a seventeenth century building in the Marais. Its large French window is directly facing the church Saint Paul that was first constructed by Saint Louis at the time of the Crusades. Again, I tried my best to furnish it, with a "guéridon," which is a round elaborately decorated table, and chairs with red velvet upholstery in the style of Louis XV, but also a modern, comfortable queen-size sofa bed in Italian leather. Both the kitchen and the bathroom with its shower are small but the whole studio still strikes me today, years later, as really charming. It is like a dream come true to own a piece of Paris, in its oldest neighborhood, only a few minutes of walk to some of the most beautiful and romantic places of the capital. To the Bastille it takes five minutes, the Seine five minutes, Notre Dame ten minutes … a real delight. I travel to France as often as I can find a reasonable round trip ticket that will not upset my tight budget, but usually at least twice a year. I hope the recent elections which were very disappointing for me, will not dampen my enthusiasm for France. The strong euro has already cut into my plans to buy a slightly larger place so that I could invite family, especially my grandchildren. I may have to wait for the next elections and another government on both sides of the Atlantic that will restore the strength of the dollar.

Paris from my window

In the meantime, I continue to enjoy the lively buzz and the genre painting that unfolds to my eyes each morning when I open my curtain. The view is typical of the Marais and most of the days quite enchanting but the steps and large gates to the church have also been attracting the homeless who huddle there in the coldest of nights, some with their dog, others just keeping warm with a bottle of wine. Relief sculptures of Saint Louis, Saint Marie and Marie Magdalene carved into the roman-style facade look down on this refuge. An old clock, whose handles have been stuck at half past midnight ever since I have moved in, is like a wishful thinking of so many of us to stop time.

One of the homeless men and his old white furred dog have been sitting there for the past few years. He does not seem to be a beggar or an alcoholic and cares well for his companion. Whenever he has empty bags or newspapers which he spends much time reading, he comes down to the edge of the rue Saint Antoine and throws the refuse in the garbage bin. He is neat, but he looks bored, maybe lonely, and sometimes attracts other less self respecting homeless with their half empty wine bottles and swollen red faces, who occasionally step over to the wall of the building near the church to relieve themselves. This spring, a young woman wrapped in a big, heavy looking, dark coat and a pink bonnet on her head found a niche for herself next to a column framing one of the smaller side doors to the church. She usually buries her head in her lap, as if she were asleep or just did not want anyone to see her face and maybe recognize her. One early afternoon I was getting ready to walk down my three floors and cross over the street to talk to her when I noticed a young man with a bag filled with plastic containers and some apples and bananas that he deposited next to her. She briefly lifted her head as if to thank him but quickly hid her face again. After a while, when he was gone, she opened the bag and started to bite into a chicken leg and then slowly munched away on French fries and the fruit. When it got dark I suddenly noticed her next to the wall, in a squatting position, with her big coat pulled up. Why do these people not walk the few steps over to the public toilet facilities where they could benefit from some privacy and not pollute the church area?

On weekend mornings I often see young attractive fathers pulling with one hand a sweet looking little girl who seems to trot happily after him while "papa" is holding a baguette in his other hand. Friday afternoons, I frequently notice orthodox Jewish dads dressed in white shirts, dark suits, hats and heavy shoes, holding little girls by their hand, seemingly rushing home after having picked them up from nearby schools. They appear more serious than other children on the street, wearing gray, long dresses and aprons, while their brothers, dragging their heavy schoolbags, looking a bit rebellious, try to keep up with their father's quick steps.

On Thursdays and Sundays, I often notice older couples carrying bags with groceries back home from the market place at the Bastille where I do my shopping as well. They usually come bye in the early afternoon, just before the market closes, when vendors, many of them North African, liquidate their left over goods for ridiculously low prices.

Then, sitting at my window, I have seen beautiful young brides, in narrowly fitted white dresses, their veils floating behind them, blissfully making their way down the centuries old church steps on the arm of their new husbands, surrounded by their admiring family and the priest.

At funeral ceremonies, there are guards men holding flags forming a path through which the pall bearers will carry the casket usually to a waiting black SUV. It is an older crowd that stands around at those occasions maybe hoping that the same honors will be bestowed upon them when it will be their turn to be driven to the cemetery.

Since I am close to the Bastille, the traditional rallying place for manifestations and strikes of all sorts, my street is frequently inundated by a huge crowd. Once a month, hundreds of roller skaters and skate borders dash by after sun set not to interfere with daytime traffic.

Recently, one roadway was closed to vehicular traffic and two attractive benches were installed in the space between my building and the church. It did not take long for lovers to discover them who, like two pigeons, seemed happy to have found a place to sit down and neck, tenderly glued to each other. The other day, I saw a young man reading his paper who was soon joined by another. When they arrived, they sat down at opposite ends of the bench, but the next time I looked out the window I saw them walking away together. Little children love to frolic on the open space as do sometimes groups of teenagers. Recently some were scaring each other, and me, by running after their friends with lit cigarette lighters.

If it were not for the firehouse a few buildings away, which sometimes interrupts the quiet with its shrieking sirens, this stretch of the rue Saint Antoine would be quite idyllic, probably not very different from what it must have been many years ago when I first set foot in Paris. It fills me with great happiness every time I arrive at this place which since my retirement I call home for several months a year.

My routine promenades

Whenever the weather and my time permits, since I do not have a car there, I walk sometimes for miles, taking big detours before doing my shopping for groceries or flowers, passing by many of the historic sites of Paris that I love. My changing routine takes me often on Saturdays in a few minutes to the Place des Vosges whose galleries and new exhibits I like to check out. In about seven minutes I can walk to the Opera of the Bastille whose performances I try to enjoy at least once or twice a year; sometimes seated on one of the "strapontins" to cope with the high cost of tickets. In ten minutes I can cross the bridge Saint Louis over the Seine to reach the romantic Isle Saint Louis and in a few more minutes arrive at the Parvis Notre Dame. From there, on Sundays, I may take a leisurely walk alongside the *bouquinistes* all the way to the Café des Deux Magots in the heart of the Latin Quarter where I sip my customary *citron pressé*, or stop at the Quai de la Mégisserie for an always delicious meal with my friends. Paris has been offering such magic promenades for centuries free of charge.

My pied-à-terre in the Marais District of Paris is a small refuge from disappointing people and politics. It provides me with a lovely window seat opposite Saint Louis-Saint Paul that is perfect for two of my favorite activities: reading and writing.

Was it love?

No wonder that it was also in Paris where I believe to have understood what so-called "love" means and where, not surprisingly, I believed to have found it. For me, it was an extremely complex experience that in its perfect beauty could not possibly last forever. But after an emotional bankruptcy due to a painful divorce and years of demanding professional activities and struggles to make it in the U.S., "love" could happen to me only in Paris. It actually started in New York but then took momentum in Paris, and finally crisscrossed all of

Saint Louis-Saint Paul

the United States and several countries of Europe. It spread to Hungary, Austria, Germany, a dreamy castle in Normandy, and the shores of San Francisco Bay. Wherever it flourished, it felt like the perfect synthesis, the total embrace of two beings. He was French, in Paris, and I was American in New York, but we completed, fulfilled each other's dreams of the other city. He also loved Budapest as I did and could understand without resentment why, after having lost Budapest I immediately felt that Paris could be my new home. I love bridges and large rivers and several will forever be connected to our togetherness. We crossed the Danube on the Erzsébet Hid and the Lánc Hid, while I shared with him my childhood dreams about living in the castle on the Buda hills overlooking the stream and its banks on the Pest side, ennobled by the impressive parliament buildings, just as in Paris Le Pont Neuf, the oldest bridge in Paris, and Le Pont des Arts with its young crowd picnicking and playing jazz and well known French chansons on weekend evenings, or the Pont Saint Louis taking me from my apartment on a typical Sunday promenade to the Isle Saint Louis will forever remind me of our walks and enchanting dinners in nearby cozy restaurants. Driving over the Bay Bridge from Oakland to San Francisco after a successful, very animated conference has left an unforgettable imprint on my mind which was later deepened by a similar event I organized in honor of René Wellek. The majestic Hudson and the George Washington Bridge I can see sitting on my living room sofa and the sprawling New York skyline to which my balcony offers a view from the WG Bridge all the way down to where the Twin Towers of the World Trade Center used to stand before I saw them crumbling in fire and smoke shortly after the second airplane, which I followed with my eyes as it was flying low downstream over the river until it reached its fateful target on 9/11; Manhattan with the tower of the Riverside Church and just behind it, a bit further South, Columbia University with its Maison Française where we met, and across Central Park to my East Side Apartment where he came to visit me and my daughter on a day that may have marked the half way post of my life, March 7, the day of my birthday, all this has taken a deeper meaning for me after we set eyes on each other for the first time. We bridged national divisions and religious and ethnic borders that we enthusiastically crossed hand in hand because we both wished to eliminate such evil in the world. We saw people as individuals, not representatives of a group. We both thought of the same person that he was a "mensch," and of another that he cannot be trusted. Speaking German, we knew, did not make someone a Nazi. Belonging to a specific race or ethnicity does not automatically turn someone into a criminal or a victim. There were no conflicts between our values and tastes, but physically, we were like two opposites molded together. His dark eyes, brown hair, trim body and smooth skin with a light olive hue, seemed to be the perfect match for my gray-green eyes, blond hair and fair skinned lanky limbs. Both of us, because of a certain physical charisma people sometimes perceived, had to deal with unfairness and envy. People deemed physically unattractive often have it easier to be credited for even the least amount of intelligence. Not just so-called blue blood aristocrats, but maybe more so those who hate them, seek ways to discredit each other. In our unconditional appreciation of each other, we seemed to have benefited from an amazing grace.

But this love remained self-contained. No fruit sprung from its beauty even though, at some moments, the desire to make it live and last, to celebrate it in the continuity of life itself, was alive and probably increased the intensity and truth of the emotions. This love which has left its reflection in so many places in fact remained in some sense outside society and had no other history than its own. It became like a diamond that shone in the sky and in memory, immaterial, extraterrestrial, never spoiled, never damaged, because never down to earth. Only in its abstraction from everyday reality could it last, be inspiring, nourishing, and faithful. The magic of this love belonged to the realm of the unicorn. Its existence was like a dream come true, the fulfillment of a subconscious desire, a generous gift of love from a finally merciful Venus, but it could not have been without the complex emotional and intellectual relationship I have had with Paris and France.

21
People Who Matter

*O*ther emotional attachments, infatuations and desires, whose force just slightly diminished with age, remained torn between East and West, often strained by the three thousand or so miles that separated the East and West Coast of the United States or by the mighty Atlantic Ocean that imposed itself as a barrier time wise and financially between me and the people with whom I longed to be.

Both of my parents have been dead for a long time. Even before my mother's death, I lost my only brother. He died from a heart attack after a long poorly treated illness at a school in Southern Bavaria where he lived and worked as a Franciscan Brother. I had not seen him in years and could not make it to his funeral because I had no money for the rather expensive roundtrip from London and more so because I was in the midst of administering and correcting final exams at the Britannia Royal Naval College where I had taught for a year and prepared my impending return to Annapolis to resume my regular teaching at the U.S. Naval Academy, scheduled for the week ahead. I have never quite forgiven myself for this but I felt overwhelmed at the moment his death occurred. I tried to honor his memory by talking to my friends about his uniquely difficult life, his brilliant memory for facts, his love for my little daughter when we saw him the last time and he looked at her admiringly while she sang American folk songs and accompanied herself on the guitar. He even recorded her truly cute performance on an audio cassette that I still cherish.

My sister, who is eight years older than I, and since our flight from Hungary during World War II has often played the role of surrogate mother to me when it was too difficult for my parents to see to my needs, has become even closer to me now that I can see her more often due to the free time gained after my retirement and the small studio I have been able to maintain in Paris. My tiny "pied à terre" has allowed me not only to spend several months a year in my beloved city but has given me easier access to my family in Europe whom I had not seen much during the forty years I lived and worked full time in the United States. As a medical doctor with a specialty in Internal Medicine, my sister also became mother to three children, her oldest daughter, a pharmacist and gifted, very attractive young woman, married to a judge; her youngest, a son, a tall dark successful veterinarian with a specialty in equine cardiology, married to a colleague who treats and operates on small domestic animals and for her intelligence and charming personality has won the undivided admiration of the whole family; and my sister's middle child, born after only six months of pregnancy, whose positive attitude toward life and cheerful, gentle nature has, despite the many hurdles she had to overcome in her life since infancy, became a skillful medical technician and loving wife to a doting husband. Four grandchildren enliven and reward my sister's life which she has mastered beautifully through hard work and the determination to make it even in moments when personal and very serious health problems brought her close to despair and even death.

My sister.

Representing the younger generation of the family in Europe, my sister's daughter, a pharmacist married to a supreme court judge, with her two children in Weimar, Germany.

My sister's son, a veterinarian specializing in equine cardiology, doting on his two sweet daughters who seem to adore him as well. With his wife, a veterinarian for small domestic animals, the family lives near Karlsruhe, Germany.

On the U.S. side of the Atlantic, even though born in Paris, France, my daughter, a real estate attorney in New York, with her two bundles of joy. She has been the most constant manifestation of "grace" in my life.

My U.S. born son-in-law, a partner in his mid-town Manhattan law firm, is seen here as proud father admiring his splendid son. He also continues to surprise me with the breadth and depth of his culture.

Today, after more than four decades in the U.S., my daughter, her husband and three beautiful children are my only family this side of the Atlantic. Having retired from teaching, I am now free to live closer to them and enjoy with enormous pride what they have all become so far. Both parents are successful attorneys in New York after having graduated from Law School at Columbia University, which is also my alma mater for my Ph.D. in the Graduate School of Arts and Sciences. All three children are quite different but equally handsome and talented in their own right. I could fill hundreds of pages with observations of their charm and accomplishments. Watching them grow up, I can now understand the sorrow I caused my parents when I left them behind to immigrate with my family to the United States.

Among my happiest moments in life has been the time spent in the witty, loving company of my family. It started when I was still a child, over dinner with my parents and siblings, then our spouses and acquired families and friends. Since most people in my family, despite the upheavals in our lives, have managed to become quite well educated adults and chose liberal professions, most of them in medicine and several in law, discussions tended to be spirited and wide ranging and still are at the rare moments those of us who are still alive manage to meet, either in New York or somewhere in Europe.

I have also been able to attend a few class reunions and was surprised how well most of my classmates have done in life and have not lost the wonderful spirit we enjoyed in class, much of which has been recorded not just in occasional "entries" in my Latin manual, which I recently discovered among old notebooks, but also in brochures created to commemorate our school years together and especially our final graduation.

While the family I remembered in Europe has considerably decreased in the last decades with the deaths of the older generation, I still have a small "adoptive family" in Paris who has played an essential role in my life. It was my best friend who invited me into her home soon after I arrived in Paris and started a friendship that lasted until her terribly untimely death from melanoma nearly twenty years ago. Her two young sons were devastated by the loss of their mother and, since she was divorced from

Of my immediate family, now living on two continents, this is the last complete family picture in Europe after the three of us had immigrated to the U.S.

Family surrounding my mother at my sister's home a few years before she passed away in Germany.

My daughter's family at their weekend home in Connecticut, the only family I have this side of the Atlantic.

their father, each of the boys went his own way to overcome his grief. One rushed into a marriage that ultimately did not make him happy but he has done well in business. The younger one drifted away from his studies and never quite found his professional calling. It ultimately was a cousin who kept the family together. His caring, generous nature and especially his concern and affection for the children created a stable pole to which they could converge and find unconditional support and comfort. Over the years, we have become a bit like brother and sister, and I always look forward to his and his wife's kind, intelligent and cultured company. My life has been greatly enriched by the long enduring friendship with this wonderful family. Since my own mother has been dead for many years, I have taken comfort in visiting my friend's mother who is close to one hundred years old now but still finds joy in life with her grandchildren and great-grandchildren. I try to see her whenever I am in Paris. We usually spend the time refreshing joyful memories. Again, it has been the thoughtful cousin, the lady's nephew, who has provided the charming old lady with much selfless care and emotional comfort. This man has been practicing what we all should do: help and be good to other human beings. It is therefore the most inconceivable crime I can imagine that as a small child he should have cruelly lost his mother and little brother to Hitler's gas chambers in Auschwitz.

With members of my "surrogate family" in Paris, France.

Among people who still "matter" in my life are two other friends from my student years in Paris. We were all friends of my best friend as well and enjoyed good times together. They are now married to each other and have created a beautiful family. I am glad we can see each other from time to time and refresh memories which warm our hearts.

The first friend I made soon after World War II, after we arrived at the refugee hospital my father directed in Germany, has maintained a touching affection for me. So have some of my classmates from my German high school. They provide me with a feeling that I have left roots in that war torn country as well.

Among my newest friends is a man who puzzled me at an exhibit of avant-garde paintings, Rue de Rivoli in Paris, when he promptly offered me his digital camera when he noticed that mine had suddenly stopped working. He had no idea who I was, a foreigner in a big city, but he did not hesitate for a moment and trusted that I would return his camera after I had downloaded the pictures. I did not accept his generous offer but took one picture which he soon after we met forwarded to me, and we have been exchanging e-mail now for several years, encouraging each other to pursue our activities: his hobby is painting and I have been trying to write this book. About once a year we meet for coffee at the Place des Vosges, and apparently find comfort in each other's company, built on spontaneous friendship and absolute trust.

All these people in Europe are my friends and I know I could turn to them if I needed help. In just under a year, while teaching at BRNC, I developed similarly trusting relationships with people in Great Britain and also with some of my neighbors in Annapolis and a few Rotarians in Cambridge and Boston during my sabbatical. But, in other parts of the United States, and particularly in New Jersey, I have experienced a marked difference in what people call "friend." There are probably thousands of people I have met in the U.S., and many would not hesitate to call themselves my friends, just because we spent some time together somewhere. For me, as I believe for most Europeans, the term "friend" has a much deeper meaning. I have lots of acquaintances and former colleagues, whom I sincerely like and some of them also admire, but would not call "friend." Nor would I ever feel free to ask them for a favor, even just to drive me a few miles to the airport.

I have usually tried to integrate in each of the many different communities in which I have lived. I organized dinners and receptions but with the exception of neighbors, mostly European natives, and colleagues at the colleges and universities at which I taught, rarely benefited from a similar gesture. Americans like to have parties, congregate in large groups over barbecue, chips, soft drinks and beer, or even invite to ever so popular potluck dinners which I would be too embarrassed even to propose. In the U.S., it seems much less customary to share even just a simple meal in the intimacy of a family home. In the seven years that I have been living in New Jersey, only two European ladies, a Belgian and an Italian, who had been to my place, invited me to their home as well, one of them even for dinner. Whenever I am back in the U.S., it is not surprising that I do miss the warmth of European hospitality. It may be that Europeans of different countries in general just like me more, are less suspicious, and don't see me immediately as a foreigner, as is too often the case even after my more than forty years of living and working as a citizen of this country. As I wrote at the beginning of my book, the first thing they usually ask me is: "Where are you from?"

22
Rotary

First female member of Annapolis Rotary

Besides my personal and academic life, I have also been a Rotarian for now nearly two decades. I was introduced to Rotary by the President of the Rotary Club of Dartmouth, Devon, during my year as exchange lecturer at the Britannia Royal Naval College. He often invited me to be his "lady companion" at dinners and on boat trips, such as the one when Queen Elizabeth's yacht, "Britannia" sailed into the waters near Dartmouth and we were circling it to greet her. I did not fully realize at that time what it meant to be a Rotarian. I thought it was a club in which the rather successful people of the community congregate to enjoy each other's company once a week over dinner or lunch. Only back home in Annapolis, when I talked enthusiastically about my experiences in Dartmouth, the director of research of the Naval Academy explained to me Rotary's "service club" functions and asked me immediately whether I would want to join the Annapolis Rotary club of which he was a member. I accepted enthusiastically, but did not expect it to become a real adventure. There were still no female members in the Club even though Rotary had recommended their admission worldwide. The director of research looked upon it as a challenge and started inviting me to their weekly lunches. The male constituents were nice to me but were not easily swayed. It actually took six months for them to say OK and accept me, in 1989, together with another lady because for whatever reason they felt I should not be the only woman Rotarian in the Club. They have been extremely nice to me ever since, as were Rotarians in all countries where I "made up" whenever I could not be at my own club's meeting. During a year long sabbatical leave, I scored a nearly 200% attendance record by joining Rotarians in Cambridge and Boston at their weekly meetings.

Rotarian service and privileges—Study Tour to Hungary, Austria and Slovenia (1997)

From the beginning, I took the "service" aspect of my membership quite seriously and tried to engage in the organization of youth exchanges, encouraging tutoring of children from poor families, working on a literacy program and finally, joining the entire Washington D.C.–Maryland Rotary District, becoming the first (naturally also the first female) team leader to take a group of four young non Rotarian professionals on a five-week tour to Austria, Hungary and Slovenia after the fall of the Soviet regime. The reason for electing me to team leader had much to do with my familiarity with two of the three languages we would need and also my so-called "leadership experience" as professor at the Naval Academy. What reassured them as well, was that I had already organized two study tours for mid-shipmen to Germany and France a few years earlier. The preparation and even the tour itself required much work and energy but turned into a once-in-a-lifetime experience. Rotary has generally been good to me. I was awarded a Paul Harris Fellowship from my Annapolis club in recognition of a job well done in my international work, just as I later was awarded a "Service Above Self" certificate by the Englewood club which I joined after leaving Annapolis. Everywhere I traveled I was allowed to join Rotary meetings and "make up" for the lunches I had missed at my home club. This took me to the wonderful Rotary Club of Paris, Porte Dauphine, at which I have been warmly welcomed for many years and was invited to become a member, as I also was at the Rotary Club "Academies" that meets at the famous Coupole Restaurant at Montparnasse, Hemingway's former "hang out" with his fellow writers, or still another club that meets near the Beaubourg. I also visited Rotary in Budapest and in Karlsruhe, Germany, which is the only one I know that still has no women members, unlike Rio de Janeiro in Brazil, Boston, Cambridge, and the Westminster Club in London among many others at which I have "made up."

It is a true privilege to find wonderful Rotary friends all around the world. This becomes particularly noticeable and rewarding at international conventions that take place in different cities, countries and even continents

With members of the Rotary Clubs of Budapest during the Group Study Tour through Austria, Hungary and Slovenia for which I was team leader representing the Washington, D.C. - Northern Maryland Rotary District.

I am one of the helpers at the Annapolis Rotary Club's famed Crab Feast, a fund raiser that attracts several thousand visitors each year to the Navy-Marine Corps Memorial Stadium in Annapolis.

On the sandy beaches of Montauk with two exchange students from Germany whom I hosted that summer as International Service Director for my Annapolis Rotary Club.

Brother and sister, two top students from the Dwight Morrow High School in Englewood, New Jersey. As International Service Director for the Englewood Rotary Club, I was able to arrange youth exchanges for both, one with Spain, the other with France.

each year, of which I attended three: in Mexico City, Nice, and Copen-hagen–Malmö. Ever since I joined Rotary, I have also had opportunities to meet the various Rotary International Presidents, which added inspiration to my work in the international activities in which I had engaged.

As team leader of one of the first Rotary sponsored Group Study Exchanges with Eastern Europe after the fall of the Soviet Regime, I am greeted by the President of the University and his spouse at the University of Maribor in Slovenia.

The mission of Rotary and my personal ethics

My decision to join Rotary was similar to the enthusiasm I experienced when I first began to work for the United Nations and the short lived hope in Paris to associate with an attorney who apparently tried to help the victims of World War II. My enthusiastic commitment to Rotary persists. I have been trying all my life to help those who had suffered unjustly and were in need of support. I have also tried to reach out to other nations and make friends with them, even with those who were enemies of the countries where my family and I lived during the war. I don't believe in generational vengefulness or inherited guilt. It has been a privilege to have been associated for nearly two decades now with people who share similar ideals.

With Rotary International President and Mrs.King in Budapest, Hungary, during one of my visits "back home."

With R. I. President Estess, a former Rotarian from New Jersey. His official visit to the Paris Rotary Club, coincided with one of my frequent Rotarian "make ups" at the Paris Club's beautiful Pavillon Dauphine location.

With R.I. President and Mrs. Boyd on "Rotary Day" at the United Nations in New York.

With R.I. President Carl Wilhelm Stenhammar at the R.I. Convention in Copenhagen, Denmark.

23

Sabbatical at Harvard

An intellectual dream

After teaching full-time for thirty-two years, seventeen of which at the Naval Academy, I was finally granted a sabbatical year which I had the great fortune to spend as visiting research professor in the Romance Languages Department of Harvard University. It was the most inspiring, rewarding and stress-free year of my life in Academia. I am grateful to the faculty and students in the department who so readily accepted me in their midst. The journal I kept that year is filled with expressions of the joy and excitement that filled my days. I spent hours at the Library and attended numerous lectures scheduled all over campus but most of all in my own department and the Barker Center that attracted an endless flow of brilliant scholars from around the world. My small but bright and comfortable apartment on the top floor of a Massachusetts Avenue building provided an inspiring view over parts of the campus. Halfway through my stay, I read an article entitled "Quit to succeed," which I could not get out of my mind. In the end, my sabbatical year at Harvard indeed changed my life.

Too many rewards and privileges?

Since the time I joined the faculty at the USNA, following the rule of seniority, several of my colleagues became chairpersons of the department. Naturally, they seemed to enjoy their sudden power and did not always escape the temptation to make the most of it for themselves. I had not realized how envious and resentful some of my colleagues had become toward me. I believe it started with my enthusiastic and successful involvement with research and the publication of two books which contributed to a seamless promotion all the way to full professor. Some of the envy

242

seemed to increase each time I was elected delegate or member of an executive committee of the Modern Language Association. I also had the privilege at the USNA to participate in, and even organize one of two, five week study tours for midshipmen to Germany and France which turned out to be very successful and much appreciated by the Administration. A few years later, I was selected to serve for a year as exchange faculty at the Britannia Royal Naval College, at Dartmouth, in the U.K. At least one of the chairpersons, I know, envied and tried to use against me my successful integration into the Annapolis Rotary Club as their first woman member, which was followed by my selection as team leader for a five week Rotary study tour to Eastern Europe. To top it off, I benefited from a dreamlike sabbatical at Harvard University.

Quit to succeed

In the year preceding my sabbatical and again when I prepared to return to my teaching position at the U.S.NA, it had become obvious that the current chairperson was not forgiving all these honors and privileges that had come my way and would not hesitate to make my life quite miserable with unfair, capricious decisions affecting class assignments and the like. I did not think I deserved such treatment and decided to hand in my resignation, asking the administration to let me take an early retirement. It was the right move for me, even though a bit bold at the time and, as I was told, upset the Dean but not for long since I was able to recommend a highly qualified friend quite happy to fill the sudden vacancy I had caused. The Dean and other members of the administration were aware of the situation in the department even before I left for Harvard and, I believe, understood my reasons, but it was pointed out to me that by retiring early, I would sacrifice part of the pension to which I would have been entitled had I stayed at least one more year. All things considered, I still think it was the right decision. The following year, I was invited with the rest of the retirees to a moving, impressive retirement ceremony at Memorial Hall and a parade by the four thousand midshipmen in our honor.

24

Freedom and Happiness at a Cost but, Oh! So Worth It

Free at last

The greatest benefit from my retirement was an incredible feeling of freedom. After my daughter had grown into an adult, and that I did not settle down into another marriage or even enter into a binding relationship that would have limited my movements and decisions, my professional, social and often charity activities became my life, an exciting intellectual and also emotional journey that has not stopped. I still meet wonderful, distinguished people with great minds and accomplishments. But contrary to my past, my thoughts and choices are now freer, really my own. I no longer feel that I have to conform to the views of a boss or other controlling agent. I can finally think, say and do what is in accordance with my own personal ethics and views. Like all freedom, mine is at times impeded by circumstances beyond my control and by people who simply do not like me, for whatever reason try to oppose or hurt me, or are little concerned with fairness and justice. Today, I have at least the freedom to speak up if I so chose. I had longed for such freedom ever since I was a little girl when I delighted in humming my favorite song, "My thoughts are free, no one can control them or take them from me . . ." The exercise of my intellectual freedom has made me walk through many doors, real and imaginary, where I have found beauty and ugliness, happiness and despair, but also a general satisfaction with my life's journey so far, and I still journey.

"Borrowing" happiness from life but not trying to "possess" it

The price I have paid in my life for some extravagant choices has been that I may not have fully exploited my potential. I do not like to fight for privileges, especially financial ones. I have fought for my students,

244

their admission to great schools and for scholarships, and have always tried to write strong letters of recommendation on their behalf, but for myself I just "borrow" from life the happiness I am allowed to experience, that often just seems to come my way as I pursue my normal activities. Maybe therefore I dislike hasslers so much. In Europe it is in bad taste to ask for a raise, to market oneself aggressively, as some doctors and attorneys in the U.S. do, placing ads about their professional "services" in local papers. New Yorkers do not hesitate to advertise themselves even in European publications. I was brought up to believe, somewhat naively, that rewards we deserve are dealt out by whatever just authority has control over us. My reluctance to fight for favors has been true as well when it came to places or people to whom I became attached. When I notice that I cannot have or can no longer have whatever or whomever I would have loved to get or keep for myself, I withdraw and move on. I do not try very hard and for a long time to possess whatever or whomever I dream about. I am sure this attitude has often been misunderstood. On the other hand, I usually try to transform close relationships into lasting friendships, an enchanted souvenir, or cherish even the longing that forever seems to tie me to secret feelings of warmth, satisfaction, even triumph over the vulgarity, platitudes, boredom and loneliness of ordinary life. At my advanced age, life is often still surprisingly generous toward me and acts like an accomplice from my more youthful years, sharing secret smiles, glances and affection that shower me with warm feelings.

Catastrophes and difficulties but always jumping back on my feet

My life has not been free of catastrophes. I escaped death in World War II and an onslaught of polio. I survived my painful divorce alone in the U.S. with my daughter, the loneliness and financial hardship that followed. There were the frightening revolts of 1968, the eruption of Mount Saint Helen, 9/11 which I watched from my balcony and that has traumatized me to this day. I saw the second plane flying low down the Hudson and finally hitting the second tower. Since then, I follow each plane flying low and close to any building with clear trepidation. What made it so much worse for me was that for hours I could not reach my family in Manhattan while phone calls from Europe kept coming, inquiring about us. I was horrified by the student murderers at Columbine and at Virginia Tech and today fear for my grandchildren living in Manhattan. They are growing up rapidly, and as they will soon be leaving the protective nest of the family, could be drafted into wars or be exposed to murderers. More recently, I felt my heartbeat accelerate when I saw on TV a school bus near the geyser spouting in the air after the eruption of a hot air duct in mid-Manhattan. It happened on the road on which my grandchildren sometimes travel to and from school. I have lived quite near to where many other catastrophes occurred, some manmade, others natural.

In addition, like most people, I have had my share of professional and emotional hardship to endure. But stress, unfair pressure, envy, jealousy, insults, disappointments no longer have the same power over me today as they had in my more youthful years, a more cruel, less generous past. I have had to cope with many unkind people and numerous incidents of discrimination, mostly by other ethnic groups. On the other hand, I have frequently benefited from the support of generous, successful, distinguished human beings. The people who noticed me and were most willing to recognize and reward my hard work or whatever qualities and talents I brought to the task, were usually those who had reached the top of their professional and social ladder, unlike my peers who competed with me and frequently tried to undercut my efforts and accomplishments.

Without family in this country, I had to struggle for several decades to establish myself in the U.S., to "make it." But having finally tasted success, admiration, affection and love, I now depend much less on the opinion of the "other" who, as Sartre said, is, or at least can be, our "hell." I walk through my days with open eyes which, even purely physically, has become easier today than it was ten years ago. After my retirement, quite unexpectedly, I regained my near normal eye sight, maybe because my eyes no longer had to cope with reading hundreds of pages each week in preparation of my literature courses and could finally afford more rest and sleep. The elimination of constant stress lowered my slightly elevated blood pressure and, after several months, alleviated the debilitating head aches from which I suffered almost constantly for many years. Today, walking for hours through the enchanting streets of Paris or alongside the banks of the majestic Hudson River, admiring the New York Skyline from my balcony, I sometimes feel like a sponge soaking up beauty and all these new positive experiences that I hope will strengthen me for the years I still have ahead of me. I now am able to chose and experience freely many of the riches, never monetary, to which I have had the privilege to gain access because of good luck, hard work and having learned to overcome the hardship I often had to endure.

I grew on what I learned from my parents and at school, from my personal and our collective history, my own interests and activities, but also from the distinguished company of people I had the privilege of meeting, who intrigued me when they crossed my path, sometimes became my friends and some of whom I even grew to love and admire. In this flash back on my past, to all the events and circumstances that determined my being, the fact that I lost my home to war and exile when I was eight years old and, as I like playfully to pretend, lived the nomadic life of a blond Hungarian gypsy in six different countries on two continents and in seven different states of the United States remains significant. Despite all the difficulties I had to endure, my journeys and sojourns in the East and the West of both Europe and the United States have taught me much. Unlike representatives of some other nations and ethnic groups, I have always tried to integrate linguistically and culturally because I yearned to feel at home.

PART SEVEN

The Search for Answers

25

Beginnings of a Book

A manuscript long in making

The novelists, autobiographical writers, literary scholars and critical philosophers whose works I have been reading, whom I met or even just listened to, led me finally to start working on this present manuscript which may or may not become a book. It has had several beginnings.

When I was about twelve years old, I had the need to start a journal. I recorded, for instance, my admiration for the Danish student who spent the summer with us on an exchange program. I wanted so much to be like her, unburdened by the ravages of war, with a real home and country that she could love and be proud of. Later, sporadically, I filled lots of notebooks about my thoughts and emotions, especially at the time of my divorce or at other moments of disappointment or joy when there was no one in whom I could confide.

I wrote letters in response to newscasts on television or articles in newspapers, some of which actually got published, including in the *New York Times*. Among these critical pieces were letters and articles about gambling, discriminatory behavior of judges in white-men-only clubs, where they were served by Blacks and women but did not allow them to become members, or the threat to eliminate French from the local high school curriculum that to me seemed totally unwarranted and unwise.

When my granddaughter was two years old, the age of my daughter when we immigrated to the U.S., I thought I would write for her about our family and dedicate the book to her since in her sweet nature she reminded me so often of her mother as a baby while her father thought her older sister was following in his and his family's footsteps. My grandson, who reminds me of my daughter as well, was not born yet. I soon abandoned my project to write exclusively for my granddaughter but continued occasionally to record some thoughts and experiences in my notebooks. I taught a seminar on "autobiographical fiction" in preparation of which I did considerable research and presented papers on related literary topics at professional meetings.

A few years ago, I decided to write a sort of fictionalized autobiography not so much of myself but of my time and major events of the political and literary history as it filtered through my awareness. Since I have started this manuscript, I have not done much research and am writing as I remember things. I do not claim to write the absolute truth, not only because I do not feel capable of doing so but also because I do not believe anyone can pretend to do so. For the same reason, it is absolutely not in my intention to write what I would know is untrue. I certainly do not wish to be unfair to anyone.

In his so-called "anti-auto-biography," *Roland Barthes by Roland Barthes,* Barthes used mere fragments of his writings and photographs instead of attempting to "write the truth about himself." Since he considered language to be an arbitrary system of linguistic signs, he distrusted any form of *doxa* or the possibility of writing the "truth" into a discourse. I agree with his approach. In that sense, much of what I write must also be looked at as fictionalized fragments of my life and times that passed through my mind and that I am trying here to "inscribe" into the English language.

The way I am perceived—do I have a "specificity"?

In my teenage years, while still attending school at a "Humanistic Gymnasium" in Germany, I used to take afternoon lessons in painting, piano, swimming and tennis, and all my life regretted not to have inherited my mother's beautiful soprano voice, but I never gained true distinction in any of these activities. Only my piano teacher used to praise and encourage me in my early teens to nurture what he felt was a talent.

For me all these pursuits remained pleasurable activities and vehicles for dreams. None led to any direct professional gain but may have provided me, in addition to my intellectual formation, with an overall culture, what some call "sophistication," that helped me in my association with some socially or professionally distinguished people and their select milieus. One of my bosses at a fine institution which combined academic excellence with occasional glamour wrote in an evaluation of my performance that he could put me in any situation and trust that I would know how to behave in an exemplary fashion. This "general know how," with which my former boss kindly credited me, was actually a direct outcome of my father's early educational principles, his encouragement to develop all our skills and intellectual potential, which may have led to a kind of "social and cultural intertextuality" that has marked my education and background. "Your mind is the most precious thing and it is the only treasure you can take with you wherever you go," he used to say remembering that our family lost houses, land and all other material possessions to World War II. Because I have experienced war, hunger, poverty and homelessness, I often feel attracted and grateful to writers who have had a similar background and evoke in their literary universe situations that may help explain what I and people around me have perceived as my "otherness."

26
Distinguished People Crossing My Path

Part of the fabric of my life

If I have written much about the distinguished or at least well known people I have met, at both sides of the Atlantic, it was because I feel that they all have contributed to the fabric of my life, intellectually, professionally, and in some sense also personally. They "accompanied" me on my career path, just by being there in my space at the same time I was, physically passing through my life, not just informing me abstractly by the content of their works.

Like flash images of their faces, gestures, sentences, fascinating ideas, gazes, warm smiles and in many other wonderful ways they still exist in my mind and enrich my life. My father was right. I learned much from being in the presence of talented, interesting, inspiring people who could teach first hand about life, inspire me and provide models to imitate and directions to pursue. Even when I am not in their presence any more, it is somehow stimulating to encounter their works, or just their names mentioned in a discussion or publication. Having met them, provides an added dimension to certain moments in my life, reinforces the experience and my understanding of what they had contributed to my time in history.

It is not the same at all merely to watch people through the media, or, rather, as I was able to do in many cases, listen to and observe their presence in real life. As I am writing down their names today, they come alive again in my mind: Colin Powell whom I recommended to one of my midshipmen to take as his model, John McCain who visited several times at the USNA because he was the Superintendent's friend, Mrs. Thatcher cheered by the midshipmen when she appeared in a bright red suit on high heels to deliver a political retrospective lecture in Alumni Hall. It said something about the business acumen of Steven Spielberg when he jokingly remarked that the laundry business in Annapolis must be flourishing since they took care of the four thousand impeccably starched and pressed uniforms of the midshipmen lined up in front of him while he himself stood on the podium addressing them in a dark brown, somewhat wrinkled suit. A few years ago, Hilary and Bill Clinton waved to us when they drove by my friends' house in the Georgica section of East Hampton after having been Steven Spielberg's guests down the street. I looked into their eyes as they looked into mine—a human connection that lasted only seconds but provided an impression. I admired Queen Elisabeth's perfect complexion enhanced by her red outfit when she came to Dartmouth, and the smiling King and beautiful young Queen of Jordan's patience in answering a myriad of questions after a lecture at Harvard Business School. Jackie Kennedy and her children John Jr. and Caroline I remember from several encounters on a bicycle near Central Park, at the Dalcroze School of Music or crossing East 86th Street around midnight, all by herself, and years later John Jr. rushing down Fifth Avenue toward Jackie's apartment building the day we learned of her death from cancer. I remember president John F. Kennedy in Paris arriving in an open limousine from the airport of Orly for the notorious meeting with Khrushchev, and presidents Reagan, Bush and Clinton shaking hands with thousands of midshipmen at commencement ceremonies and at the end leaning down from the podium to shake hands with us faculty. Secretary of State Madeleine Albright, a fellow C.U. graduate, exchanged a few words with me at one of the USNA's yearly Foreign Affairs Conferences, as did political commentator David Gergen at a lunch table. I saw him again later at Harvard. I recently met the ambassadors from Palestine to the United Nations at a small breakfast meeting, and only days later listened, at a Rotary meeting in Paris, to the Iraqi ambassador to France whose speech seemed to echo President Bush's statements at press conferences. After four years in France, the ambassador still felt not secure enough to deliver his speech in French which therefore had to be translated from English. At a conference of the association of Philosophy and Literature, I had the opportunity to converse with the post modern architect Frank Gehry, to whom I jokingly suggested he should create one of his famously post modern structures, possibly representing a ship, for one of the still open spaces at the USNA. Just as jokingly, he responded that he found my idea inspiring and would love to follow up on it. At a reception at the Maison Française of Columbia University, the famous musician Pierre Boulez took some time to chat with me, telling me, in answer to my question, that his computer assisted concerts could not function in nature. The integrity of the music would be lost, he said, sort of "evaporate" in open air. I also remember John Cage who gave a "concert" at Columbia University after 1968 with his non-traditional instruments, stressing rhythm over harmony, mixing poetry and music. It was a revelation of a new art form. Several times in New York and also in Paris, I met the philosopher Bernard Henry Lévy whose intellectual integrity I have particularly appreciated at the time of the recent election campaigns in both France and the United States.

I feel privileged to have been able to listen to and meet many of such great critics, philosophers, writers, artists and politicians of our times, and

At the Maison Française of Columbia University, in a conversation with renowned composer and musical director Pierre Boulez about his computer assisted concerts.

especially those I was able to interview for my book on Lukács. Some may judge it frivolous to attach importance to such chance, sometimes distant, relatively short encounters, handshakes or merely polite, necessarily a bit superficial verbal exchanges. I feel that I gained an additional dimension to understanding their works and at the same time got to know the human being a bit by observing their gestures, facial expressions, speech patterns and relationship to the audience or the way they talked to me personally.

Now that so many of the people whose world used to be part of mine have passed away, like Lucien Goldmann, René Wellek, Edward Said, Michael Riffaterre, and Jean Baudrillard, to name only a few in literature with whom I was associated through my work, I feel their loss in my own life. These were people whom I knew and followed in their thought and writing. I served as their "reader." It was also satisfying to be recognized and often encouraged by them personally. They were witnesses to my life as I was to theirs. They left a void.

With Bernard Henri Lévy after his recent lecture at the New York Public Library. I first read his philosophical work at the time of his enormous media success in France in the 1970s. More recently, he emerged again as one the most visible and committed French intellectuals in the twenty-first century.

27

Who Am I Today?

Forever a question mark

On these pages I have tried to respond to the question which has been put to me so often and which I finally put to myself: "Where are you from?" I have tried to retrace what I remember about my origins and the personal and intellectual "individuation" that I underwent and that has made me what I am today. But who am I today? What has become of the privileged, blond little girl, shielded from danger and the outside world, playing with frogs in her beautiful garden in Hungary, who was then abruptly thrown into the cruel world of war, homelessness, loneliness and alienation but seems to have survived and "made it" in her world? Who is she today?

Interest in deterministic theories

As a graduate student, I became very interested in theories and philosophies of genetic, social, political and linguistic determinism. I read works by Freud, Marx, Lukács, Bakhtin, Foucault, Derrida and many others. I studied literature and poetry for its beauty, its rhythm and enchanting metaphors, but also, maybe most of all, for the "truth" I could glean from them. Since I have never subjected myself to psychoanalysis, I tried to piece together the puzzle of my own individual make up determined by my genes and a multitude of influences and personal experiences. Once I had passed my exams and obtained my diplomas, "union cards," as we sometimes called them among colleagues, I enjoyed the freedom of indulging in my own research about the fabric of reality and what many modern philosophers have mockingly dismissed as "the truth." During my sabbatical year at Harvard, I audited seminars in psychoanalysis hoping to better understand myself. I do not pretend to have found absolute truth, not about myself, not about the world, but I will probably always keep trying. I think it is the only means to arrive at and maintain one's personal ethics and integrity. Like so many other traits I have inherited from my father there may also be this need and drive to discover my individual truths and then simply do what I think is right for myself and also for human society in general.

Witness to three quarters of a very imperfect century

If I live a few more years, I may claim to have been a critical witness to nearly three quarters of a century. Since my childhood in World War II, I vowed to combat what I felt were the greatest evils in our history. I have never forgotten what Jóska and I saw that terrible morning in the forests of Sopron, or the photographs, I saw when I arrived in Paris, of the innocent little children horded toward the gaping gates of the gas chambers. All this has no doubt shaped my politics which synthesizes what I think of the world today.

Disappointments

György Lukács entitled his autobiography *Gelebtes Denken*, "Lived Thought," which inspired me to follow him in this attempt. As I expressed in my papers and publications, I have admired Lukács's theories ever since I encountered them with the help of Lucien Goldmann. After presenting a paper on Lukács at an MLA session, a young man came to congratulate me and asked me whether I identified with Lukács and maybe for that reason spoke with so much conviction and enthusiasm about his work. I did so for many years. His indictment of inauthentic bourgeois values based on money, the fetishism of merchandize that characterizes our modern consumer society, where young people kill for a pair of sneakers or a plasma TV, capitalism as ally of imperialism, human exploitation through prostitution, pedophilia and drug trafficking, all these forms of abuse had become targets of my own intellectual struggle for a better society. I felt attracted to critics and philosophers who upheld similar ideals.

It was therefore distressing to hear from Georg Steiner and more recently from György Konrad, who, like my aunt Manci, had met Lukács at his luxurious apartment on the banks of the Danube in Budapest, that Lukács was a "great bourgeois" himself who had his meals served by butlers wearing white gloves and did not turn down his rich, ennobled banker father's money while prohibiting other, non-Jewish bourgeois sons to benefit from an excellent education at the University of Budapest and tried to prevent their privileged access to cultural events such as the theatre and the opera, taking away their tickets and giving them to cleaning ladies and street sweepers. Konrad, an openly self-described bourgeois, was helped by Lukács with the publication of his first manuscript. Even though it did not last long, Lukács's violent anti-bourgeois activity apparently created havoc among the student body in 1919, at the time when my father was a medical student at the University of Budapest. I believe it says much about my father's intellectual open mindedness and ultimately his humanistic concerns, that he did not resent my study and enthusiasm for some of Lukács's theories. To the contrary. While I was doing research for my Ph.D. dissertation, my father sent me books and critical articles about Lukács whenever they came to his attention in Europe.

Other disappointments occurred, for instance, as I have reported above, when I accepted a position of secretary to a lawyer who attempted to get money for Hungarian Holocaust victims but did not refrain from harassing me, groping my breasts with his creepy bony fingers and propositioning me to agree to his disgusting advances.

Even the situation at the United Nations in the 1960s, when I worked there for the duration of a General Assembly, turned out to be a bit disappointing because many of the delegates seemed more interested in having fun and pursuing sexual adventures than the interests of their poor countries. It was distressing.

Among the many other disappointments I have had to deal with in my mind and quite often in personal situations have been provoked by national, racial, ethnic and religious discrimination and, very disappointingly, even in so called "well meaning" circles and charitable organizations.

28

More Wars—Devastating Politics

The shock of the Golf War

Here is what I wrote in my journal on January 16, 1991:

"War has begun, at 1900 this evening. I am watching TV in bed. The horror has begun. Bush went ahead. They are now killing, butchering each other. Aggression is met with aggression. Bombs, like fireworks, are falling over Baghdad. *Desert Storm* has begun. My head is pounding. Memories of the other war, nearly fifty years ago, are coming back. My father standing outside our basement apartment to which we had fled in Sopron. He is watching the chain bombs flying over his head. I am sitting on my mother's lap, in a winter coat, my mother told me I was sweating, in December, afraid for my father, for all of us. I am now afraid again. This is absurd. Not war again! Please! If Bush spoke Arabic, maybe he could have called, negotiated. This is horror, déjà vu. My family lost everything in the war. And what for? Crazy mankind. Vulnerable human beings victimized. We did not stop Bush. We are guilty, as Germans were. Mitläufer, collaborators. I work for Bush at the Naval Academy. He is my boss. He uses my students, midshipmen. They may die. Children will die. Reporters at the Al-Rashid Hotel in Baghdad are joking that they haven't had the time to have dinner, they may never have dinner again. They are scared. I feel so helpless, impotent. What if I yelled, shouted, cried, roared!? I hate this. Where is my child, my life, and my sweet little granddaughter? What a world will they inherit? Bush is going to speak in half an hour, followed by Cheney and General Powell. In Baghdad bombs are falling. There is anti-aircraft fire. It's awful, crazy, unreal, this "Operation Desert Storm." Suddenly a commercial interrupts the fiery images of war: "Anti-Acid." How grotesque! One reporter asks whether "'it has been successful'? What does he mean? This is a catastrophe! Hell burning in this world.

Bush apparently has prepared for this for two-three weeks. The climax has come, now the tragedy unfolds."

On the next day, the 17th, I wrote in my journal that "they feel that the optimism of last night is dissipating. (What optimism?!) In Israel, in Haifa and Tel Aviv, they are wearing gas masks against the nerve gas. They are locked into sealed rooms. It's lethal to breathe the air."

"But rapidly, within a few days, this horrible war has become routine. The networks have gone back to their silly soaps. Prévert's poem comes to my mind: 'le père fait les affaires, la mère fait du tricot, le fils la guerre' (the father does business, the mother knitting, the son war)."

The election of G. W. Bush

After the Clinton years, which resentful Republicans tried to turn into a hell not only for the President but the entire country, soon another tragedy happened with the election of the presidential son, George W. Bush, elected by the same vengeful Republicans. I felt like escaping from this country for the duration of his presidency. It is then that I bought my place in Paris. Especially after 9/11, the horrors of which I witnessed from my balcony. I was convinced that it came in retaliation to the first Golf War, when Americans invaded the land of Moslems and Arabs. Soon thereafter, having been unable to capture the master mind of the 9/11 terror attacks, Osama Bin Laden, emboldened by a slight victory over the Taliban in Afghanistan, G. W. Bush started the preemptive war in Iraq to take out Saddam Hussein because he allegedly had arms of mass destruction, a war instigated for years by Wolfowitz, Cheney and his friends at the Pentagon, in Israel and no doubt also the first President Bush who had not been able to do so during his own Golf War. It soon turned into possibly the greatest tragedy for Americans. Anti Americanism spread like wild fire across much of the world and gave this beautiful country a bad name. Those of us who opposed the war were called unpatriotic, anti-Semitic. The vicious anti-French campaign that followed after Dominique de Villepin's powerful anti-war speech at the United Nations turned even Rotarians in my club and district into nasty calumniators. Some took it out on me, a Francophile. I received hostile e-mail and was denigrated, fired from my position as youth exchange chair because I praised the French host families of one of my exchange students. I was told that I had "offended" other Rotarians. When the war in Iraq soon turned into a huge tragedy for the U.S., Wolfowitz quickly tried to dissociate himself from what he had helped create. He made an attempt to escape possible accusations for human rights violations by seeking refuge at the World Bank only to be forced soon thereafter to resign for violation of professional ethics. I sometimes wonder whether those anti-French militants have changed after the election of the new pro-American French president, who decided to spend his first presidential vacation, just a few months after his election, with his wealthy neoconservative, ideological friends in New Hampshire, as one of the few remaining "friends" of G. W. Bush and who seems to have begun propaganda for an attack on Iran?

Afghanistan, Iraq, Lebanon, Israel, Palestine and will there be an Iran?

All these recent wars, almost equally devastating for all concerned, for me brought back the horrors of World War II. I thought the world would never again have to experience such violence against human beings and the destruction of their homes and countries. I felt particularly guilty and impotent in my, I know hopeless, desire to save the children in all these countries. Among so many other young Americans, Mr. Bush's war in Iraq killed a former midshipman from the U.S. Naval Academy, Jennifer Harris, a brilliant young woman, shot down while she was piloting a helicopter in the war zone.

Recent electoral campaigns in France and the U.S.

I used to believe that France, maybe because it had a more socialistic government, fared better than the United States with regard to human rights, but since the recent elections, I fear, as I did in 2000 when George W. Bush was elected president, that the same humanistic values that had been so attractive to me, may be endangered, lost forever. The boundless ambition of a ruthlessly aggressive, materialistic president and his allies not just in France but also in the U.S. and other countries, seem to seek imperialistic domination not limited to their own country but, considering their moves, over Europe, Africa and maybe the rest of the world. As the French president exclaimed (*New York Times,* 24 August 2007): "Tony and I have just made a decision. We're going to conquer Europe." The president and his self-appointed government officials act as if they had been chosen to lead the world and, most of all, to live the good life among their ideological friends around the world. As was the case after the election of G. W. Bush, the French president at present enjoys a strong following, but the opposition has begun to raise its voice, among them a few outspoken women.

Several French politicians attracted by the new president revealed their selfish political goals. One of them, who still capitalizes on his former association with a charitable organization that a few years ago received the Nobel Peace Prize, was among the few French men who declared themselves in favor of the war in Iraq. As I am writing, he still feels, as he affirmed after a recent visit to the war torn country, that France, too, should have "a place in Iraq." He did not elaborate, but having offended the Iraqi Prime Minister, he soon had to submit apologies. Another talented but extremely vain man, who in the past did not hesitate to spend huge government funds on programs by which he could promote himself while professing social concerns for the poor, did not hesitate long to betray his Socialist Party in order to gain a place in the limelight of the new right-wing, neoconservative government. I was shocked while listening to Radio Israel in Paris that its declared mission is to put the welfare of Israel ahead of the welfare of any other country, even the one of which they enjoy the privilege of citizenship. This could explain why previously declared socialists in France have chosen to follow the politics of the new president in France and why former U.S. Democrats switched to support the neoconservatives who precipitated the country into the most devastating wars in recent history. If the same treacherous attitude were encouraged by Moslem religion, it would explain the perversity of home grown terrorism. As I am writing today, I hope such ideology will not lead to more terror, violence and war.

The new French president elect, similar to George W. Bush, does not seem to believe in transparent politics. Already during his electoral campaign, he did not refrain from kissing babies (like most other politicians do) but also embrace Arabic youths he previously called "scum," and even stroke cows from Normandy in front of TV cameras, to convince the French electorate to vote for him.

It was a great disappointment to me to witness the victory of a person who went from France to Washington, even before he had won the elections, to seek support from notoriously wealthy interest groups and confess admiration rather than condemnation for George W. Bush's politics. It became clear already at that time, that the neoconservatives and certain media groups on both sides of the Atlantic were sympathizers of the French candidate. His election was quickly followed by hand-picked members for his government who were willing to betray their former political allegiance and follow the new president on ethnic or maybe religious, but certainly not formerly upheld ideological or charitable grounds. These defectors, mostly ambitious men and women with big egos and a questionable integrity, were bought with the promise of awarding them visibility and power in the new government after their former party had lost the election.

I nevertheless still trust that the French people, with their keen critical minds and Cartesian reasoning powers, who are now ridiculed by the current government for "thinking too much" instead of just following their brash new leaders, will ultimately regain the upper hand and eliminate the scum that is currently endangering the values of their centuries old humanistic tradition. There are signs of such awakening in recent publications, particularly by an Emmy Award winning writer, which make the headlines of not only the most prominent French but international media including the *New York Times*. Obviously, the French president also has his supporters in the U.S., especially in the G. W. Bush camp and the tireless instigators of more war in the Middle East, this time against Iran.

We have witnessed political treason in the United States as well, after a senator who lost the elections to vice president and his hopes for power and a place in the limelight, did not hesitate long to turn around and kiss, in front of TV and the whole world, a president whom he just weeks before pretended to oppose politically. In the current electoral campaign, the same untrustworthy politician refused to support a candidate, still hoping that his friend would ultimately declare his candidacy so he could follow him and, if elected, have a chance at a high position in his government. This man has already once become a traitor to his party and could well become one to his country if the circumstances presented themselves.

29

The Integrity of Individual Human Beings vs. Members of Interest Groups

A critical distance

Living "on the margins" of so many different countries, and amongst so many different races and ethnic groups, I believe, has helped me maintain a critical intellectual distance from the mainstream and other dominant groups. A "critical distance" has often been said to benefit journalists, writers and even politicians (the catholic Kennedys?) by providing them with a more judicious judgment. A good critic, it is said, who writes "on the margins of society" is not easily swayed by blind allegiance to a majority in the center and its potentially nefarious cause. I have many years ago decided, even when I found myself in delicate situations, torn into different directions by people, some of whom pretended to be my friends, that I will not be in support of any groups, schools, parties, ethnicity, race or whatever entity that regards itself superior to the other.

I have found inspiration in this thinking in Martin Luther King's dream, as I interpret it, to judge human beings according to their character, their human individuality. Few today would speak up in favor of Hitler's belief in the superiority of the Arian race or Nietzsche's "Ubermensch," but there are ethnic and religious groups who maintain that they are God's "chosen people," and others who pretend that their God asked them to engage in a religious jihad against those they consider faithless, infidels. It is distressing that in the 21st century quite undistinguished individuals are called to govern major countries because they are ruthlessly supported with enormous funds by their ethnic, religious or political camps who vie for power and influence.

I have spoken up about such abuse wherever I observed it on both sides of the Atlantic, without consideration of the consequences it might

267

have on my personal or professional life. As I mentioned above, my interventions have been purely intellectual, I do not have the temperament to manifest in the street, but I intend to live according to my ideals, views, ethics and integrity as long as my body and mind will allow me to do so.

Is there a decent country in the world unlike any other?

In recent years, I have been wondering whether there was a country on this earth where evil political practices do not exist, or at least are condemned rather than condoned or even enforced by elected officials. Having visited Scandinavia in 2006, and looked into some of their governmental systems and programs, I have the impression that these Nordic countries have found ways that may eventually lead to a more decent human society, if they are accepted as models. At my age, I must not forget that I may eventually become dependent on the help of others. It is too late for me to make major changes in my life or significantly affect the lives of my descendents. At this point, however decent the country and its inhabitants, I could not create a new home, none that could compare to Hungary, Paris, and some parts of England and the United States where I have found relative happiness and activities that allowed me to act in accordance with my conscience. It may also be more beneficial to the common good to continue living and speaking up in a country that needs reform and a more positive direction.

My puzzle

I have looked at my existence as if trying to complete a puzzle, weighing each piece to make sure it would reflect who I am. This puzzle received input from all aspects of my life on two continents, in six countries and seven U.S. states in which I and some members of my family settled at least for a while to make a home after the war. It also was shaded by the different ethnicities, nationalities, and characteristics of my friends, colleagues and inhabitants of the various places. I would not be who I am today, and the story of my life would be incomplete, if I lost one piece of the puzzle or were forced to restrict my existence to only one part of it. Naturally, the last piece, presently in the form of a question mark, will have to be inserted by time.

30

In Search of a Conclusion

Climbing back on my rock for more answers

I went back to my "half-way rock in Montauk" to find a conclusion to this "book" if ever what I have been writing gets published as such. This time again, I was alone at the beach. It was in the middle of June 2007, sunny but cool even around noontime. I felt much less enthusiastic about the future than I had, more than thirty-five years ago, when I first sat on that rock, the day I purchased my little house which is still surrounded by Japanese pine trees but no longer belongs to me. Also, after the recent months that I have immersed myself in observing election politics, both East and West of the Atlantic, the phrase that has come to my mind and would not let go of me was Claude Lévi Strauss saying, in one of his most recent interviews, that he does not like the world in which he is finishing his existence. There is much I do not like about it either and wish I could change but in the end I nevertheless believe that in spite of all the bad things that exist today and that I have had to endure in the past I have had a relatively good life.

A life lived in exquisite places

I still do like Montauk, its blue waters and white beaches in the fall and in the spring, when the wealthy New Yorkers who years ago took over the tranquil fisherman's village and turned it into their glitzy playground have not yet arrived for the summer or have returned to the city after Labor Day. I still love Paris, always, and dream of Budapest that I cannot visit often enough. I am also grateful for the beautiful tranquil place I found on the Hudson that allows me to concentrate undisturbed on my writing or look across the river where my children live.

My apartment on the Hudson.

Dazzling moments

There have been dazzling moments in my life, such as working with the "top guns," those "knights in shining armor" at the USNA, to be "On Her Majesty's Service" and have lunch with Queen Elizabeth with only forty other faculty members and administrators, the subsequent chat with the Duke of Edinburgh, the ceremony when I was awarded my Ph.D. degree by Columbia University, or the Excellence of Research Award I received at the USNA from the Dean and Superintendent, the birth of my sweet daughter at the Hôpital Port Royal in Paris, her graduation from Columbia Law School, the enchanting festivities at her wedding at the Plaza, the birth of each of my beautiful grandchildren and the moment when they first opened their eyes to look at us, or the experience of teaching so many brilliant students during my career. Crossing the U.S. twice in a U-Haul, all by myself, or another time in a small Pinto with my daughter, have left me in awe of this beautiful vast country. There have been lots of thrilling moments in my life that still make me smile, most of all the time spent, East and West, in the company of people I loved. I cannot list nor rank them according to what they have meant to me. Even though I have mentioned a few, I do not wish to dwell on events and people who have distressed me or that I found to be a disgrace to humanity. After all, this is no doubt just a fictionalized account, in the Barthesian sense, of events in my lifetime that simply came to my mind, popped up in my memory, when I finally sat down to write about them, but I did so in good faith.

A life in awesome company

I feel that I have lived in awesome company that started with our dinners in my family "back home," continued in the company of my intelligent, kind daughter, and later branched out to include her erudite husband and so many others. Also, I have accomplished so much more both personally and professionally than I would ever have dared dream of as a child and even much later when I was struggling to make it all alone with my young daughter in the United States. My child is still the greatest gift I have received in life, the only true "grace" I have felt ever since she was born, but I have been showered with a myriad of unexpected rewards once I had learned to survive what at first seemed unbearable hardship, the worst of which was loneliness. All the while people would tell me that I looked like a million and was seemingly surrounded by lots of so-called friends. As Nietzsche promised, what did not kill me made me strong. Indeed, I became stronger each time I succeeded to jump back on my feet.

Epilogue

What is there left for me to do?

As I reflect about what I would still like to accomplish in my life, I am reminded of several of my colleagues who one day compared me to the character of "Julia" in a movie about World War II, played by Vanessa Redgrave. She tried to have Hitler eliminated but was in the end herself murdered by the Nazis. I find her act and sacrifice admirable. She lived and died for her purpose, even though tragically.

As to myself, I wish I could do something to unite nations, establish peace and freedom and prevent future wars that are cruel and arbitrary as we have known them in my life time. I wish I could guarantee all the children of my dispersed family around the globe a peaceful, rewarding life. It was particularly devastating to me that the same people whose children were savagely murdered by the Nazis did not have it in their hearts to refrain from killing just as beautiful and innocent little children in a recent war in the Middle East. It is incomprehensible to me.

The least I can do, which is not much, is to speak up against such violence and inhumanity. I am trying to do it right here, on these pages. I believe that our dignity as human beings requires us to do as much good for humanity and the world as is in our power, despite all the odds and all too often limited success of our efforts. I used to say to my students who were fearful and insecure about what they could accomplish in a test or in their future: "Just do your best, that's all you can do."

Against ruthlessness and greed

I try to speak up against people who abuse others on national, religious, ethnic, political or other arbitrary grounds. I have observed so many such people, whose selfish pursuits of monetary, professional or social ambitions made them unfair, vicious and even turned them into criminals. Because of their ruthlessness they often manage to get away with it while good people are relegated to a more modest life, all too often marked by want and suffering.

Arrogant religions

The exclusionary pursuits of human success and the greed for earthly rewards is encouraged by the biased interpretation of certain religions and thus contributes to the evil that too often surrounds us. This has been happening for centuries. It is not a popular thought in America, but I believe one does not have to believe in Jesus, Allah or maintain thoughts of belonging to a superior "chosen people" to be a positive, decent member of the human race. No one should be called an "infidel" or be treated like a "shiksa." Decent human beings whatever their background should be equally respected. Unfortunately, there have always been people who have tried to denigrate and subjugate others and force them to conform to their beliefs. To have peace in the world, we must combat any such tyranny.

My "spirituality"'

I believe that I will not have another life after this life, but I am not fanatic in this belief, nor does this idea distress me, contrary to what people might think. Rather, it just encourages me to do the best I can in the life I still have. My "spirituality" does not really go beyond the human. I cannot at this point of my life believe in heaven, hell or a personified god. The realm of my imagination and my perceptions are the limits to which I commit. Classical music is perhaps the media that takes me the farthest, but also my idealism toward life in general, human life in particular, and my deep affection for the tender life of children, most of all. I would consider myself lucky if I could alleviate the suffering of children, protect them from evil. Such values are like stars in my idealist heaven but remain bound to human existence. On the other hand, it probably seems contradictory to people who are either religious or atheistic, that I like churches, and attend services of various denominations, just as I like some spiritual music, Gregorian chants, some national hymns, art and aesthetics which all help me, and I hope will help my daughter, grandchildren and, as I used to hope, also my students, to pursue goodness and "purity"—I do not mean this in a goody-goody, corny sense. Even though such ideals and "spiritual" goals appear forever elusive, I believe they nevertheless have a positive function in the lives of human beings. The abolition of slavery, torture and mutilation, movements against violence and war, the practice of equal rights, the protection of life on earth and earth itself, assistance to the poor, the sick, the old and the handicapped are ideals that I connect to my spirituality even when I cannot be of much help.

Can goodness ever win over evil?

I am sure that many people would call my idealism exaggerated, even ridiculous. "Why should we be good to others"? some one asked me recently. "People don't deserve it." "Most people look out for themselves," they say. "So far, even the most 'civilized' countries have engaged in terrible injustice, aggression, violence and exploitation of others." I know that we shall never succeed in eliminating evil altogether as I had hoped we could when I was a little girl, when my nanny told me that goodness would ultimately win over the bad. All we can do, as individuals, is to "continue," as Sartre said, trying to uphold our integrity. So that is all I am doing. I try to live according to my own ethics, my "spirituality," developed over the years on the basis of a comparative search for my own values.

After I am gone

Once I am dead, I hope my ashes will float in the Atlantic, between East and West. I will be free of my body and mind but my Odyssey will continue as long as someone still remembers me. I will live for a while in some people's minds before I finally vanish to make room for some other form of life. At this point, my journey still continues. Wherever I am, I am never just from there, I am also from somewhere else. In the end, it is in this exciting journey between East and West itself that I have found myself and my home.

A NOTE ON THE TYPE

This book was set in Caslon, a typeface originally developed by Nicholas Kis (1650–1702), a Hungarian, whose work permitted William Caslon (1692–1766) to create his own incomparable designs, such as the typeface used in the first printed version of the United States Declaration of Independence. — ELC

Book design by Judith Pendleton of
Annie Graham Publishing Services, Chattanooga, Tennessee

Cover design by Eva Livia Corredor

Printed by Thomson-Shore Inc., Dexter, Michigan